T0195999

THE TROUBLER

Joseph A. McCaffrey

authorHOUSE®

AuthorHouse™
1663 Liberty Drive
Bloomington, IN 47403
www.authorhouse.com
Phone: 1 (800) 839-8640

This is a newer version of the book published by AuthorHouse in 2006.

This book is a work of fiction. People, places, events and situations are the product of the author's imagination. Any resemblance to actual persons, living or dead, or historical events is purely coincidental.

Published by AuthorHouse 01/27/2020

ISBN: 978-1-7283-4176-7 (sc)
ISBN: 978-1-7283-4175-0 (e)

Print information available on the last page.

This book is printed on acid-free paper.

Cover Design: Sally Paustian

In memory of: Velma Forret and for
her devoted daughter: Monica

CHAPTER I

'Roberta Chamberlin!!!! – 10 a.m.'

This is what Mark Hennessey saw when he opened his appointment calendar. He ran his left hand through his thinning brown hair, already speckled with whiteness. He shook his head back and forth a few times and said, "Jeez."

After Roberta Chamberlin's phone call two days ago, he concluded that she would be big-time trouble, a truculent know-it-all who would probably make outlandish demands on the Chicago Police Department. He would listen with feigned concern and send her on her way with hope, he hoped.

Homicide Detective Hennessey spent four full days looking into Regis Chamberlin's murder. Every rock he picked up exposed a new cluster of smaller rocks that in their turn exposed more of the same, but smaller still. In his experience, a successful murder investigation was a matter of eliminating suspects until only one stood out; at that point it became necessary to concentrate all resources on that perp. Roberta Chamberlin's son's murder went the other way, every effort opened a whole new matrix of possibilities. It was a treadmill case, with an obvious start but no end.

In just four days, Hennessey had decided that the case was pretty much a clunker. The entire file was headed for deep, deep burial, even if he had to go through the pretense of interest.

Whitey Bennett came trudging into the over-lit olive green office area that housed sixteen desks in what was once a six desk space. He looked as though he hadn't shaved or changed clothes in a decade. "What's up, Hennessey?" he said gruffly.

Bennett, through all the years that Hennessey knew him, had never used a first name. He wondered what he called his wife, 'Hey, Bennett' or when he was romantic, 'Hey, Bennett dear.' "I've got this victim, Chamberlin; his mothers' coming in at 10. She's on a horse, let me tell you."

Whitey came over to Hennessey's desk, pulled up a seat, and plunked down all of his 250 plus pounds accompanied by a hugh sigh. "That's a fucked up case."

"You only know a fifth of it. I told you about it on, when, my second day? Here's the problem – who wouldn't want to kill the bastard? The list of suspects keeps expanding. Like the universe."

"What?"

Hennessey was going to explain an article he had read in the *Chicago Sun Times*. He caught himself before embarking on the useless voyage. "After talking with mommy dearest, I can see why the son was screwed up."

"Yeah, you know what they say. The tree isn't far from the acorn." He gripped the arms of the chair and brought himself to a standing position. Whitey trudged back to his desk and picked up his phone.

Hennessey looked at him closely. Whitey was just two

years from retirement. He wondered how addled Bennett's brain was before he became a detective some 10 years or so ago. Or was he genetically dumb? Hennessey still had another eight years to go. He hoped he could leave the Department with his mind still reasonably intact. Whitey, however, was leaving the Department, genetics or not, dumber than a boulder.

The single ring of his phone indicated an inside call. He picked up the receiver, "Hennessey."

"Lieutenant Hennessey, this is Commander Miner. Do you have a few minutes?"

"Sure, sure I do."

"Why don't you come up right now … and bring along some of the info on this … Chamberlin case you're working on." He hung up abruptly.

Commander Miner was a black guy who had been foisted onto the station three years ago by the Daley administration, anxious to muscle up its statistics on black advancement and opportunity. He had been brought into the Department, originally, as a consultant, having served in military intelligence and enforcement for 20 years. Hennessey detested him. He saw him as an uptight freak who sat up on the top floor of the stationhouse acting like he was in the papal palace. He was sure that the animosity was mutual.

Somehow his secretary, Elizabeth, was cloned from Auschwitz-administrator DNA. She was a tight-assed bitch with arrogance as her calling card. This 40ish black-haired woman with face too thin and face too long, was on the phone when he arrived. He waved; she looked away. He cursed himself. Why wave to her when there was only a one-percent chance of any kind of reciprocity?

"I'll pass it on to Commander Miner. I'm sure that he'll be interested. Thank you," she said insincerely as she turned her attention in his direction. "Lieutenant Hennessey?"

"I'm here to see Commander Miner."

"His schedule is pretty tight. Try to keep it brief for me."

Not for him, for her. Like you could see the mutt, but don't stay long. "That's his call, isn't it?" It came out wrong, churlish.

She pursed her super thin lips and caught him nastily with her squinty gray eyes. She didn't respond except for that unmistakable body language that held Hennessey in disdain. She got up, positioned her right hand outwards motioning him to freeze in place, and entered Miner's open doorway. "He's here, sir. Are you ready to see him?"

He heard a muffled, "Send him in." She did so with a forward wave of her fingers, that directed Hennessey to advance into Miner's office.

It was a sun-bathed corner office on the top floor of the three-story building. Miner stood up and pointed to the seat in front of his gargantuan desk. They sat at the same time. Miner made no effort to close his office door.

He began, "You know," he looked down at a piece of paper in front of him, "you have a real stinker on your hands."

"Sir?"

"This Chamberlin affair. Come off of it, Hennessey. You know what I'm talking about. I asked you to bring your notes. We're having a conversation for God's sake. Don't play stupid with me, sir."

He wondered if Elizabeth heard the exchange. If she did, she'd love Miner for what he just did to Hennessey. "Chamberlin – a real stinker? It's a tough case if that's what you mean, sir."

"His mother is coming to see you this morning. What are you going to tell her?" Miner, small faced, had a tiny, toothpick-like mustache. His brown eyes were both intense and judgmental.

"It's a tough case," Hennessey knew that he was being a disingenuous jerk with Miner.

Miner let the insipid comment just lie there for about 15 seconds. He finally said, "You should know that she has huge connections in the state of Illinois. She could hurt you and the Department."

"Oh?"

"Hey. You know Illinois better than I do. You know the score. Don't give her a hard time when you see her today."

"Who said I was going to?"

"I didn't need a rat on this one; your record of obnoxiousness is long enough to let me guess. I'm sure that I wouldn't have to go far to confirm, would I? Like your personnel record."

"Commander Miner, I'll be as nice as I can with her. Is there anything else, sir?"

"Give me a synopsis of the case – clear and to the point Hennessey."

"He was drugged and hung underneath I-55 on Cicero Avenue."

"Suicide?"

"No, crime scene gave it away. If anything, it was a showcase killing."

"Tell me more."

"The victim was 350 pounds of sheer piss and vinegar. He ran what might come out to be hundreds of websites, every one devoted to tearing down a group, an individual, or an institution, you name it."

"You know this for a fact?"

Hennessey opened up his folder. "Ben Ross – one of our go-to computer specialists did the work. All sorts of correspondence in Chamberlin's computers and his files. Answer – affirmative."

"Suspects?"

"Yeah – sure. Each group or individual he screwed with. Start working the groups – talking thousands, millions I guess to be accurate."

There was a long pause. "Any hot prospects?"

"No. The next inquiry always looks better than the last one. It's like the universe – it keeps expanding."

"What? What the hell does the universe have to do with this case?"

"Excuse me sir, just a manner of speaking." Unlike Whitey, who was just plain dumb, Miner was a literalist. He probably knew all about the expanding universe, but he was unable to connect one idea, the expanding universe, to another, the murder case. Hennessey decided not to read any more stories about the expanding universe. He clarified, "The list of suspects is extensive."

"So, go through this again. What exactly are you going to tell this man's mother, an influential and powerful mother?"

"I'm going to try to explain that this case is very difficult because her son was so deeply involved in the political process and wasn't afraid to take on tough issues. How's that?"

Miner tried it on for size, or at least his eyes indicated such as they swiveled up to his right. "Well, that's better than what you might have been inclined to do, I guess."

"Excuse me, sir?"

"You heard me. You don't have a reputation for delicacy, after all."

"I guess I don't. Doing homicides is not like AWOLs or shop-lifting from commissaries," Hennessey said sarcastically, while wondering whether this military dig scored.

"That's enough of that, Lieutenant. I'll just give you fair warning. Get your job done on this quickly, and treat her carefully. If it comes back to me that you've been an ass, I'll make your life difficult. Believe me. Keep me informed; you are dismissed."

Hennessey got up quickly and walked out. Elizabeth caught him with a disdainful stare. "I made it easy for you. It was a short meeting, wasn't it?"

She rose and headed for Miner's office. She didn't respond to him.

Hennessey wasn't sure about what to share with Brunhilde, AKA, Roberta Chamberlin. In his occasionally sympathetic heart, he felt for her. A son was a son, a huge loss by any standard. Regis, the youngest of the family, was the only son. She also had two daughters, the eldest in Istanbul with the American Embassy. Her name was Iris. The other, Sybil, was a local who lived in Aurora, Illinois, employed as a buyer for Nordstrom's Department Store. Roberta was married for 30 years until her husband died nearly two years ago. No one in the family was hitched up at this time. The murdered 29-year-old Regis had attended Harvard, but he dropped out after his sophomore year. From there his history became rank; and his personality, always somewhat problematical, started its descent into hell.

Surely the mother was onto all of this. But he did wonder how she might massage it. Parents were frequently aware of general problems but unknowing about the ocean of specifics.

What Miner said about the mother's political influence was noteworthy. His relatively unobtrusive checking on Roberta came up with her being associated with the democratic party in the State of Illinois. She lived at a downtown address – town home, probably she and it worth millions. So far, no connection with the Daley machine came up, but the call to Miner hinted at some extensive connections to someone, somewhere. The worse that could happen, he thought, was that he'd be pulled from the case. He would consider that a blessing, provided that it wasn't done in a disrespectful way. He'd try to be civil, but he wasn't about to take a lot of crap from her. He had already taken too much when she called two days ago.

By the time she showed up, the desks and noise level of the second-floor detective area were at full throttle. The call from the desk sergeant on the first floor came through at 10:05. "You expecting a visitor, Hennessey?"

"Yeah, a woman, Roberta Chamberlin."

The sergeant lowered his voice, "Well, this is your lucky day, buddy. She has enough airs about her to win an Oscar. I put her in C. Do me a favor and get down here. I don't want her on my ass."

"You owe me. I'll be there in a few minutes."

It must have cost her a fortune in cosmetics to be so severely overdone as to affect such an underdone look. She was probably in her sixties, although she was desperately hanging onto a below-fifty look. She had short, blonde hair, at least three layers of makeup to create a slightly faded tan look, pale red lipstick, and impeccable grooming around her eyelashes and plucked brows. When she stood, her two-inch heels barely brought her over the five-foot mark. She couldn't have weighed more than 110 pounds, maybe 10 lighter. Her brown eyes held him and they both sat.

"Mrs. Chamberlin, I'm Detective Hennessey. I'm the lead investigator into your son's death."

Up close her mouth was infiltrated by tiny wrinkles. They got more noticeable as she spoke, giving her a touch of meanness.

"Detective, I know about you."

Whatever the hell that meant. He let it go. "I'm pleased that you came down here. You're on my short list for an interview. I waited for the funeral to be over. But, of course, there was your call."

"Oh? Is that right? I guess that makes us alike."

"I'm sorry?" he said querying.

"You're on my short list also."

"I see," he said as he opened up his casebook. She was trying to make him feel uncomfortable. "Do you know of anyone who would try to murder your son?"

She looked at him with a slight smirk before saying, "Detective, such a question. Isn't it beneath you? Regis may have had a few unfriendly acquaintances. Who doesn't? But murder? Hardly the same thing. He was politically active, but what serious adult isn't?"

The woman was wrapped in questions. Already Hennessey was concluding that she was ignorant of her son's proclivities to mix hatred with the Internet. "So, his murder was a complete shock?"

"Are you kidding? Why wouldn't it be?" Her probably once pretty lips were now coiled tightly, the many small mouth-lines fully visible. Her eyes manifested a mixture of disdain and, was it, surprise? She continued, "I loved my son very much. Get that straight. I will not sit back and watch this case get swept under a rug. Do you understand?"

"Is that your impression?" he asked carefully.

"More than an impression, Detective. It's a hard cut assessment on my part. I have three places, Detective. I usually split my time in all three: Chicago, Naples, Florida, and Davenport, Iowa. Three very different environments. I have very few good impressions of your city and how it operates. You are overworked and underpaid, aren't you? As far as I can make out, you're no exception." She stopped abruptly, glaring at him as she gave a once-over to his wrinkled and too worn clothing.

Hennessey wanted to slap her across her pessimistic, opinionated face. Instead, he let a silence come between them. "You know, Mrs. Chamberlin, this is not an easy case. I need all the help you can provide, for example, those acquaintances your son had – those who might have disliked him. I need names."

"Conjecture on my part. I have no names, I know of no individual who hated my son. Do you understand?

Furthermore, he was not into making friends. Too smart by half for almost everyone."

"Very well." He held out the palms of his hands. He decided that it was time to toughen things up. "When was the last time that you saw your son?"

"Three weeks ago, we had lunch, three weeks to the day."

"Your son had a weight problem," he said flatly.

There was a delay. Hennessey waited for the coming blast. "I see your observational powers are really attuned, Detective. Do you want a gold star? Is this your idea of good police work?" she said bitterly.

He held fast. "Not in itself. But a number of fat people are dealing with issues such as self-love, self-hate, and assorted psychological problems. Don't you agree?"

"No, I don't. Are you some kind of psychologist? Are you telling me, Detective, that you've come up empty, and that's where you're going with this case? Because if that is your best theory, I demand someone other than you on my son's case."

"I'm asking for your cooperation. All I see is someone in denial. It won't help me solve this case."

"I'm being fully cooperative. All I see, to echo you, is some amateur psychologist, as off the mark as can be. All I have are the details of my son's murder. A gruesome death. What a terrible way to die. And, you, what do you have? Nothing. My son was overweight. Gee – Detective! Is this supposed to impress me?"

Her undraped, upper arms showed some loose-hanging flesh as her arms became animated. He stared at them, hoping to get her on the defensive. He said, "Anything else you want to say?"

"Whom do you suspect? Why is this so hard for you?" she said, slightly mellowed.

"Mrs. Chamberlin, you do know that your son was involved in politics. You said as much. Are you aware that he was very active on the Internet? That he had a number of devoted sites?"

"As I said, he was politically active."

"Would you say mainstream politics?"

She allowed a slight smile, inward as it were, as she reminisced. "Well, yes and no. I'm a rare species, among my friends, I've been a lifelong democrat. I don't fit the profile. But my son, given his youth, was a bit more, let's say, pointed than I am. What's your angle here, Detective?"

Hennessey was baffled by this woman. Insanity, if it was genetic, clearly issued from this crackpot whose own obnoxiousness was only outdone by her screwed-up son. Poor old Regis never stood a chance under the care of this goofy cow. "There are some specialists in the Department who work with and on the Internet. They make judgments about the hatefulness of some of the content. The FBI also does this. Some of the sites run by your son are classified as hate sites. Were you aware of this?"

"What are you talking about? What a terrible thing to say to me. My son is, … was, firm in his beliefs."

"Are you a user of the internet, Mrs. Chamberlin?"

"No," she said dourly. "I see it as impersonal, as terribly lonely. I don't do it."

"But your son, you know that he was into it."

"Yeess … so?" she said guardedly.

"Are you aware of the fact that some sites can be pretty negative, pretty vicious?"

"Yes, but not my son's. He was a man of opinion, not a man of hate. It sounds to me as though you're trying to attach blame onto him. Aren't you?"

"No, not blame. But your son seems to have been stirring up some trouble with a variety of groups. Do you know of any reason why he'd start sites that would state some pretty radical views of religious groups, ethnic groups, races, sexual orientations, just to name a few?"

She stopped looking at Hennessey. She had a way about her that clearly indicated that she was going inward. Hennessey tried to figure it out but couldn't put his finger on it, except that he knew, at least for the moment, that she wasn't there. She came back, "I need an example."

"Do you know how to use a computer?"

She blushed slightly. "I can have it done, don't you worry."

He reached into his folder and took out a list of 25 website addresses. "Here are some examples. Why don't you go home or to some place where someone can do it for you, Mrs. Chamberlin." He let this last comment drip out sarcastically. "When you look at some of these, perhaps you'll understand the difficulties around this case. The simple fact is this, your son's murder could have been from any number of enemies that he himself cultivated. One of them may have decided to take action."

She gazed at the list. He wondered how ignorant she was of the Internet. She looked back at him and said, "I'll study this and get back with you. But, I'll tell you now, you leave me unimpressed."

"Those things happen, Mrs. Chamberlin, those things happen." He got up and walked out of the room. He felt that he had gotten in one solid gut shot against the mean-spirited bitch.

CHAPTER II

Hennessey was given two more detectives, Whitey Bennett being one of them, by the divisional Chief of Detectives, John Kiernan. He was told that he had two days to advance the investigation. "If you can't, we'll have to put it out for someone else. Burying this one is out of the question, Mark. Sorry." Kiernan said. Kiernan was a holdover from the old school. He was unemotional, straightforward, and had the sense of humor of a polar bear. Hennessey wondered whether Kiernan liked or disliked anyone; life seemed to him to be a matter of moving pieces to and fro. Then, again, he had to coordinate his efforts with Commander Miner and his scorpion bitch Elizabeth.

Whitey burped as he came into the conference room on the second floor of the station. He sat with a thump, nodded his head at Hennessey, and stared flatly at Eddie Jones, the newly-made, black detective. Hennessey watched Jones duplicate Bennett's glare. Great, a team made in heaven. "I'm sorry about your drawing this case, you guys. There's a lot of political spin moving through it. So, we've got to show something, or we all take a hit on it."

"We means you, Hennessey. It's your case." Whitey said abruptly.

"I suppose that's right – ultimately. But I need your help. I sent out a summary sheet on this to each of you. Need any clarification?" He eyed Jones who sat there quietly and sullenly.

"I'll do whatever you want me to do on this. But it seems like a waste of time. This Chamberlin had some kind of death wish if you ask me." Bennett said.

Hennessey didn't respond to the comment because he didn't ask Whitey for his opinion. "You OK on this, Jones?"

"Yup. Guy was a maggot. What am I supposed to do? Interview all of the black groups he dissed? That why I'm on this detail?"

"Kiernan assigned you, I didn't" Hennessey said defensively. "Who would you like to interview? The Cardinal? The Chief Rabbi? The guy was a universal hater, not just blacks. So please, check the attitude."

Whitey snarled, "Yeah, Jones, what gives? Maybe you should interview the Gay and Lesbian Alliance?"

"OK, Whitey, that's enough from you," Hennessey said. "Jones, I thought you'd have the best chance of getting some kind of response from the three black groups that we've identified. But, …"

"That's profiling crap, Hennessey, and you know it."

"How about just common sense?"

"Yeah, sure, that's what they always say, common sense, common sense. But, if that's what you want, I'll head off to the south-side and see what I can dig up."

"Thanks. So, you'll sniff around the NAACP, Urban

League, and the Black Muslims. I'd appreciate an immediate call if you get something hot. OK?"

"Yup. That it?"

"No. I want everyone to know what each is doing. Whitey …"

Jones cut him off, "Have *him* do the Klan. Is that on the list?" He glowered at Whitey Bennett.

Whitey Bennett laughed ugly. "Go screw yourself. The only reason you're even here is because you cheated on the promotion test and you're black."

"Hey! Guys! Come on, will you? I'll make sure that neither of you have much to do with the other, but please. Time to focus on this damn case."

They looked at each other with sheer hatred but said nothing. Hennessey went on, "Whitey, I'd like you to do Churches United, Peace for Life, and Environmentalists United. Same thing, keep me informed." He slid across a folder to each of them. "Here's the latest stuff from his websites about these groups. As you can see, he could really manufacture hostility."

"What are you going to do?" Eddie Jones asked with surprising mildness.

"I'm going to hit the ethnic stuff, the Irish, Mexicans, and Poles. Let's meet back here at about two. Then, let's talk."

They sat there for about five minutes. Jones and Bennett read through the material in their folders. "Got a question, Hennessey. What was this guy trying to prove?" Bennett asked.

"He's just a bigot. What's the big deal?" Jones added.

"Yeah, he's all of that. But something else is going on.

Some of his stuff is so bad, so mean, I don't know, comic bookish, that it's funny, humorous almost. Did either of you pick that up?" Hennessey remarked.

Neither of them said anything. Hennessey felt a twinge of regret at having used the word humorous especially with Jones in the room, who seemed the type to use political correctness to advantage. That, of course, wasn't the issue with Whitey Bennett. With him it would provide permission for a misuse of the case materials, making over-the-top comedy of serous things. He decided to cut his losses. "OK guys, here about two. Thanks." Neither of them got up. Hennessey did finally, which caused Jones to do likewise. Whitey kept reading the file. He was just a few pages into it. He probably wouldn't move his fat ass until two. Hennessey and Jones split directions at the door. He drew two jerks, one with horizontal stripes, the other with vertical stripes – but striped jerks nonetheless. The chances of either of them pulling up something were almost nil. But if he hadn't used the two he was given, Kiernan would be unforgiving.

He worked at his desk for another 15 minutes before heading to his car. While descending the staircase, from the corner of his eye he caught Whitey Bennett leaving the conference room. Big Whitey was on the move, the problems of mankind were about to take a positive turn, he thought ruefully.

Hennessey was given names by Captain Harris at Central Command. Central Command acted as the head of a huge octopus that kept track of the disparate groups that swirled around the underbelly of Chicago. Hennessey briefed Harris on the case, and, in turn, he was given three names: Mickey Mullins, Pedro Tapia, and Stephen

Wysnowski. All three could lead Hennessey into the web of their respective ethnic sensibilities. Of course, not the center of the web, but rather enough of the periphery to understand how and if these groups had a marker out for Chamberlin.

He found Mullins in the Bridgeport section of Chicago, an Irish ghetto that had held its own against the black tide that swamped ethnic neighborhood after ethnic neighborhood in Chicago. It was the Daley home base. Hennessey had once dated a woman from there. He thought that he was transported to Dublin. It didn't last long. Her Irish didn't resonate with his as she was fanatical about her Irishness and she didn't give a damn about any heritages other than her own. He agreed with his father, who used to say, "You're American, kid. American. When you go to Europe, they won't call you Irish. You're a goddamn American, and don't forget it." What exactly these Bridgeport characters were trying to prove with their Irish flags and stupid signs such as 'Parking for Irish Only' in front of their garages, he knew not.

He went into Finnegan's Wake Bar – a dark, damp, smelly, and smoky place along the outer fringe of Bridgeport. The meeting had been arranged by Captain Harris at Central Command. Mickey Mullins would be wearing a blue hat with ND on it. "No, it doesn't stand for Nostradamus, Hennessey," Harris said in response to Hennessey's wisecrack. By the time his eyes had adjusted the bartender, a beefy guy with huge eyebrows, said, "Can I help you?"

"Yeah. I'm looking for Mickey Mullins."

"I meant, can I help you to a drink?"

A subtle putdown, Hennessey thought. This bartender

was telling him that he didn't know anyone in the place; he wasn't going to compromise anyone's privacy. He probably also smelled a cop. Hennessey looked back toward the windows and saw a booth with a guy wearing a blue baseball cap. He walked towards the individual and finally read the faded and soiled yellow letters overlaying each other, ND. He said, "Mickey Mullins? I'm Lieutenant Mark Hennessey."

Mullins eyed him suspiciously. He looked to be in his sixties; he was fat and small of size with a face configured as an almost true circle. His glass of beer was almost empty. "You have it right, I'm Mullins," he said in a virtual whisper as he looked around furtively.

Great! The bastard thinks he's in some IRA conspiracy. It would probably take a full day to get something out of him. "Can I get that glass filled again for you?" Hennessey asked nonthreateningly.

Mullins looked to his right and left before putting his hand over his smallish mouth, "OK."

Hennessey went back to the bartender, whom he noticed had kept his eyes glued to the two of them. "Mister Mullins needs another glass of beer."

He drew another draft, placed it on the counter and said brazenly, "Six dollars."

"What?"

"Well, only two, but I figured that you were paying for the other two he's already had."

Hennessey gave him six dollars. On another day and in another circumstance he would have brought the bartending bastard to his knees, with a stomach shot. He went back to the booth, sat down and placed the full glass in front of Mullins.

"Friends call me Mickey," he said.

That's a good reason to call him Mullins, Hennessey thought, then said, "Nice to meet you, Mickey, call me Mark and we're even." Mullins nodded almost imperceptibly. Hennessey continued, "What did they tell you about why I'm here?"

"They, being Harris, told me it was about some Irish stuff. That's it. Oh … a homicide, that too." He spoke just above a whisper while constantly brushing his hand across his mouth.

Hennessey leaned forward in order to hear him. So far the fat bastard was giving him nothing, but he was acting as though he was surrendering some international drug ring. He drove right to the point, "Have you ever heard the name Regis Chamberlin?"

Mullins looked down at his beer and then to his right and left. Eyes still down he said, "Murder victim, a few days ago. Sure, read it in the papers."

"Anything else?"

"Don't think so. Should I?"

"It's come to my attention that he ran a pretty nasty website – full of hate for the Irish. Ring a bell?"

"Not yet. But keep talking," Mullins' blue eyes now took on more of a focus.

Hennessey pictured Mullins as a huge catfish in the middle of some river who once every year or so would attack some bait. It had to be the anti-Irish thing that got his attention. "The website was called, 'Irish: Bluster, Blarney, and Drunkenness dot com'." He stopped and waited for Mullins to react; he didn't. Hennessey went on, "There were chatrooms for a variety of Irish haters. For example, there was one on drunkards; it drew a big crowd of haters. There was one for Irish jokes; some of them were pretty rank. One for Irish priests, Irish nuns, Irish stupidity …"

"That's enough," Mullins pounded the table. "I know this site. It's been talked about. Tell me again what Chamberlin had to do with it?"

"He birthed it. He maintained it," Hennessey said evenly. He decided to wait out Mullins.

"We've … I mean, some of the boys have been trying to get a fix on the site. They thought it was some kind of wise-ass out for fun."

"And?"

"Well – we just didn't know. It drew out a large number of hate-filled bastards. Some of them were stupid enough to give their names, addresses, phone numbers. Not a smart thing to do. I think that some mayhem might have found its way into their lives, if you get my meaning."

"Meaning that they've had some unpleasant surprises, in their mailboxes? Their email? Their lives?"

"So it's been said," now switching back to his conspiratorial whisper.

"No acting out, I hope," Hennessey said noncommittally.

"Heaven forbid," Mullins said coyly.

"Back to Chamberlin."

"I didn't think that we had left him," Mullins said sharply.

"No, no I guess not. It's all related. So you're saying that no one successfully tracked the site back to Chamberlin?"

"No, no one did."

"Are you sure that you'd know?"

Mullins sat back as though he'd been struck. "Well, it's

not absolute. But I know what's going on among the Irish in Bridgeport, and elsewhere" he said defensively as he leaned back in to drain his glass of beer.

"Need another?"

"Sure, why not? I'll be spending the day here keeping my ear to the ground."

He means keeping his fat ass on the seat, Hennessey thought as he walked to the bar and asked for another two-dollar fillup. He was pleased that he didn't have to pay Mullins for his information; this being a relatively new policy for the Department that when an informant was controlled by Central Command, they took care of the payoffs. Technically, buying the fat bastard a beer was probably a violation of some sort. He took the glass from the bartender who shot a knowing look at Hennessey. Just what the hell he knew was beyond Hennessey, but it left him wondering. Did everyone in Bridgeport know that Mullins was a snitch? Did Mullins know that everyone knew? Was the whole thing a charade to bleed money from a Central Command that thought of itself as omniscient? In fact, it was omniscient about everything except for its probably being taken for a long ride by a bunch of tricksters sucking at a regular and bountiful dole. As he walked toward Mullins he felt that such was probably the case. However, Mullins had achieved his purpose, he established that he knew things, thus he was worthy of a continuing dole; but he also gave him nothing by way of names, or footholds, yet.

He put down the glass by Mullins and said, "So Mickey, how about a name of one of these guys who has been on the hunt for the website author?"

Mullins didn't hesitate. He knew that it would come to this. "Paddy Doyle was a man to be sure."

"Was?"

"Well, he's gone you know. He went back to Cork a few days ago. He'll be gone for some time." His blue eyes emitted a look of coyness and celebration.

Hennessey wondered whether the sneaky bastard would yell, 'Checkmate!' "This Doyle – got an address, phone number?"

Mullins reached into his pants pocket and pulled out a small, rubber banded black address book, which had more loose pages than bound. After a minute of studious fumbling, he gave Hennessey an address in Cork, Ireland. "The U.S. phone number is out of commission, so you won't be needing it."

"How about his email address?"

"I have no idea. I don't do email; it's so impersonal, it's really un-Irish in a way."

Maybe for fat drunks on the dole it is, Hennessey said to himself. "This isn't all that helpful to me. This case won't end until we nail someone."

"I'm sorry this is all that I know. It's a back-pocket issue among the Irish here."

"Back pocket?"

"Definitely. If it came our way and Chamberlin's name had gotten out, he'd been spoken with – you know? But murder? That is too much of a stretch."

Pedro Tapia was about 40 years old. He stood on the corner of Cicero and Cermak. When Hennessey pulled up to the fire hydrant beneath the street sign on the northwest corner, Tapia entered the car quickly.

He was a heavyset man with large, sad, brown eyes. As Hennessey drove, he felt Tapia's gaze on him. "I'm Mark Hennessey."

"Yeah … I know. What do you need?"

"There's a website called, 'Mexican Trash dot com'. What do you know about it?"

"Nothing. News to me. But I do know that there are a number of those racist sites out there. What's the point? Where are you going with this, man?"

"The site had a creator. He was murdered. There's the thought that some Mexican evened the score."

"Forget it. There's nothing there. If I never heard of it, it doesn't exist in our community. There's so much crap out there. Just forget it. We the only ones?"

"What?"

"Mexicans! We the only ones that this guy was on? You know, man, this usually spreads out, Dominicans, Haitians, you know."

"There are other groups, but not those."

They drove around for another five minutes. Hennessey thought that the Mexican was telling the truth. If a Mexican was involved, Tapia just didn't know. He dropped him off at the same spot from where he had picked him up. The interview didn't remove Mexicans from the expanding list, but it certainly didn't suggest anything unusual. He wondered how much Harris and the Central Command had to cough up for this chat.

Stephen Wysnowski had a shaved head, squinty eyes, and a nose and ears that had been flattened and expanded in a boxing ring. Hennessey took a quick look at him in the back of the Polish Deli and Eatery on the near west-side of

Chicago. Unfortunately, he knew Wysnowski, whom he had questioned some years ago relative to a homicide-beating that had been given to a Russian mafia figure. It was a territorial thing, and Hennessey was just going through the motions, wishing that the bastards would kill each other off once and for all. Needless to say, they didn't. He wondered if Wysnowski even knew what the world wide web was given that he had an IQ of a pitbull.

"So, Mister Wysnowski, we meet again. I'm Mark Hennessey. Remember?" He sat down across from him.

Wysnowski sized him up before, saying, "What's your name again?"

"Mark Hennessey."

"Don't know you," he said convincingly.

Hennessey figured that the dolt probably didn't even remember his own address. He told himself to tell Harris that he could do a lot better finding a rep from the Polish community probably by just placing a finger across names ending in 'ski'. He noticed that Wysnowski had aged badly in the last five years; his movements were restrained and slow like he had to pre-think every gesture and comment. But he pressed again. "There's a hate group on the internet saying some nasty things about the Polish. The guy behind it was knocked off a few days ago. Any ideas?"

"I'd kill the bastard just for that. But you say he's dead already? So what do you want me to do?"

Great! He thinks that this is an arranged meeting to kill the murdered man, Chamberlin. Dumb bastard. "I'd like to know if a Pole killed him."

"How the hell would I know? And … if I did, you think that I'd rat them out? I'll tell you what I know about the fucking Russians, but I'm not in it for anything else. What did you say your name was?" He curled his hands into fists.

"Ernest Hemingway."

"Well, I don't know anything about this, Hemingway. If somebody was doing the Poles, he had it coming. That's all I'll say."

Hennessey got up. "OK, Wysnowski, thanks for the help. I'll let Harris know how useful you were."

"Yeah, yeah, I'd appreciate that."

Hennessey arrived back at headquarters at 1:50 p.m. To his surprise, both Whitey Bennett and Eddie Jones were at their desks. They were ready to go by 2:00 p.m.. They went into an empty interrogation room.

Bennett started, "I'm glad that I'm getting out, I'll tell you that. Two of the groups laughed me out of their place – Churches United and Peace for Life. Environmentalists United insulted me. But at the end, I'd have to tell you – I got a big zero. None of them even heard of Chamberlin, and only Environmentalists United knew that there was a website aimed at them. You know what they said? They said they love the attention. Those kinds of websites help them to raise money. They said they'd say a prayer for Chamberlin, telling me they considered him a friend."

"What did you get, Eddie?"

"What do you think? The Black Muslims said that they'd kill Chamberlin if he had even come into their sights. But, he didn't. The NAACP gave me a 10-minute lecture on racism and denied any knowledge of Chamberlin or the website. The Urban League – their attitude – what's new? Who cares? This all seems to me like a wild goose chase."

Hennessey didn't respond to Jones' observation. He went on to give his report that, as he talked, sounded more and more like the others.

He concluded the meeting by assigning four more Chamberlin target groups or individuals to each of them. "So, two p.m. tomorrow – OK?"

"OK, OK, but we're wasting our time," Whitey said in exasperation.

"Amen to that," Jones said.

'Great,' Hennessey whispered to himself. 'These two bastards are in agreement, just what I need.'

CHAPTER III

Bertrand McAbee was exhausted when he finished the half-marathon. He looked over at his running partner, Judy Pappas, who exclaimed, "Jesus! Am I glad that's over with." As was their custom, the pair began to walk.

McAbee checked his Polar watch, which was designed to receive the signals from a heart monitor attached to a strap that circled his body at chest level. It read 155 beats per minute. He would walk until it was in the lower 100s or upper 90s. "We did OK, Judy, 2:29."

"Not bad considering that we've been out of practice." She had just come back from a two-and-a-half week hiatus, taking a one-week vacation in British Columbia and then participating in a week-long conference of the American Association of Statisticians in Houston. She was A.B.D. at the University of Iowa – a dissertation her only obstacle to receiving a Doctorate in statistics. She and McAbee had been running together for a few years. They had completed their first marathon the year before.

"I take it that those two runs in Houston kept you sharp?"

"Oh sure. If you like to run in 100 degree humidity.

Glad I wasn't wearing one of your heart monitors; it would have blown up."

McAbee looked at her. There was a slight smile on her lips, but just barely so. "Well, it's good to have you back, partner."

"Good to be back. I need to get my corrupt ways corrected."

McAbee thought, generally, she was too serious. She was a highly disciplined woman. Corruption would not be in her profile. "How's everything at Iowa?"

"Yeah, OK. They speak about the impossibility of herding cats. That's what it's like when you have five statisticians and/or mathematicians on your committee. But I'll get there, and you'll have to call me Doctor, Doctor McAbee," she said lightly.

She was referring to McAbee's doctorate in classics, which had determined his career for many years as a professor of classics and an occasional administrator at St. Anselm's College in Davenport, Iowa. He had given up that career to become a private investigator, a most unlikely career choice. His agency, ACJ Investigation Agency, had carved out a pretty lucrative niche, and even more so in a field that had burgeoned since 9/11.

McAbee was persuaded by his brother, Bill, "to do something useful and challenging in the real world". Bill funded his entry into the field of investigatory services, a field in which Bill himself was a major player with extensive national and international connections.

But it was Bertrand's call as to the title of his small agency, ACJ. It was a saint thing. Saint Anthony, the patron saint for finding lost objects; Saint Christopher, the patron saint of safety; and lastly, Saint Jude, the patron saint of hopeless causes. Bertrand thought it was a great acronym; Bill-the-ever-practical thought it was part of Bertrand's wrong take on life and meaning. While he loved Bill very much, he thought that perhaps one of them had been parented from divergent DNA. Who that was was the question for the centuries.

He remembered that a comment was expected from him, "Ah yes, I will gladly call you Doctor Pappas, but only if you don't call me Doctor McAbee – bad for business, as you know." He looked at his monitor; his heartbeat was now down to about 125 per minute. The bike path that ribboned through Davenport and Bettendorf, Iowa was approximately 13 miles long. This morning it had been virtually empty, with only a stray cyclist on it.

"Time for coffee?"

"Not today, Judy. I have a meeting in my office in about 45 minutes. Sorry for cutting this so close."

"Hey, no problem. I know when I'm being snubbed. I can handle it," she said teasingly.

When McAbee returned to his condo in Davenport, he was greeted by his white German Shepherd, Scorpio, who resorted to his friendly yelp/bark of welcome. Scorpio assisted him upstairs as he laid on the bathroom floor while McAbee showered and shaved. The aging Scorpio became more and more pronounced in his one-man-as-an-owner attitude. McAbee worried about his dog's increasing territoriality and unpredictable reaction to strangers. His vet said that this was normal for the breed. McAbee wasn't convinced.

McAbee brought him to his run into which Scorpio

walked with a resignation and sadness that stood in contrast
to his loud barking and protest in previous years. As he
pulled out of his driveway, he shot a quick glance at the
dog, who gave him a parting yelp and a downtrodden look.
McAbee felt sad as he headed for his office in downtown
Davenport. He concluded that it was probably time to
get the dog back running on the bikepath. Scorpio was
depressed and needed a change in his life.

His eleven o'clock meeting was with a former colleague
from St. Anselm's College – Marion Innis. His knowledge of
Innis was mixed. While they had always gotten along, he saw
Innis as a aggrieved man who was wont to pick fights with
his own department members in the business school. Innis
was a economist who bemoaned the reduction of economic
courses in the business department at St. Anselm's. He did
not endear himself with the management faculty when
he announced that the reduction of mandatory economic
courses in the major meant that their students were being
denied access to the only true science in the business school,
their management courses being a mixture of junk-science
and intellectual pretence. A predictable civil war occurred.

Pat was already in the office. She had been with Bertrand
from the very beginning of his new enterprise. He considered
her to be a friend, colleague, secretary, office manager, and
wizard. Without her, he felt that his agency would sink to an
abominable level of inefficiency. Red-haired and razor thin,
she had fox-like features. He couldn't be positive, but he felt
that she hadn't aged a day since he had met her.

Her one huge vice that kept McAbee in a perpetual
state of concern was that she was a chain smoker. He never

brought it up because she was too astute not to know about the inherent dangers thereof.

"Good morning, Bertrand. You ran today; how did it go?"

"Hi Pat. Yeah, OK. Got it done before the heat came on too hard. 13.1 miles. You impressed?" he said ironically.

"No. I think that you're addicted to endorphins. Why don't you just take a Xanex and be done with your craving?" she said smilingly.

Bertrand was tempted to turn the tables on her by referring to her smoking but caught himself. "Pat – as you know, I'm in a permanent state of atonement for my sins. The punishment that I self-inflict is good for the soul. It's like the Shiites who flagellate themselves on the streets of Iraq and elsewhere. And be assured, I feel that my atonement is so great that I'm doing it for you also. How do you like that?"

"Hey brother, atone for yourself. I do my atoning in this office with some of the characters who come through here."

Bertrand smiled. In a way, she was right. It was a sometimes daunting place peopled by some odd characters. "Is Marion Innis still coming in? Not to change the subject."

"When people say things like 'not to change the subject', I am pre-warned that that is exactly what they're going to do. As to your subject-changing question, the answer is yes. And speaking of not-to-change-the-subject characters, he sure sounds troubled. He couldn't contain his thinking within a sentence; it was like an audio tape on fast forward."

"He was a pretty combustible guy when I knew him. Very dynamic, very determined. Combative, I guess, would be apt."

"I thought these academic types were thoughtful, serene,

rational, somber. It seems that most of them have huge issues going on in their lives. The image doesn't fit the reality."

"But I'm all of those things, aren't I? Serene, somber?"

"Sorry, this is where I say I've got work to do."

Marion Innis had changed in many ways. He had grown a full beard that came in 90% white, his head was shaven, his face rounder than McAbee remembered. He was a short man, no taller than five feet six inches. He had picked up a huge amount of weight. McAbee wouldn't be surprised if he took a 240-pound hit on the scale, up considerably from the time when he had last seen him.

Bertrand ushered him over to a small circular table in his office; they both sat. "Marion, it's been so long. How have things been for you?"

Innis looked at McAbee in a way that appeared confused, but also with a tinge of suspicion. He said, "What have you heard?"

"Nothing Marion, nothing. When Pat told me that you were coming in, it was the first time I had heard your name in years. Why? Is there something that I should have heard?"

"No, no, just wondering. Your question suggested something, that's all."

His voice was too loud, given how close they were in a pretty contained area. "Marion, you've always been a man of straight talk and getting down to business. Why don't we start there? I know that you didn't come here to pass the time of day." While saying this, McAbee noticed Innis' face morphing into a series of unpleasant poses.

"Someone's trying to kill me, if you know this let me know. Do you?"

"Marion, what I said to you is the case. I really don't

know anything about you, believe me. Tell me, how do you know someone's trying to kill you?"

Both of his hands slid across his bald head in unison. "What do I have to say to convince you? It's been going on for the last five years. It's unbearable."

McAbee said, "Try to be specific with me Marion. Please, what has been going on? I need data, instances." McAbee was also wondering if Innis was on the edge of a mental cliff.

"I've had notes. I've had messages. Things have happened to my car. I'm not really here to discuss these things. It's a matter of what do you charge and can you find the guilty party."

McAbee paused the conversation for a minute as he weighed the sanity of Innis about whom a case of paranoia could already be argued. If McAbee determined that such was the case, he would cut him off and get him out of his office with dispatch. He had enough familiarity with paranoia to know that he could easily become part of the persecuting team that preyed on Innis' mind. "Let's start with the notes. Tell me about them."

"I get messages on my answering machine all of the time – at the office, at home. They hang up right away. They say things like, 'You are dying,' 'We are dying to kill you,' 'You're too fat to play,' 'You're done, over with.' You see? All those messages! I . . ."

"Marion, written stuff first, notes. You mentioned notes. Did you bring any with you?"

"No, I had my car damaged. Another message, 'Kill economists.' Oh …and another, 'Death is awaiting you, my son.' Are you following me, McAbee? What are your rates?

You haven't said anything about that. Why? You are in the private detective business, right?"

With patience, not one of McAbee's great strengths, he persisted, "Back to the notes. Did you or did you not keep them?"

"Of course not. What if they were found? They'd give people ideas," he said as though he were talking to a dense child.

"How many notes, over the years?"

"Hundreds, hundreds. Don't you believe me?" His look was slightly hysterical.

"Why wouldn't I believe you, Marion?"

"Because, no one else does. They all look at me like I'm crazy. But let me tell you, I'm not." He hit the tabletop hard with an open hand.

"I'm still not clear about the notes. Why did you throw them away?"

"You don't believe me, do you? I can't go through this with everyone. I'm being boxed into a corner by my enemy."

McAbee decided that Marion Innis was indeed crazy. For whatever reason, the man had fallen into a world of chimera. He was saddened as he watched his fidgety body language. But he was determined to get Innis out of his office in short order. "Marion, I'm at a deep disadvantage in the investigating game when the evidence is compromised. It is not a question, therefore, of believing or not believing. It's a question of what can be done, and there's damn little that I can do given what you've said to me. It makes no sense to me that you'd destroy notes that could give a giant advantage to an investigator. Sorry, but that's the way I see it. The messages, did you tape any of them?"

"No, of course not. Their very presence unsettles me. Only when they're out of my sight and hearing do I feel some kind of safety. Don't you see this?" His harsh look was unwavering.

"That sounds like magic thinking, not the kind of thinking that a hard-headed economist would take to. Don't you think?" There was no response except for a look from Innis that showed disappointment and surprise. "What has happened to your car?"

"My brakes went out, a flat tire, bad gas – how's that for evidence? Those things just don't happen to most people, you know? And I have proof of these things. I had them fixed."

"Is that the sum total of these things? Anything else?"

"My car was keyed a few years ago too."

"All of these things could have happened through the natural span of a vehicle. Don't you think?"

"No, not with the messages and notes under consideration – no." He stopped and looked closely at McAbee, probably for the first time. "Look, no one believes me, and now I can see in your eyes – the same story. I thought that maybe, just maybe, you'd listen. But you're just like the others, aren't you?"

"Marion, I don't mean to disrespect you, but given what you've brought to the table, I'm at a loss. But if you can get me hard data, like keeping the notes and taping the messages, I'll listen and read. Then we can go from there. If you won't do that, I'm afraid I can't and won't take your case."

Marion Innis, tears welling up in his eyes, arose and walked hurriedly from McAbee's office. The session was over.

McAbee went to his window and looked out over Second Street in Davenport, Iowa. To his left was the Mississippi River – lethargic, brown, and still. Straight out he could see the Centennial Bridge that spanned the great river between Davenport and Rock Island in Illinois. Beyond that, he could make out the rebuilt first railroad bridge across the Mississippi that again spanned Illinois and Iowa. It was a controversial bridge, fought adamantly against by the riverboat interests who foresaw the dangers of rail traffic. Those interests lost the case against the railroads, who had been represented by a lawyer named Abraham Lincoln.

He thought of Innis as he broke away from his reflections. Innis was not an easy guy to like, and in reality probably had his share of enemies. But his reasons for not keeping tapes of messages and copies of notes didn't hold up. Something was amiss. Perhaps the matter would eventually clarify, but until then nothing could be done.

Pat came through his door, "I take it that we're not opening a file for Doctor Innis?"

He turned, intent to find out whether or not she was speaking ironically. He couldn't tell. "No, no file on him at this juncture."

"He didn't say goodbye, and the door is still rattling."

"No, I imagine he wasn't happy with me."

"You have a noon lunch with Augusta Satin at Bennigan's in Rock Island, and this afternoon is stacking up pretty high; two, three, and four."

"Thanks."

She left with no further comment. He closed his office door.

By the time Pat was back at her desk, she knew that

Bertrand McAbee had sunk into one of his moods – distracted, removed. It had to be Marion Innis, since before that meeting he seemed to be fine. Often and over many years, she felt him drift away after a meeting with a client. In this case, there were three likely reasons: Marion Innis' craziness distressed him; McAbee felt a sense of despair because he couldn't help Innis; or lastly, McAbee felt that he didn't handle Innis well and he was down on himself for doing so. McAbee had shown past difficulties on all these fronts. He was terribly prone to thinking too much about himself and mazes.

CHAPTER IV

Sybil Chamberlin took another personal-leave day from Nordstroms. Two days after the murder of her brother, she had received four CDs in the mail. The note that accompanied them was terse, 'Syb, my diary. If something happens, open and read. All OK, otherwise. Love – Regis.'

For reasons seen only darkly, she refused to look at the files on the CDs. On five distinct occasions, she had put one of them into her Dell computer only to remove it and place it on the top shelf of her computer desk. But this time, now five days after his murder, she dedicated herself to her brother's materials. Her decision to open the files on the CDs was hastened by a visit from Mark Hennessey, who seemed to be pissed off at Regis and the world in general.

"So, Ms. Chamberlin, what you're saying to me is that you are surprised that your brother was murdered?"

"Why wouldn't I be?" she said with purposeful antipathy; Hennessey had already shown himself to be an arrogant son of a bitch.

"I've interviewed your mother and your sister in Istanbul on the phone. It seems that you're all in denial. Your brother, to put it mildly, was a pain in the ass. Yet all three of you act as though this was new news. I can't believe it. It takes a long time to develop the viciousness that he had." He ended with a provocative sneer.

She knew what he was up to. He was trying to raise her anger level. It wasn't hard to do that to a Chamberlin. He succeeded.

"Listen, Detective. My brother and I weren't all that close. But if you're suggesting that he had it coming or I should know his killer, you can go screw yourself. Just catch the killer and stop wasting my time." She ended by pointing a finger at him as they sat in the empty employee dining room at Nordstrom's in Oakbrook, Illinois.

"That's the point, Miss. I can't solve anything without the help of the family, and I'm not getting it. You're all in denial. Your sister in Istanbul? It took me 10 minutes just to get her to admit that she had a brother, no less own up to any suspicions about a murderer. Some help! Why, she didn't even attend the funeral," he said tauntingly.

She said nothing, getting control of herself, a new way to get under the bastard's skin.

"And your mother! What gives? Is there something I should know? Some deep family secret?" he said sarcastically.

To be honest, she had no idea about her brother's murderer. But Hennessey was so annoying and belligerent that she had no intention of helping him. The thought that he might be credited with breaking a case coupled with any help from her was simply and unalterably unacceptable.

"Let me repeat. Your brother, problems and all, did not deserve to die in such a gruesome and vicious manner. Your help is really needed," he said with a slight plead.

"I told you. We weren't close. He was into his own life.

Daddy left each of us a large lifetime annuity. This helped us, but it also created the condition for us to go our own ways. Are we done?"

Hennessey snapped his book shut. He got up and stood over her, "Just on the off chance that something comes to your mind, here is my card. Call me, please." He handed her his business card and left with an ever-so-little more of a slouch than when he had started the interview some 25 minutes previous.

Absentmindedly, she placed the card in the bottom of her purse, and there it ended. But he'd had an effect. She was rattled enough to take this day and finally find out what her crazy brother had put on the CDs.

The CDs comprised a diary that went back five years. She scanned some sections quickly and ascertained that Regis was true to daily entries. She did the math – somewhere near 1800 entries awaited her. Some were merely the length of a short paragraph, some were treatises. All were typed by her disturbed brother. She really didn't want to go into this, but she knew that he considered her his closest family connection, another distressing fact, for she felt that her knowledge of Regis was scant at best. A messed-up family, to be sure, all victims of a crazed mother who surely sent her husband to an early grave, after having successfully twisted her now fully-grown children.

She wondered whether to begin at the beginning or to start at the end. Part of her pleaded for still another reprieve, tempting her to remove the CD, place it on the top of her desk shelf, and perhaps just pedal the day away on her bike. 'Come on, come on, do it,' she muttered to herself.

Regis really was demented out of his skull, a conclusion drawn from his fifth entry. It read:

> There's no greater pleasure than that of a provocateur who is able to break down the phony facades that people build up around themselves. I intend to bring it to an art form, reducing the imbeciles around me to a state of frantic confusion. Thank you, Daddy, for enabling me to pursue my new-found profession on a full-time basis. For I have discovered in myself that supreme joy is achieved by provoking others. It is joyous and very, very funny. I had my first great experience today in my new avocation. I went to a coffee shop in Willowbrook, Caribou Coffee. They had a musician playing a saxophone off in a corner. He was a fat guy, like me. I knew his insecurities because I know my own. But besides his being fat, he had a touch of Tourette's Syndrome. He'd stop playing, awaiting the applause. Oh how funny, there were two or three people present, the rest driven out by the crazy bastard. Then the marvelous weakness. He would bark! "Woof – woof" real loud. People would jump in fright or bewilderment. I did – he scared the hell out of me at first. Then he'd play again. I studied him. He'd act as though he did nothing, like it was normal

to bark like a fucking dog! I felt that it was time to prey on the sorry bastard. It was important to me to do this right since it will become for me an art form. So, I awaited his next ending. The two people applauded the overly loud and obnoxious fat fool. I sat and waited. He sipped his probably free cup of coffee – I doubted whether they paid the sorry sucker – and then he did it. He barked! Immediately, I started on my wolf howls. He looked at me puzzled. I howled again as he knitted his Tourettish eyes at me, stunned and sad. I howled every 10 seconds as I looked at my watch feigning some kind of obsession. He picked up his sax to play again, but he froze. He couldn't play it. I had gotten into his skull. I was delirious with joy. I kept howling every 10 seconds, finally causing him to go to the manager to ask for relief, I believe. The manager, a young, stupid-looking thing, came over to me and asked me if I had a problem. I said, "Yes, I have Tourette's Syndrome which I usually can keep under control. But your fat fucking saxophonist has brought it to the surface." I howled some more. The saxophonist started to bark. It was great fun. The poor girl was about to cry as I howled again. She asked me to leave, and I said that I was handicapped, that the fat fuck with the saxophone should leave. He heard me between his barks. He started to cry. Can you believe it? He started to cry. She went to him and tried to console him as he hurriedly put his sax into his case and came over to me, tears streaming down his face. "You are a bad man." He was a fag too; I knew from the way he talked. Oh, what fun. I howled again and called him a fat fuck of a dog. He ran out of the shop. The girl went to the telephone – cops? I don't know; I left. I got into my car and laughed all the way home. The provocateur had scored his first victory! Here's to the beginning of a long and happy career. My humor is as sublime as it is low, as edifying as it is vicious. I see so many ways to express myself in this art form. Maybe someday I'll see this Tourette maggot-dog again. He is set for pure destruction!

Sybil sat back in her chair. She said, "Oh Regis, how crazy you were." She hoped against hope that this new-found art form lived and died on that very same day. If it didn't die, it was bound to get Regis into trouble with someone who did not see the humor in his practice of ridicule.

She bit the outside of her forefinger as she wavered about going on. It was entirely possible that the unfortunate sax player could be construed as a possible suspect by the likes of someone like Hennessey.

She went on. A week later another entry caught her

attention. He had called a night-time sports show on WGN radio in Chicago.

This show is run by two primetime goofs. I find them to be very irritating. So little time is spent on sports and so much time is spent on gibberish. They are neither fish nor fowl to use one of mother's favored expressions. It's not that hard to get through for a call. When they would focus on some sports subject, which was rare, I'm sure that the producer tries to get callers in who will focus these two goofs on a sports question. They had been talking about the Cubs, a team as low down and as incompetent as the two goofs. So I call, and this voice comes at me, the producer in all likelihood, "WGN Sports, what would you like to ask Dan and Gary?" In my friendliest of voices I say, "I'd like to comment on the Cubs." "Specifically?" he shot back. "About the left-side of their infield." "Go on." "Well, I think they need a new shortstop, and the third baseman needs to be taken out in the later innings, that's all," I said politely. "Name?" "Russell." "OK, Russell, you're scheduled to be third up. Lower your radio. There's a three-second delay." "OK." So, I got through their screener. Now the question was, how could I get into the flesh of the hated Dan and Gary, who had now wandered off the Cubs and onto a new hose that Gary had bought for his lawn, proving once again that they had A.D.D. I waited 10 minutes. This allowed me to edit and re-edit my come on to the sorry bastards. An audio of this conversation is in my basement, but here's a faithful transcription:

Dan: "Yeah, yeah – so's your mother, Gary. Let's get to the next caller. Russell, what kind of name is that?"

Gary: "Don't they make sweatshirts and pants?"

Dan: "Good evening, Russell."

Me: "Hi."

Gary: "You into sweatshirts?"

Me: I laugh (HA HA) "No."

Dan: "Did you get beaten up in high school walking around with that kind of name?"

Me: "Yes, how did you know?"

Gary: "Dan used to beat up kids when he was young. Now he's reformed. He just beats himself up. You should see his face."

Me: "You guys are rough."

Dan: "What's up, Russell?"

Me: "I called about the Cubs."

Gary: "Oh no, not another. Hey, Russell, I have news for you. The season was over before it started."

Dan: "Hey, let the man speak."

Gary: "Me? You don't let anyone get a word in edgewise for Pete's sake."

Dan: "Yeah, yeah. Russell, You're up. Don't blow it, man. This is your big chance; your 15 minutes."

Me: "Our third baseman, Ramirez. His defense? I think it's wanting."

Gary: "Wanting? Hey, Russell, this is a sports show. Wanting? Wanting what? Popcorn, a Budweiser?"

Dan: "Hey, leave him alone. He's right. Ramirez is a sieve. Every ball hit to him is an adventure on the high seas. Good observation, Russell. But what would you do without his offense? He's the only consistent power this sorry team has."

Me: "In the late innings I'd use Towne for defense."

Gary: "You're just repeating what those Cubs announcers have been saying for three years."

Dan: "Better than repeating something you'd say. What else, Russell?"

Me: "The shortstop, Perez. He's almost as bad as Ramirez. Between the two of them, why they're like you guys."

Gary: "What?"

Me: "Assholes. Fucking freaks who have no brain."

Dan: "Uh! I'm glad we had a three-second switch. Russell, you're a nasty little rat. You think he led us on?"

Gary: "Yeah, I do. I want to know how the little freak got through. We'll be back in a few. Is tonight a full moon?"

I have listened to these two freaks long enough to know that they were both frosted. Every phone call after me was answered with wariness. I only wish that the three-second delays would not interfere with this art form. If anyone's reading this, make sure that you listen to this tape. You'll see. It's a great laugh.

Sybil didn't have the tape. Maybe the cops had it by now; maybe mother had it. She went on in the diary. He got through this particular month without further incident. His daily notations were brief and non-committal. She wondered whether Regis was like some kind of dormant volcano. Underneath the non-threatening exterior, there were huge movements of plates and molten lava shifting in some process of pregnant violence. The beginning incidents as delineated on the CD were scarily formative.

Her phone rang. Her caller ID signaled her mother's name and phone number. She hesitated before answering. She didn't need a conversation with her – this one-way conversation with her dead brother's diary was more than enough.

She picked up on the third ring, "Hi?"

"It's me. I called Nordstrom's, and they said you took a personal-leave day."

"They're not supposed to do that."

"I'm your mother, not one of your supposed friends."

Sybil's entire body tightened. Her goddamn judgmental mother was back in business. But she didn't want this conversation to end like all the others, fractious and spiteful. "What is it that you wanted to talk about, mother?"

"Well, to begin. Are you all right?"

"Yes, I'm fine."

"It's 10:30 in the morning. On a personal day, I figured you'd be biking by the lake or something."

'Judgmental bitch can't help it,' she said to herself. "Nope, just hanging, mother." She held herself back from asking about her health and well-being, fearing the fallout from such.

"I miss Regis," her mother said gently.

"So do I. But there's nothing that we can do."

There was a lengthy pause. With exasperation her mother said, "Now you sound like that detective-bum, Hennessey. If he had his way, he'd call off the investigation. I'll remind you that Regis was murdered. There's much that we can do."

"I meant, mother, about bringing him back. I wasn't talking about the murder case. Must you always misinterpret and twist everything that I say?"

Another long pause. "Just in case, young lady, just in case."

Sybil had no idea what exactly her mother meant by that cryptic comment. Whatever was meant, she wasn't going there.

Her mother said, "Have you met with Hennessey?"

"Yes, yesterday. He's an ass. Why do you ask?"

"That's what I'm calling about. He called me yesterday, three times after I met with him. Wanted to know if I knew of any notebooks or diaries. Like I was concealing evidence."

"Do you? Are you?"

"I should say not. I have my memories, I have my mementos, and I have the things in his apartment. But I don't have any secret papers where the murderer's name lurks. I talked with my contact in the mayor's office. He'll do what he can to get Hennessey removed from the case. I knew from the start that he'd do nothing. He was more concerned with blaming me for Regis. And where does he get off saying that Regis was doing dangerous things? He never hurt anyone. So gentle, so sweet." She stopped and then went on with a hint of doubt in her voice. "You don't have anything like that, do you?"

"Like what?" Sybil pretended.

"Papers, diaries?"

"How would I get anything like that?"

"I don't know. That's why I'm asking."

"If I had any notebooks or writings, I'd let you know. I don't." She told herself that a CD was not a writing or a notebook, not that she wouldn't lie to her boorish mother at the drop of a hat if such were necessary.

"Did Hennessey tell you about the web pages and chat rooms?"

"Yes. It was all news to me."

"Don't you think there's a good chance that someone was using his name to frame him?"

"Mother, I don't know what to say. Regis always had an odd sense of humor."

"What does that mean?"

"Just what I said. Maybe he was pulling people's legs."

"Hate sites? Regis? Yes, he had an unusual streak in him, but not for racism and defamation of different nationalities. Did Hennessey tell you about that?"

"Yes. He thinks that Regis made it a point to offend people. He thinks that if that's true, that would make for a lot of suspects. I don't know anything about this, so I had nothing to give him. The less I see of him, the happier I am. I have to get going now, mother. Is there anything else?"

"Have you heard from your sister?"

"Two days ago – email. She's OK; that was about it. We should go to lunch one of these days, mother. Goodbye." She hung up before her mother could invent some other reason to continue this useless discussion. The fact was that she wanted as little to do with this crazed woman as possible.

CHAPTER V

Commander Lee Miner returned to the station house at 10:45 a.m. His meeting at City Hall with two assistant-chief Chicago PD types and some smarmy Daley aide had amounted to a psychological gang rape of Miner. Only because of his years in the U.S. Army, and the discipline that it taught him, had he been able to withstand the gnawing and badgering that had come his way by this trio of white bastards. They made it clear that he'd had the Regis Chamberlin case for almost six days, that it had been incompetently handled, and that it was necessary to remove the case from his jurisdiction. Furthermore, he was to discipline his "outrageously stupid lead detective," meaning Hennessey. It was also obvious to them that he was the ultimate villain since all of this had happened under his watch and in his station house. It would not be forgotten.

"Good morning, sir," Elizabeth said in her most professional of ways.

"Not good, Elizabeth, not good."

She looked at him warily as she said, "Oh, I'm sorry. Is there something that I can do?" She stood.

"Just give me a few minutes to think it through …

well … yeah, OK, call up John Kiernan and see if you can talk him into seeing me, ASAP."

"Yes sir."

He closed his office door – a known signal to Elizabeth to be careful around him. He had no love for Kiernan, the know-it-all divisional chief of detectives who probably already knew about the reaming that Miner took at City Hall. Kiernan had contacts all over the city and never seemed surprised by occurrences. Then again, maybe his practiced nonchalance was due to an etched hardness acquired by a career spent in this city of hidden agendas.

Elizabeth buzzed him. He picked up, "Yeah?"

"John Kiernan is in the station. He'll be here in a few minutes."

"Send him right in."

He wondered if it was an accident that Kiernan was around. After all, he oversaw four stations in the region. He wouldn't be surprised at all if Kiernan had been tipped off. But he'd never know with Kiernan.

Kiernan came into his office with that unchanging look about him, blue eyes, white haired, tall, thin, and with an overly-long nose. His bearing exuded intelligence and composure.

"Lee, good to see you. I was here for a meeting when Elizabeth called. What's up?"

Kiernan may have been telling the truth about a meeting, but then again maybe not. The fact that he brought it up made Miner suspicious. "I just got back from City Hall."

"Oh … oh," Kiernan said consolingly.

"Why do you say it that way?" Miner responded.

"Meetings in City Hall usually don't go well for one, and two, you don't look too happy Lee."

Miner had to give him that, "Yeah, well you've got that right."

"So what's the deal?"

"Tell me what you think about the Regis Chamberlin murder."

Kiernan removed a small black book and thumbed through it until he found what he was looking for. "I have a team on it. Mark Hennessey is the lead. Doesn't look good, to be frank with you."

"I know, I know. I've known that for a while. What's the deal with Hennessey?"

"Hennessey? He's good, a bit abrasive, but able. People don't put much over on him."

"He's had the case for six days. You gave him two men. I don't see anything happening."

"No, I know. It's not for lack of trying. This Chamberlin was an odd duck. He used media – the phone, faxes, the net, signage, you pretty much name it – to irritate people. No one was immune from his mean humor. I'll give you an example. He'd put up a Palestinian hate site and draw all sorts of vicious comments about Palestinians, Hamas, the whole bag. Then he'd create an Israeli hate site and the same there. Then he'd take the most vicious comments said about Palestinians as lead-ins to kind of whet pro-Palestinian appetites. It was like, 'See what the Jews are saying about you?' So, all sorts of brutal stuff would pour into that site. Then he would use them to stir Jews into a frenzy. That was his shtick. I think that he probably just sat back and howled. He did it over and over again to group after group. It was his M.O."

"Where does this leave us? Ok, sounds like the guy was a sorry son-of-a-bitch. But that's not the point. Lots of murder victims are sorry sons-of-bitches." Kiernan's blue eyes registered an ever-so-slight change. The comment threw him off, but how so was unclear.

"I don't know what to say now to you, Lee. The list of suspects is still enormous. My men are stretched beyond themselves, and other cases are being neglected. I guess I need to know what happened at City Hall. What do you need from me?"

Miner looked at him and suspected that he was just another one of the white bastards who controlled the city, and yet he wasn't quite sure. "Regis Chamberlin's mother, Roberta, is a bull dressed as a cow. Apparently her husband, now dead, was a first cousin to one of Daley's inner circle. I was reminded this is a clan. Loyalty is a big thing."

"More than that, Lee. An article of faith. Excommunication, seizure of property, and permanent banishment are all likely when you cross this clan." Kiernan said this with an earnestness that sent a slight shiver through Lee Miner. "Who was at this meeting?" Kiernan asked.

Miner took out his wallet and withdrew three cards. "Assistant Chief Patrick Walsh, Assistant Chief Otto Schnick, and Aide for Community Affairs Barney Murphy. Know any of them?" He placed the cards neatly back into his wallet.

Kiernan's face gave away no secret thoughts. He said flatly, "That's a tough crew. They've come up together, and they work like a wolf pack. Did you feel like a wounded moose?"

Miner laughed loudly, instantly, and against his will. It was his first encounter with humor on that otherwise brutal day. "Since you put it that way, yes. I felt like I was being worked on by a group of well-trained hunters."

"And tell me, Lee. What was the message? Is there any way I can help?"

Miner looked upwards toward the ceiling. Then he said, "They're pulling the case out of here, and they want to see Hennessey punished."

Kiernan sat awhile. He finally said, "Let them have the damn case. It's intractable and probably unsolvable."

"Have they ever spoken with you?" Miner finally found the right place into which he could insert this question.

Kiernan came back resoundingly. "No."

"I didn't mean to question your honesty on this. I just wanted to know if there were any warnings."

"No. They were aiming at you on this, not me. It's a perennial problem we have, as you know. I'm over four station-houses of detectives, but those assigned here have a dual-reporting role. It puts you, me, and the detective in a bad place some times. I'll tell you now, Lee, I'm glad it was you and not me. That pack had at me a few times before you ever got the job here. They're nasty down to their bones."

Miner believed Kiernan, and yet something told him not to even try to find a comfortable zone with him. He must be forever on his toes. "So you don't have a problem with them taking this case?"

"No. But even if I did, it would be futile. They've already

decided. Time to pull off Hennessey and transfer the files downtown."

"Yes, and I'll do that. But they want lashes on Hennessey's back."

"That's another story. That's a personal thing. They're already humiliating him by taking the damn case away from him. Roberta Chamberlin will find her way into hell because of her dirty play."

"I warned Hennessey a few days ago about this. He knew the score."

"What the hell was he supposed to do? Kiss her ass?"

Kiernan was showing more emotion than Miner ever saw from him. Maybe Kiernan didn't know beforehand what was going down at the City Hall. "So, I take it you support Hennessey to the hilt in this."

"What I think is this. Mark Hennessey is honest and capable. He's in a no-win situation. Do you think those wise-asses who are inheriting this case are going to reach any answers? That they can do better than Mark? Hey, I know them. Most of them at central are there because of whom they know. The case will regress under their care. Then, we'll see what Roberta Chamberlin will do. It'll be a cousin versus a cousin. Fun to watch." He sat back, his blue eyes fastened onto Miner who was beginning to finally like John Kiernan.

"I have to punish him, John. What do you suggest?"

Kiernan went silent for a moment before responding, "Tell them that you gave him a bawling out that he'll never forget. That will probably appease them. They can tell Roberta, and everyone will be happy. If this is all sufficient, in a few days it will all be over."

"And Hennessey?"

"When you tell him you're taking the case from him, tell him that he is being officially bawled out. Pat him on the back, and send him on his way. You'll have touched every end of the square. That's my advice to you."

Miner thought it over. It felt right. "Unless something else happens, I'll take your advice. I probably should be happy about this cancer morphing into another body."

Sybil continued her foray into her deceased brother's computer diary. It became no better, her apprehensions about Regis being fueled the more she went on. No groups, no person, no religion, no ethnicity, no sexual preference, no physical handicap went unnoticed; and if there was opportunity to attack, Regis went after it with zest and fervor. He began to refer to himself as the master of hatred. His commentary on the foolishness of people was as elaborate as it was trenchant. She agreed with some of his insights when it was directed to hypocrisy in general. He hated haters, but ironically he nurtured and cultivated them.

At 10 p.m. she dialed Istanbul, where she figured it was six a.m. Iris had left a message on Sybil's answering machine earlier in the day when Sybil had shopped for groceries. Iris, the perpetual early riser, would be available.

She heard the double buzz of the Turkish telephone system, once, twice, and then it was picked up.

"Yes?"

"Iris, Sybil. Got your message."

"Hi, Syb. Yeah. What's the deal with mother? I've had four long conversations with her in the last two days. Last one at midnight over here. She thinks that you're freezing her out. Tell me that's not the case."

'Great,' Sybil thought, 'we'll have a war over a 5000 mile

expanse.' Iris, as usual, was on the edge just like mother. Sybil took a deep breath. "Iris, what are you talking about? Things are hard enough around here without you coming at me like this." Maybe she was too confrontational, but Iris would run over her otherwise.

"She says that you've been dismissive and abysmal. No help for her with Regis' death. This true?" It was said in a manner that already held the answer, an elder sister routine.

"Listen, if you're concerned about mother, take a personal leave and head back here. I do what I can, but she's a hard case for me. I can't stand to be around her for any length of time. What do you want me to do?"

"Well, sympathy might help. You know that the sun rose and set with Regis."

"For Iris too," Sybil said snappishly.

Iris went silent for some seconds before saying, "Same old crap with you. Listen, I didn't call to get into an argument."

"No? It sure sounds like it."

"I called to tell you that I think you should really lighten up. Please."

"OK, back to where we are. Why don't you send for her and bring her over to Turkey? You tend to her. You didn't even come to the funeral for Christ's sake."

"I think that you're being really pissy, Sybil. Mother, for all of her faults, loves you deeply; and yet you come across to her as a bitch."

Things were going as she figured that they would. "OK, so we understand each other. You come over and tend to her, and get off your high horse, Iris. Don't lay her off on me, it won't work." Nothing like nice sisterly chats.

"Do you want to know something? Every thing we just went through has nothing to do with this call."

"Oh? You wouldn't know it."

A long silence from Iris. "Mother says that the Chicago PD has been useless. If anything, they've orbited away from the case. Hold on …"

Sybil heard some papers being handled.

Iris came back and said, "Hennessey. Mother said that you spoke with him?"

"Yes. A real jerk."

"Praise to the Lord! You and she agree on something."

"What's the point?"

"Well, she used her muscle and apparently he's being tossed off the case."

"Good for her."

"It will be kicked downtown to some other department. Sounds like the public relations branch of the PD. They made a big fuss about the case, you know. They spent all sorts of time holding mother's hand, but I'm thinking that they're probably a bunch of bullshitters. Have they been in touch with you?"

"No."

"Regis? What was going on with him?"

"Nothing of note. He was on the weird side, as you know."

"Well, he had a different way of looking at the world," Iris said defensively.

"Iris, look. You can color it any way you want to. I loved Regis, but he was an oddball. Never could quite get himself in sync. I don't know who his friends were. I don't know much about him. We were close, but distant." As she spoke, she knew that she was dissembling. The CDs caught her gaze, sitting there in mute judgment.

"Sounds like mother is prepared to take it another step."

"They'll just keep playing with her down there in City Hall. She's using every card in her deck. Everyone knows that they're a bunch of lying jerks down there." Sybil was angry. She wondered why she was so mad, and towards whom she was so mad? Her mother? The cops? Regis? Or, Iris?

"Here's the deal. Father was involved with a New York firm, an investigation firm. High powered, but I sense they really played hardball. Dad would use them when all of the official channels were closed off."

"Sounds like a perfect place for mother to work."

"Please, Sybil. I need you on this. Stay with me. Mother spoke with them yesterday. The boss of this firm remembered father fondly and consented to get involved. He's going to have someone on the ground soon."

"And?"

"What do you mean 'and'?" Iris said sharply.

"OK, let me try again. So?"

"And? So? Great. The objective here is to find who murdered our brother, your brother. Hello!?"

"I've got news for you. Our brother had a list of enemies, as tall as the Sears' Tower."

"Where's this coming from?"

"Hennessey, for one. The Chicago detective."

"Oh? So now he has credibility? I thought they were all a bunch of jerks?"

"In terms of finding a killer, yes. I don't think that Hennessey could find his way off of a barstool. But he knew enough to know that Regis was challenged to the hilt with trouble."

"Mother thinks that you know more than you're letting on. Another reason I'm calling. Just in case you do, would you please be upfront with this private firm. Besides costing an arm and a leg, we really need your help, Sybil." There was a long pause. "By the way, do you know more than you're letting on?"

"Right, Iris. You have to be kidding. You can't be serious. I don't know anything. Period." She looked again at the CDs on her desk.

"Sybil, I have to beat the rush and get to the embassy. Please, try to help if you can. Mother, quite frankly, feels that her asking would only make matters worse. She is sensitive enough to realize this."

Sensitive my ass, thought Iris. Bitterly, she said, "OK, you called. I got the message. Is that it?"

"Jesus, Sybil. Get more therapy, will you?"

"To hell with you too, Iris. Why don't you take a swim across the Hellespont, and don't wear a life jacket!" She hung up.

The Chamberlin family was in full battle colors. No matter how she construed what had happened in the family, it always came back to her mother, the center of all that had gone wrong in the family. Regis, coming up through all of this clutter, was outgunned by dysfunction.

She wondered what her father had done with a private investigation agency in New York. Another family secret that was probably best left in the ground with father's lifeless body.

Well, at least she had been forewarned. Some private

dicks would be headed her way, and from the sounds of it they may be the types to break into her apartment. Briefly, she thought about the CDs on her desk. Should they be shared with anyone?

CHAPTER VI

Bertrand McAbee had a hard night. He awoke with a start on four different occasions, staying alert after each episode for at least 15 minutes. Each dream had the same urgency and much the same message. He was driving on winding narrow streets in a valley town with Mediterranean characteristics, two and three story buildings beside each other in an array of colors that included yellow, blue, tan, and pink. A storm was on the horizon, coming in from the mountains that surrounded the town. The sky had turned into a black menace. There was little wisdom in trying to get across the mountains. Every window in the village was shuttered and in its own way as terrorizing as the mountains. He drove in fear. This was the point where he awoke. He felt that it was a dream where either option available to him was without much hope. After the fourth dream, he wrote in a notepad next to his bed, 'Mountains, village, black sky, Plato's cave?'

He finally went to sleep again when his telephone rang – too loud, too shrill. He looked at his clock radio, which read 6:05 a.m. He picked up after the third vulgar ring.

"Hello."

"Bertrand, Bill. Sounds like you were sleeping. It's 8:05 out there. Let's go, up and at 'em."

"Thanks for the wake up call, Bill. After a hard night, you're just what I needed. And don't give me that crap that it's 8:05. We're an hour behind you, not an hour ahead, and you know it," Bertrand tried to keep the irked edge off of his tone.

"Yeah, yeah. Whatever. Hey, you live in Iowa, the land that time forgot. Right?"

"Yeah. OK, Bill. You're not calling to say hello. What do you want?"

"Younger brother getting a bit cynical, judgmental."

"Bill, what do you want?" Bertrand picked up his glasses, put them on, swung his legs down to the floor, and while sitting on the edge of his mattress he picked up his pad and pen. He saw the jotting about the dream and turned the page. Maybe this dream was not about the present at all but a warning about the future.

"I'm in Chicago."

"Same time there as here. I'm only 170 miles or so, and it's still 6:05."

"Well, so what? You can always sleep. You can't always meet with me and a client. Need your help on a case. A real thorny one. It's a friendship favor, asked and no way out. It's a case that has your name written on it."

"What's it about?"

"Chicago murder about a week ago. Your future client's son was murdered. The Chicago PD has struck out, and now it's your turn to come to the plate."

Bertrand had tangled on occasion with the Chicago PD.

They did not manufacture a valued experience. "I've had my problems with Chicago, Bill."

"Who hasn't? You know all about dysfunctional families. Just make believe that Chicago is a huge extension of it."

Bertrand was starting to wake up, all the while wondering if he was not better off in his dismal dream sequence. Bill was alluding to their own family matters that led to Bertrand's mantra, 'Dysfunction is our middle name.' Bill would laugh at the statement. Bertrand's take was that Bill felt that there was no such thing as normal functionings anyway, Bill once saying off-handily, "The world is built on dysfunction. Because of that, I'm a wealthy man." And he was that. His investigatory services had a worldwide reach that Bertrand knew first-hand had few reservations at hitting below the belt of morality and legality if necessary.

Bill had successfully avoided three assassination attempts over the years. The latest attempt, however, had caused injury; his left leg had hosted two bullets. He now walked with a nasty limp. The would-be assassin was captured in the Cairo Hilton and inexplicably disappeared before the Egyptian police could make an arrest. Bill, though not given to share very much information with Bertrand, did tell him that the man was alive, at least five months ago when it was discussed, and was a guest of Bill in a house outside of Saratoga, New York. The word 'guest' was used flatly and harshly. He wondered whether Bill's guest was still alive and/or in one piece. Bertrand was quite sure the man would never again see the land of the pharaohs in this lifetime.

"So how are you arriving?"

"Private plane out at the Davenport airport, wherever the hell that is."

Bertrand laughed. The Quad Cities was served by a regional airport in Moline, Illinois. Davenport, Iowa had a small, private airport on its north perimeter in Mount Joy. It wasn't much, and he was sure that Bill would exercise full scorn when he saw it. Generally speaking, Bill felt that everything west of the Hudson River was in some kind of terrible freefall from his New York City.

"And the time?"

"I'm at Midway now for a meeting in a few minutes. I intend to leave here by 7:30 a.m. and be there at 8:20 or so. At least that's what they're telling me. I will be accompanied by your future client, Roberta Chamberlin. Ever hear of her?"

Bertrand was now convinced that his nightmarish dreams were omen-like. The gods knew that Bertrand would meet Bill and Roberta Chamberlin, neé Roberta Van der Berg, a well-known harridan of the Quad Cities. Her family roots went back to the founding of Davenport by Colonel Davenport in the nineteenth century. Her family was deeply entrenched, at first, in the lumber business and then in river traffic, barges and shipping. She considered herself to be a blue blood who should be treated as some type of local royalty. On three distinct cases, Bertrand had reason to investigate matters that touched her: one, a divorce case involving one of her friends; another, a hit-and-run case involving still another one of her friends; and lastly, a 'kidnapping' situation where a separated couple was preparing their child for a lifetime of hurt as they fought out the custody game in Iowa courts. One of the parties in this last case was an enemy of hers, thus her involvement. Bertrand had met directly with her; it lasted five minutes, and it was at least six or seven years ago. He wondered if she even remembered. It was not a good meeting. He took her for what she was, a too smug, too arrogant, and too imperious horror. His distaste for her was intense and instantaneous. He figured that it was reciprocal. "Yes, I've heard of her, and I have met her. I think that she's a nasty critter." He stopped, waiting for his brother to respond.

"She didn't indicate to me that she had met you. Are you sure it's the same woman?"

"Do you know of the name Van der Berg?"

"Yes, I do, and it's unlikely that she's anyone other than whom you think she is."

"Maybe you should find someone else," Bertrand said.

"No, Bertrand, you're the man. I'm just a bit confused about her not mentioning you."

"It would be an act of the will to have to deal with her."

"Come on, Bertrand. So what? It's an act of the will for me to deal with 75% of the people I deal with. Get over it," he said in his typical autocratic way.

Bertrand knew that he was indebted to Bill. It was only under the most extraordinary of circumstances that he could say no to him. He shook his head mournfully, knowing that he would have to accept this case. It got close to some line but didn't go over it. "For you, I'll do this, Bill. By the way, how do you know her?"

"Her husband. He was a fairly serious player in oil. Used her money, but he was a skillful man. My agency did work for him on a spec basis for years. He was a good man, had a code and followed it. We had a bond of sorts. He gave me a critical stream of intelligence about Iran during the hostage crisis. It opened up some heavy doors for me and led directly to my company making a giant leap into the international arena of things. He died of a heart attack in Libya. In the magnitude of favors and reciprocity, your helping with this case and hopefully breaking it is very important."

"What does Roberta have to do with favors?"

"It's family. Gotta do it. She came to me. What can I say? I know that she's a different piece of material, but I also know that this death, this murder, has staggered her. One of her daughters is in Turkey. She's her best support. The other daughter lives up here in Chicago somewhere. Seems like she's a pill."

"She has lots of friends down here – very well known."

"Well, Bertrand, I have news for you. Those kinds of friends turn up to be pretty useless, I have found. I think she's beginning to realize this fact. She's vulnerable and doesn't seem to be sure of herself as compared with the last time I met her."

"Sometimes it's not ignorance that's the foundation of wisdom. But maybe vulnerability is a form of ignorance."

"Sounds like your classics crap."

"Yeah, Socrates."

"Gotta go. See you at the Davenport airport at about 8:20, maybe 8:30. I'm not staying long. I just want to see the two of you connect. Bye."

Bertrand shook his head again. Bill's appreciation for the classics was dismal. He looked around suddenly. Scorpio was nowhere to be seen. He yelled out, "Scorpio!" and then sat still, listening. He heard a tortured and slow movement of legs, body, and a collar whose dog license and identification medal tinkled. He had been sleeping on the landing of Bertrand's condo. It was very unusual for him not to have come up to his bedroom either to lie on the bed with Bertrand or, if not that, to respond to the sound of the telephone. As the dog came through the door, Bertrand saw a white German Shepherd who was discernibly aging. He came over to Bertrand who petted him vigorously. Scorpio's beautiful brown eyes gazed back at Bertrand, his mouth opened, and he nestled his head into Bertrand's outer left thigh. "That's more like it, big boy," he said while looking down at the dog with a touch of sadness.

The twin-engine Cessna landed at the Davenport Airport at 8:15 a.m. The pilot quickly taxied near to a squat, two-storied copper-brick building that housed a vending-machine cornucopia of foods and drinks. Such had replaced the live cafeteria that was once there. Roberta Chamberlin's take on Bill McAbee had not changed. He was as competent and edgy as he was cold and arrogant. Even his attempt at commiseration felt like hammer whacks disguised in velvet cloth.

After the Chicago PD, she had no recourse but to request the services of his firm. Her husband had been convinced that Bill McAbee alone could manage through the most daunting of fogs. As her husband's empire grew, so did McAbee's influence on his actions. Still, to this day, she didn't know whether she liked Bill McAbee. But she did trust him, she did respect him.

She was leery, however, of his desire to throw her son's murder case to his brother in Davenport, Iowa. He was another matter altogether. She remembered meeting with him for a few minutes several years back. He was representing a man who had kidnapped his small child during a custody battle. Not only did he kidnap the child, but also he made the mistake of driving across one of the five Quad City area bridges traversing Iowa and Illinois, thus according him the privilege of an F.B.I. warrant involving an interstate or federal offense. The whole incident was none of her business, of course, until she found out that the would-be felon was the one who had been engaged in a faulty wiring project that almost caused her house to burn down. It was with vindictive joy that she passed $2000 to the estranged wife to press both civil and criminal changes against him. While representing the kidnapper, Bertrand McAbee had gotten wind of her gift, thus their abortive meeting.

It was her opinion that relationship success or failure could usually be ascertained by her almost infallible first impression. Bill McAbee perhaps being the exception that proved the rule. When she met with Bertrand in her parlor those years back, she felt instant distaste and dislike. He was fifty-ish, balding, athletic, square-faced, with a pair of small, dark wire-rimmed glasses that fronted a pair of gray eyes that shifted between blue and green tinges. It was the eyes that caught her. She felt that he was taking a liberty with her, not as if undressing her bodily, but as if undressing her soul and mind. Like his brother Bill, he had some kind of eastern accent, New York, New England. He thanked her for seeing him, and got right to the point about why she was funding his client's wife. Her response, "It's America, I believe it's still a free country sir," set those gray eyes several shades lighter. She enjoyed causing a fire in his mind.

"My client thinks it's due to a wiring job that he did for you."

"Might be, you have three minutes left."

"He wanted me to remind you that you brought in another outfit against his advice."

"So?"

"So, look there for the cause of your problems. He also wants me to remind you that he really loves his child, and that you are creating havoc in his child's life."

"One minute left, sir," she was doing her imperious finger-tapping routine.

"For my last minute, Mrs. Chamberlin, let me address you on another level. There is a very good chance that Kharma will come your way some day. Only this time the funding will be metaphysical and worthy, instead of your vindictive, cruel, and vicious ramblings into the lives of good people." With a riveting look, he left her house.

She was unable to respond to his words that smashed her feigned haughtiness and nonchalance. Bertrand McAbee had struck deep and lastingly because the more she heard about the marriage, the separation, and the wife of the wirer, the more she had questioned her propriety in the matter. It was the last and only time that she had met Bertrand. At that particular time, she had not connected him with his brother, Bill. She hoped that Bertrand forgot their meeting and that if either he pretended to or actually did forget she would do likewise. When Bill had inquired of her about Bertrand, she had faked ignorance of his existence even still remembering and living with his cruel parting shot.

As the three of them sat in the makeshift lounge, Roberta gave a highly edited version of her son's murder. Bill seemed distracted while Bertrand gave her a puzzled look through much of her uninterrupted narrative. She wondered what he was thinking. Regardless of that, she saw him as someone in her employ. He would do as he was told.

"I'm going to take the plane and return to Chicago and

then New York now that I see you two connecting," Bill said taking her out of her musings.

"Oh yes, of course. I'm going to stay down here in Davenport. I have some business matters to attend to."

"Would you like something? A Coke, coffee?" Bill inquired.

"No, thank you."

At that moment Bill said goodbye to the two of them and left for the plane.

When the two returned to their seats, she looked sternly at Bertrand and said, "Do you have any questions?"

"I've got to have a totally unfiltered analysis from you. I don't feel that you're prepared to do so, and that's no good," Bertrand said abruptly.

She thought him offensive and his comment without warrant. "There's no such thing as unfiltered. What a foolish requirement to make of me. Maybe it's expected in some vicious divorce case where you're prowling around some motel for an indiscretion. But you are dealing with me, sir. And you'll take this case under my terms because your brother requires you to do so." She was now in full sail. She looked at him defiantly.

Bertrand fought all of the demons within himself that tempted him to demolish her. He kept the death of her son as a constant. "If we have to return to where we were a few years ago, I'm afraid that we're reaching an impasse. I won't be able to work with you. As to my brother, I'm not in his employ. I dislike having to disappoint him, but unless we can move from where we are at this moment, I will walk out now. There will be no charge; there will be nothing, it will be as if we have never met. Nor will I ever meet with you again on this matter or any other," he picked up his notebook, closed the cover, and placed it in the inner pocket of his tan sport coat. He looked at her with a deadly seriousness. How this too arrogant woman would handle this moment would determine McAbee's future in this case.

Her face relaxed a bit. "Would you really leave?"

"Part of me already has, Roberta. The other part is poised to do so."

"You know, you probably think that you're different than your brother. Not as much as you might hope. You seem to have a bit more nostalgia in you, and you're better with emotions, but after that you're both terribly obdurate." She smiled. "I think I'd rather have you with me than either against me or neutral to me. So, I'll not filter with you, even though it hurts my pride. Ask away, Bertrand McAbee," she said softly.

It was one of those signal breakthrough moments for McAbee. He thought that just maybe there was potential for the woman.

They spent another two hours at the Davenport Airport. By the end of the session, he felt that he had a pretty good sense of Roberta's view of her son, her two daughters, and interestingly, of herself. As she spoke, she became more human. They ended with Bertrand in full commitment to the case.

As Roberta entered a limousine, Bertrand called Pat, "Pat, just finished out here."

"Good. You have a one, a two, and a three. You'll be here?"

"Yes. I need you to call a meeting for tomorrow, about

two hours. Jack Scholz, Augusta, and Barry Fisk. We've got a tough case coming up. Open up a file for Roberta Chamberlin."

"Her Ladyship of Davenport! How touching."

"How do you know her?"

"Years ago, I helped with the Festival of Trees. You know, Davenport's love affair with decorated Christmas trees."

"Sure I do. I was at one of the first ones, the night Cary Grant died. He was going to give a talk; he died at the Blackhawk Hotel in downtown Davenport."

"A few years after that, but before I came to work for you, I volunteered. Roberta Chamberlin was the honorary chair. She came down and deigned to speak with us, the hoi polloi. What a horribly arrogant bitch!"

"You know her son was murdered in Chicago."

"Yes, I read it. Sorry for him. For her? Not! She needs some tough corrections. Maybe this will do it."

He was struck by Pat's anger. He rarely had seen it run this deep. Pat must have been rankled beyond her endurance. He made a note to remember this if and when Roberta Chamberlin ever came to his office. "I'll be in around 12:45."

"OK. Oh, Bertrand. I don't wish her bad, but I do wish her a personality makeover. That's all I meant. I don't ever want you thinking I'm a shrew or something worse," she said.

"A shrew? Never. A bit of a cat? Maybe. A bit scratchy? Maybe. But a shrew? Never," McAbee said teasingly.

"Well, I just want you to know I'm not a bitch calling a bitch a bitch."

"Pat, I know that. You're way beyond something like that. See you soon." When he hung up, he wondered how she'd take his last comment, which invited several interpretations, although he meant the comment as a positive.

CHAPTER VII

McAbee was reading Cicero's writings on the Cataline Conspiracy. The incident had the potential to alter the course of Rome's history back in the first century B.C.E. He had picked the book at random from the Cicero volumes in the Loeb Collection of the Harvard University Press. The entire, still emerging, set of nearly 500 volumes wallpapered his office. The books, jacketed in either green or red, had the original classical language on one page (Greek in green, Latin in red) with the translation on the facing page. A classics scholar, McAbee was proficient with Latin, which for some reason he had maintained nicely, while his Greek was beginning to wobble. He was buzzed by Pat, "Augusta's here, early."

"Send her in Pat," as he ran his hand through his thinning hair, straightened his glasses, and put the book aside. When she came into the doorway she caused him to catch his breath. She was the only woman who could cause that in him, a stunning African American around five feet 10 inches, athletic, with a short afro, high cheekbones, long elegant nose, and eyes to kill for. She was dressed in a pair of black trousers tight enough to show that there wasn't a pound of misplaced fat on her lower body, along with a light-blue turtleneck sweater that did not conceal the lines of her upper body. She wore turquoise jewelry that complemented her beautifully.

"Don't get up Bertrand. I know how hard it is on you," she said in full taunt.

"Well, I'm up. So, I guess I might as well stand until you sit." They stood looking at one another. Silently they hugged, she pecked him on his cheek, and they sat. He felt a rush. "Good to see you, Augusta."

He reminisced about her. She had been married to a physician who had, one weekend, left her and their kids to themselves as he fled to Wisconsin for a new career and a new woman. McAbee, hired by her, had intervened on her behalf pretty forcibly. Before her marriage, she had been a detective with the Rock Island, Illinois PD. Because of her professional experience, McAbee had engaged her services on a case by case basis. Their care for each other had grown over the years. McAbee felt that they had a very intimate relationship, even though they had never become sexually involved. There was a huge amount of current that ran between these two very close friends. As the years progressed, her involvement with the agency increased. She was his confidante as much as was the happily married Pat, his secretary.

"What's new, Augusta?"

"Not much. The kids are fine. I'm fine. I pulled down a referral from the Lewis Law Firm. They want me to track a Deere Vice President who quit over there and then suddenly went underground. No one seems to know where he is. Some stuff he signed off on that has become central to a lawsuit that the Lewis people are involved with. I got the job because he's black. They think I could pass. Don't you think that's funny?" she said with a smirk.

"Yeah, I can't believe they'd reach that conclusion given how Polish you look," he said.

"Hungarian, and get it right, Mistah," she spoke with exaggeration.

"Are you having any luck?"

"No. It's really as if he died. Like no one will be able to I.D. him because he isn't anymore."

"Maybe he's dead."

"I know."

"Did he have enemies?"

"Yeah, but no more than other suits over there. It's intriguing, but without a break I'm hitting my head against a wall. So, what brings me in this morning?"

"Not just you."

"Oh no. This a Scholz and Fisk thing?"

"Yes," he said in a low voice.

"So when do they come in?"

"Soon, in fact, any minute. I'm glad you came early. Just to touch base is great."

"I'm doing well, Bertrand. By the way, where are you taking me to dinner? Seems a few weeks ago, when we last met, an idle promise was made to me by none other than you."

Pat came to the door and said, "Jack Scholz is here."

"Send him in," Bertrand replied.

Scholz had been in the Marine Corps or some military outfit for a huge piece of his life. He was now somewhere in his late fifties. A small, wiry man who served in special operations all over the world, he had been of great assistance to McAbee on a number of difficult cases. He was very task-oriented, had extraordinary resources at his disposal, but was thoroughly unethical. McAbee always flinched when he used him while simultaneously admiring Jack's ability to cut through the most impossible of snares and traps. How Scholz managed to gain access to the most recent of military and espionage tools always left McAbee shaking his head. As a further enhancement, if men were needed, it appeared that a few phone calls from Scholz could bring forth any number of former SEALS or Green Berets.

But Jack was super-secretive and super-sensitive leaving one to guess at some of the tawdry things he had probably engaged in over those years with the Corps. For a fact, Bertrand knew that he had served in Guatamala, Korea, Vietnam, Laos, Cambodia, Kuwait, and Saudi Arabia. What he did in those environs was anyone's guess.

Augusta Satin was no fan of Scholz. She had no idea, however, that Jack had used considerable threats to make her former husband come through for her. Bertrand always hoped that she wouldn't find out that he had employed Scholz on her case. Her major complaint with him was that Scholz was a corrupting influence and that using him would corrupt all those around him. Bertrand understood her point, but when he needed muscle, Jack was where he went.

"Augusta, Bertrand," he said as he sat at the table. "This it?"

"No, Barry will be here too." Barry Fisk and Jack Scholz oozed hatred toward each other, the difference between them being Scholz as the totalitarian with Fisk as the anarchist. Bertrand spent entirely too much time managing the two of them who wished each other unequivocal misery. But, Bertrand knew they were both without peer at what they did.

At that moment, Barry Fisk entered the doorway with Pat at his side. Fisk, if he could manage to stand upright, might reach the five-foot mark. As it was, his deformed body looked like a contorted corkscrew which left him with a humped back and diagonally-angled shoulders. Fisk was a computer maven, capable of breaking into gigabytes of data at the stroke of a few keys. A history Ph.D. from Yale could not help him overcome an extraordinary impediment for the teaching profession; he was a misanthrope. Ridden out of academia, he niched onto research and the writing of articles for publications such as the *Smithsonian* and *National Geographic*. Barry was a born researcher who took pains to cultivate an enemies list. His relationship with Pat was deeply antagonistic, Augusta barely tolerated him, and Scholz in his best of possible worlds would hang him at the city gates. McAbee, on the other hand, felt compassion for him. His brains were matched by his extraordinary interpersonal inadequacies. When he had listened to Roberta talk about her son, Regis, Bertrand sometimes made an association between Regis and Barry. Both of them were challenged, their differences in approach being vindictive humor for Regis with unequivocal hostility for Barry.

When he sat down, feet not touching the floor, he said, "I see it's going to be another one of those cases," looking scornfully at Scholz who peered back at him through his mirrored glasses. "As usual, I'll try to be professional and ethical," dig one aimed at Scholz.

Scholz was quick. "Oh yeah, you're so ethical. Regularly breaking into people's personal files. Get off it shrimpy."

"At least I'm not breaking bones. Your record would have you executed in most places in this world. It's just that you're protected by a rogue country like ours where policing is controlled by the likes of you. I …"

"OK, OK, OK. That's enough. I need your help on a case. I don't need you batting the hell out of each other," Bertrand said evenly, careful not to raise the stakes.

"We were doing fine here until this deviate came through," Scholz shot out.

"OK, Jack. Enough please. You both are very good at what you do, and I need each of you. So does the mother of a dead son. Are you about ready to put things aside and listen?" Scholz nodded, while Fisk swept his right hand upwards as if to say 'proceed'. Augusta looked at Bertrand with an ever-so-slight smirk. Pat sat off to the side, eyes glued to her writing tablet. From previous experiences, Bertrand knew that she saw things the way Augusta did, which is to say, that Bertrand was attracted to exceptionally talented and exceptionally abnormal characters.

Referring to his notebook, Bertrand gave a thorough summary of the case that he had divined from listening to Roberta Chamberlin. As he spoke, he realized the downside to what he was saying, Roberta Chamberlin was hardly an unprejudicial or objective observer. There were few interruptions through what amounted to be about a half-hour recitation. When he finished he said, "Our job is to find the murderer."

Augusta enjoyed listening to Bertrand and his use of subsidiary clauses, his reliance on countless 'maybes', 'buts', 'perhaps', and assorted other verbal tactics. One thing was clear; he had severe doubts about Roberta Chamberlin and her ability to decipher truth. It sounded as though he was prepared to spend a week or two just to get an accurate picture of things.

"The kid sounds like a screwball," Scholz began. "It also sounds like his mother knew it too. I'm prepared to give you all the resources I have, but right now it looks like you don't need heavies," he scornfully looked across at Fisk as he added, "lights, not heavies."

"You're right about the heavies. That's the way I see it," Bertrand said, tactfully avoiding Scholz's sarcasm. "I'm prepared to go to Chicago for a few days. In the meantime, Barry, I see this as a case that really fits your skills. What do you think?"

"No doubt. I'm going to have to get beneath his websites, into some of the users, and then into their correspondence. I'll need the list Roberta gave you of some of the sites, but you also said that she was barely familiar with computers. Regis sounds like he was up on things. I'll try to break down his PC."

"The cops have it. Evidence."

"That's OK, as long as they haven't shut it down. If I can access it, I can get most of what I need. If that's impossible, you'll have to use some of your vulgar heavies." He sneered at Scholz. "How about his sisters?" Fisk asked.

"Doesn't sound like he was close to either of them, but that's his mother talking. The kids probably worked around her, I would guess," McAbee said.

Augusta decided that it was her turn. "She told you that the Chicago cops were inept. She had the case pulled from a local station and had it brought downtown. That's not easy. She's that connected up there?"

"Yes. She has ins with Daley. But my sense of it is that it was given over to some professional BSers. I think that she realized that the original detective wasn't all that bad compared to the ones who took over the case. Not one of her virtues, she let them know how she felt. The case appears to have been put out of existence She's convinced that it won't get solved by the Chicago PD no matter what the Daley people try to do. I take it that she feels that she used her last bullet to get it transferred, and now it comes to me through my brother who has had extensive relations with the family and especially her deceased husband. I have to give it a big try. Money is not an issue. Augusta, I'd like you to focus on the PD, especially the first detective who took the case. OK?"

"Sure. I think that I can use the Rock Island PD to open some doors up there," Augusta said.

"Barry, besides looking at Regis Chamberlin's websites, I'd also like to know about all of the hate groups that might be prone to acting out on someone like Regis." Bertrand stopped and eyed everyone for a few seconds. He went on, "Jack, I'm just putting you on notice to be ready to move if I need you. It may come down to some action in Chicago."

"Just give me a few hours notice and clear directives. I'll make things happen."

Augusta reflected that this was exactly the problem. Someday Bertrand would get stung because of his usage of the likes of Scholz. She reflected back to a case in Iowa that involved a private college, Baden, where an investigator for the state of Iowa Department of Criminal Investigation had made it unequivocally clear to McAbee that his employment of shady types like Jack Scholz and Barry Fisk was known, that he was being watched, and that his license and agency was in danger if he continued to skirt the law by engaging them. It troubled her that Bertrand, not exactly a high risk taker, was still willing to forge ahead with the likes of Scholz and Fisk. She wondered if her own reputation was not taking a hit besides the others.

Bertrand brought her out of her ruminations. "Augusta, here's the name and number of the detective who did the original workup on the case, Mark Hennessey. And here are the ones it's under now. We probably should go to Chicago together."

She took the page that Bertrand extended to her. She asked, "What are you going to do up in Chicago?"

"I'm going to visit his apartment, try to track some acquaintances. From what I can make out he had no close friends. I especially want to see his sister in Aurora."

Jack Scholz picked up his pad and said, "Well, I'm on call. There are also a few people I could contact to see if there's any chatter about this case, if you'd like me to do that, that is."

"Absolutely," Bertrand responded quickly. "Any help that you can provide."

"Anything further for me?"

"No, thanks Jack."

Scholz left. Augusta noticed that Barry Fisk relaxed his tense shoulders. She wondered what kind of hell this tormented little man put himself through.

Fisk said to no one in particular, "Once before I went into a thicket like this. This could get pricey."

Bertrand was fast to respond. "Barry, don't worry. It's all taken care of. We have deep pockets behind this. Whatever it takes, it's OK. Be as thorough as you can."

"Well, just want you to know," he said defensively as he swiveled off of his chair. He stood there and said, "Anything else?"

"No, but keep in close touch. You have my cell and, of course, call Pat. Here's the list that Roberta was given by Hennessey."

He took the page from Bertrand's extended hand and left without saying anything else.

Bertrand said to Augusta and Pat, "Things went pretty well between the two of them for a change."

Augusta retorted, "Did you ever think of meeting with them separately?"

"Yes, and I do on occasion, but not at the beginning of a case. I want to start out on the same page with both of them."

Pat said, "At least we're moving forward. They're both going in different directions for this case, so maybe we won't have to have another meeting again with them together."

Both Augusta and Pat looked at him as though they were one person.

Bertrand let the silence maintain for a long period. Finally he said, with a strong touch of temper, "Look, you two. I know how you feel about them. They're both very difficult guys, but they're on our side, and as reliable as could be. A trait they share with you two I might add. I sense that you'd both be thrilled if I dumped them, but I think that in our hard cases there are no better guys to have. In fact, without them, we would have failed on a number of occasions. So, stop looking at me as though I was employing felons."

Pat said nothing. Augusta responded, "Bertrand, it's not that. We both worry that someday you might be harmed because of one or both of them. And to be quite blunt, Jack Scholz and Barry Fisk are maybe not moral felons because they are both seeking justice, but legally they sure get close to the borders of felony. And that's based on the ten percent of their doings that you share with me."

Bertrand winced and then said, "Augusta, Pat, you're my good angels. I'm always listening to you."

"Well, if we're your good angels, then your bad angels are those two," Augusta said flatly.

"So be it. But let me tell you this, I'll never compromise either of you. You'll never be placed in a situation that would put you in any legal danger."

"But you, Bertrand. How about you?" Pat asked in exasperation.

"You two are my very best friends. Know this, I will always fly into enemy territory with what I need on my side. Sometimes that means coming in beneath the radar. Barry and Jack help me in that regard. I hate to use this comment, but I will – Trust me!"

Augusta said, "What do you think we've been doing all these years, Bertrand McAbee?"

"Amen," Pat added.

McAbee sat back and laughed. Augusta always loved to see that.

CHAPTER VIII

"Somebody pissed off the poor bastard. There's no other way around it," Mark Hennessey said as he drained his second Old Style beer in less than three minutes.

Augusta saw him as a tormented man, with the Regis Chamberlin case as just another sharp piece in his crown of thorns. She noticed that when she had approached him two hours previous that he gave no eye contact. His consent to a meeting appeared to be a way of ridding her from the station house. It could also be a black/white thing but she wasn't sure about Hennessey. It seemed that the problem ran much deeper than racism.

Whatever the truth of the matter they now sat in a booth at the Five & Ten Cent Bar, a block away from the station house. It was stashed with cops. She figured that she still had enough of a cop look to pass as one of them in that odd nether world. "How far did you get into them?"

He looked at her blankly.

She continued, "The somebodies, the groups. How far did you go?"

He poured himself another beer from the pitcher.

"Enough to know that I was in quicksand. Like Mont Saint Michel."

She knew that she was supposed to understand what this meant but she blanked on it. She joked, "Your French is beautiful but you lost me Detective Hennessey."

Finally he looked at her. He smiled almost unwillingly. "Mark. And you are Augusta, right?"

"Yeah – sounds right. Mont Saint Michel? Your point? The quicksand? Hello?"

"It's a Benedictine abbey on an island on the Atlantic coast of northern France. I went there while I was in the army, Germany. The tides come in and go out. When they're out the sand is a big slab of goo – quicksand, sort of. People get caught there when the tide comes back in. If they get the tide times screwed up – they drown; they can't move fast enough."

"So you felt that you were out in the sand flats with this case?"

He scrutinized her still more closely as if she was once a far off ship now coming close to the harbor. "Yeah, exactly. So tell me again. You were a cop in Rock Island? That place as bad as it sounds?"

"No. Pretty sizable black population. So everybody makes a bunch of assumptions," she said with the intention of smoking out some of his assumptions.

No luck. He didn't say anything for awhile. He took another long swig and then said, "OK, so Rock Island's a nice place. Sorry." He smiled ever so slightly as he leaned forward a bit.

She appreciated this slight concession. "I was a detective, got married, quit, got divorced, got on with an agency as a free lancer. We're looking into this one for the Chamberlin family."

"Yeah – Roberta Chamberlin! Good luck. She's a harsh bitch. Her kid had a big price to pay. You meet her?"

"No. My boss did. He saw her as…troubled. I think it would be fair to say troubled."

He laughed meanly. "Troubled? What a word. Ask your boss who isn't troubled? Troubled. Hah. Are you kidding me. She's a first class bitch. Tell that to your boss, does he really use words like troubled?"

"Yeah. I'm sure he'll be happy to hear about your opinion," she said airily, trying to conceal a defensiveness that rode across her shoulders in the form of tightness. She caught herself, Bertrand McAbee can take care of himself. And Mark Hennessey is Mark Hennessey, so what. "So let me get at this again. The groups?"

"I had a team assigned to me. Pack of misfits. But I'll say this – they were perfect fits for the bad asses they had to check out. Every rock we turned up had 20 snakes under it."

"Example?"

"I don't know how much you know about this. Regis Chamberlin, the sorry fat bastard, liked to play head games on some nasty fuckers. When I was a kid, I used to know this kid, Bernie Tibbets. Goofy son of a bitch. He liked to provoke animals. You know the kind. Dog comes up to a fence – stuck a stick in his face. Hurt the dog. He'd get a big kick out of it. Did it to a german shepherd – stick in the face. The shepherd jumped the fence and caught him. Ran him down like a goddam squirrel. Bit his face up pretty badly and did a job on his…genitals. Nasty stuff. So they gassed the dog. Can you believe it? They should have gassed little Bernie."

"Bernie was a friend of yours?"

"No. I said I knew him. I didn't see this by the way. I just heard about it."

"So what happened to this kid?"

"Who knows? Probably holed up in some leper colony in Hawaii," he laughed and finished his third glass of beer. He poured a fourth from the pitcher..

So Hennessey liked to talk around things through his reminiscences. That was OK as long as she could keep him on point or get him back there. "The hate games? McAbee, my boss, told me a bit. What did you think? I guess when I heard about it someone might think it was humor. That he was a crank of some sorts."

He looked at Augusta as though she was crazy. "I investigated a case once. We had a big Hells Angels gang in town a few years ago. Kid from the suburbs, Oakbrook or some lily white place out there, Willowbrook, Burr Ridge, I forget. He went down there and drove through their area calling them a bunch of fags and other stupid things. So you'd think that they'd take it as a joke. Ha-ha, very funny. He came through the next night – same crap. They caught him. They put a tire around him, poured gasoline all over him and lit him up. Poor kid was burnt to a crisp. Since you don't seem to get my point," he said in rebuke, "it's this. There are some mean sons of bitches out there and they're humorless and they intend no good. Regis Chamberlin was provoking hordes of groups. Are they as mean as the Hells Angels? Yes. In fact, was one of those groups the Hells Angels? Yes. Were they on to him? I don't know. I just don't know whether they tracked him down or not. But I think there's a good chance that one of these groups did. You see my point?"

"Yes, yes I do. It's a tough case Mark, I'm sure. By the way, what happened with the Hells Angels case?"

He gulped down a huge part of the beer in his glass. "Got nowhere. It's still an open case. Never will get solved. But the kid? Just a nice kid who got a little wild at the wrong time and place. His parents were put into hell and probably will be there for the rest of their lives. But what's new?" He took another close look at Augusta. Each time he did that he looked as though he was surprised at what he saw on the other side of the table.

"So, the groups? Can you share a bit with me."

"No," he said quickly.

"It would really help me Mark. If I uncover anything I'll get you in on the action, I promise."

"Yeah, sure," he said sarcastically. "The goddam file was taken away from me by the Chief. Roberta Chamberlin has pull. It's downtown with the bullshitters. They'll heap all sorts of garbage on her. Of course, what they'll do is break her heart with their incompetency. In some ways I was happy to lose the case, but I didn't like the way it was done. But I wouldn't mind getting a piece of the action by way of revenge."

"Give Roberta some credit. They may have been BSing her but she saw through it. Now she's with the McAbee Agency, ACJ."

"I don't know anything about that agency. I can tell you right now this is way beyond you Augusta. Mega resources might get at it. But a few gumshoes from Iowa? Give me a break." He made a pleading motion with his hands.

"The agency has some sharp pencils. Don't underestimate us."

"OK. Sure…sure."

"But Mark, come on. Just give me a look at some of these groups you hit on. You must have had some cause to pick them."

"I told you that I came up empty."

"So that I don't cover the same ground. Give me a break will you?"

"I don't know anything about you. I'd get my ass in a wringer for sharing these things with you."

Augusta was prepared for this impasse. A Rock Island police sergeant had a brother, Pat O'Neal, who was a detective in the south side of Chicago. A call by his brother to this Pat and Augusta had a Chicago cop who would be glad to vouch for her.

"Do you know Pat O'Neal on the south side? A detective."

With scrutinizing eyes he said, "Yeah, I know a Pat O'Neal. What about him?"

"He'll OK me."

"Is that right?"

"Yeah. Would you talk with him if I dialed him up?"

"No. I'll dial him up on my own cell. He removed his cell from the inside of his jacket. He ran a check on his listings and then speed-dialed. "Patty, Mark Hennessey… I'm OK too. Listen I have a question for you. What do you know about a woman named Augusta, hold on…" he looked at Augusta and said "What's your last name again?"

"Satin."

"Satin. Augusta Satin. She says that you'll vouch for her?" There was a long silence as Hennessey heard out O'Neal's reply. "Well just wanted to make sure…What?… yeah she's tall and she's black…yeah, I'll say hello to her. Thanks for the help. Stay in touch…Gotchya, thanks!" He turned to her and said, "OK. I'll give you that you did your homework. You checked out."

"Does that mean you'll help me?"

"Yeah, as long as I'm never associated with what you do. I'm hanging here by a thread. The local commander and I don't connect. If I get caught doing this, I'll be in hell." He removed from his inside pocket a five page printout which he put face down on the table by his left arm. "I'm going to the john. When I get back I'll assume that these pages disappeared mysteriously. I also would prefer that you disappear too." He wrote a phone number on the back of one of the sheets. "My cell number."

"Wait, wait Mark. Why did you bring these pages along if you didn't know that you were going to cooperate with me?"

He stared at her as he smiled, "Lady, you've been too far removed from us. Welcome back." He left.

Augusta shook her head and laughed to herself. She'd already been checked out. She picked up the pages and put them into her shoulder bag. She went over to the bar and ordered another pitcher of Old Style, paid for it, brought it back to the booth, and left. As she was leaving the bar she looked back and saw Hennessey returning to the booth. She waved, he didn't.

McAbee entered Regis Chamberlin's apartment. He didn't have to use the key given to him by Roberta. The cops had not thrown the lock. In the near northside of Chicago, it was located in a brownstone that had been converted into four apartments, two upstairs, two down. Regis' was on the first floor, right side. There was yellow police tape across Regis' door. A smell of lemon Pledge hung in the air as he entered the apartment. He threw the light switch to his right. A low voltage bulb revealed a small entranceway that had a long, thin, marble table. There was nothing on it. A picture hung above it – Van Gogh's room in Arles. He opened a closet door. There were coats in it and a vacuum cleaner. Two of the coats were winter parkas, sized extra-extra large. The other vestment was a raincoat, London Fog, extra, extra large, black, no lining. A soiled Cubs hat sat on a shelf above the wooden bar that held the coats. He put his hands into the pockets of each coat. He found three pennies in one of the parkas, and a small pencil in the raincoat pocket. The pencil had embossing, that said, 'Off Track Betting – Oakbrook.' He pocketed it and turned to find two doors ajar on either side of him. Entering the door on his right he encountered more darkness until he threw a nearby switch exposing a large high-ceilinged room. The floorlamps-lit room stood in contrast with the specks of sun that peeked through the tightly closed blinds. It was a multipurpose room that seemed to be 25 feet squared. On the south end was a large plasma television, probably at least 50 inches, a stereo system replete with small but expensive looking speakers and a sectional sofa that sat facing this equipment. McAbee tried to picture what it must have felt like to be sitting in this huge room. Impulsively, he strode across to the east side of the room and opened the blinds. The morning sun streamed in brilliantly. He wondered if Regis would have liked the room, bathed in bright sunlight.

On the north side of the room was a desk area clearly devoted to the world of computers except that the PC itself was gone. Evidence. He wondered how long it would take for Roberta Chamberlin to successfully lay claim to it. There was a recliner in front of the two windows that overlooked the street. McAbee went to one and sat. He swiveled the seat and gazed at the room in which Regis probably lived most of his life at least in recent years. It wasn't cluttered, in fact it was sparse. He wasn't a slob. But, then again, maybe Roberta had straightened things out.

He noticed a small bookshelf to the right of the door on the west side of the room. He got up and walked toward it, only now observing an oriental carpet that must have been 20 feet by 20 feet. Of the shelves, the top one was devoted to books dealing with computers, scanners, printers and hardware and software catalogs. He picked out a manual haphazardly. It had been used, clearly thumbed through often. He looked at the others and found them also to have been worked at. Regis was manifesting a geekish quality of mind. Barry Fisk would appreciate this.

On the middle shelf were a number of books that dealt with political science, sociology, and psychology. They were probably useful source books for the pot shots that he liked to take at the disparate groups that peopled America.

The bottom shelf drew a comment from him, "Whoa – Regis." He saw the satires of Juvenal, the essays of Montaigne, and back again to Cicero, Martial, Suetonius, Tacitus, and back again to Diogenes Laertius, Livy, and back again to

Jonathan Swift, Samuel Pepys, George Bernard Shaw, and lastly Aristophanes. McAbee was surprised. Regis had a classical bent in him. Not much for the Greeks, but rather for the Romans. A cynical temperament more or less. All of the authors who found their way to his bottom shelf, had attitude or wrote about those with attitude. Of them, the meanest by far was Juvenal a first century mocker whose epigrams tore at every conceivable peccadillo imaginable. A bright but nasty little bastard to McAbee. He took out one of Chamberlin's books. Not only had it been read but there were copious comments in many of its pages. The 'ex libris' nameplate inside the front cover had his signature. It matched the notations throughout the book. Regis Chamberlin was no fool even though he did things that only a fool might do.

He read some of his annotations on Juvenal. They were witty. Regis was inclined to taking Juvenal even deeper into his cynicism. Juvenal would probably have liked Regis even though he would have scorned his obesity. The two of them would have egged on each other to further degrees of viciousness. He thumbed through his other bottom-shelved books. He determined that whatever made it to these shelves had found deep resonance in Regis.

He left the great room and stepped out onto the ill-lit hallway and pushed open the door opposite. This area was also dark. He threw a switch, finding a small dining room facing the street, a long thin kitchen, and still another door which he opened, finding Regis' bedroom and bathroom. He opened the blinds. The kitchen was pretty basic, compact. He opened the refrigerator. There were condiments on the door but in the refrigerator, there was nothing except a box of Arm & Hammer Baking Powder. This was evidence that Roberta did, in fact, have the place cleaned.

He called her.

"Hello" she said.

"Roberta, Bertrand here. I'm in Regis' apartment. Did you have the place cleaned?"

"Yes. But he was very neat. Most of the work was in the kitchen and bathroom."

"So that's why the fridge is pretty much empty?"

"Yes. I told Marcia to throw away anything with a limited shelf-life. Why? Is there a problem?"

"No. Just checking. Was anything taken out of the apartment?"

"As far as I know just the computer, by the police."

"I'm walking into his bedroom. Was that re-done?"

"Just straightened out. As I say he was neat."

McAbee opened the bedroom dresser: underwear, socks, hankerchiefs. Nothing of interest there, unless the cops found something. The bathroom was the same; it had been straightened out also.

"What was his rent?"

"No rent. He owned it, he owned the building." As if to accent it she said, "Owned it outright."

"There are three other apartments. Are they all rented?"

"Yes. My lawyer in Chicago has placed the property under the family umbrella until we can get matters clarified."

"What do you know about the renters?"

"They've all been there for some time. He didn't charge as much as he could because he wanted some stability around him."

"What did the cops tell you about the apartment?"

"They asked me to leave the place untouched for awhile. Except for cleaning it a bit, I have."

"I intend to remove a few of his books. That OK?"

"Take whatever you need. To hell with the Chicago PD. If their damn police department ran as well as their political machine, this case would already be solved."

"Thanks Roberta. I'll be in touch," he disconnected, intent on avoiding her anger.

He spent about three hours going through each and every corner of the apartment. He concluded that Regis couldn't be that much of a minimalist. There had to be other materials, other personal items. But, if they were in the apartment, they were well-hidden. Except for a few audiotapes, which McAbee pocketed, the basement was empty of personal items and very dusty. It seemed that Regis avoided it.

In a closet, he found an empty hunter green shopping bag with Marshall Fields written on it. He placed some books from Regis' bottom shelf into it. About to leave the apartment, he heard a knock on the front door.

He opened the door and saw staring at him a very heavyset man with bulging brown eyes, a mustache and jaw that suggested he didn't have his teeth in. He had a large goiter on his neck. In a raspy and slightly suspicious voice he asked, "You have reason to be here?" He was mouthing an unlit cigar as he spoke.

Before answering Bertrand was surprised as he looked at a Boxer dog who stood looking up at him with bulbous and deadened eyes. His nose and muzzle were white. He was a woefully old dog who like his owner was weight challenged. They were quite a pair. "Yes, I'm here on behalf of Regis' mother. Thanks for asking. Are you a neighbor? By the way my name's Bertrand McAbee," he held out his hand.

The man, less suspicious now, took Bertand's hand and shook it once vigorously. "Rufus O'Hanlon," he nodded behind him, "I live across the hall. I really miss him, you know, he was a swell guy. Full of piss and vinegar," he looked down at the floor.

Bertrand could not stop looking at the dog who returned his gaze with a sad, sad demeanor. He looked back at O'Hanlon and said, "Would you like to come in? I'm looking into the murder. Seems the cops are sitting on their hands."

"Sure. Let's go Duke."

McAbee stepped aside as Duke the Boxer and Rufus O'Hanlon the neighbor came into the apartment hallway. Rufus went through the doorway on the left, entering the kitchen. O'Hanlon and Duke went to the dining table, they sat, both letting out a big sigh. It wasn't the first time this sequence had happened. Rufus was somewhere in his sixties, Bertrand surmised. McAbee stood by the small counter that separated the kitchen from the dining room. "I'd offer you something but his mother, Roberta, pretty much ridded the place of all foodstuffs."

"Ah! Good old obnoxious Roberta Chamberlin. What a royal pain she was to Regis."

There was something about the man that attracted Bertrand, perhaps a potential to humor. But maybe it was just a simple matter of him and his dog. A combination to end all combinations of man and dog. "You see her a lot?"

"In absentia mostly. Regis made it clear to her that she was not a favored guest, you know. I met her twice, formally.

We didn't get along. Duke tried to take a chunk out of her. The bitch, you won't believe this but it's true, growled back at him. He backed away. She scared the living dickens out of my dog." His hand reached down, patting the dog's head. The dog showed no response.

Bertrand would have paid dearly to have seen the scene between Duke and Roberta. He forced himself to get his mind as far from the scene as possible lest he burst out laughing at the whole thing. "She has a rough edge to her," he said, languidly.

"Ha! Do you make your living as an advertiser? Do you put dresses on pigs? Diamonds on sharks? Listen to the man Duke," he patted Duke's head to no noticeable effect on the dog.

It was going to be a three-way conversation with Duke, playing hard to get. Bertrand smiled, Rufus didn't. In order to maintain appearances and some kind of standing with Rufus and Duke he said, "She's a very good friend of my brother. We're both in the PI business. Whatever help you could provide would be appreciated."

"Ask away," he said with a softened tone. Duke remained unchanged.

"I'm trying to understand Regis. I never met him. What was he like?"

"He was the funniest man I ever met. But you'd have to get by his initial impression. His humor was 24/7 and it could be scathing." He stopped and looked off into some distant space outside the dining room window. As he gazed McAbee said nothing. He came out of it again, "Regis could find a scab on anything in existence. He knew exactly where they resided. You could put piles of clothes over them, bandages whatever – he'd find them."

"What do you mean by a scab?"

O'Hanlon looked at McAbee as one would look at a fool in a Mensa meeting. Even Duke had a peculiar look in his face. "Weakness, problems, difficulties. Anything that could be belittled, torn into. Did you ever pick a scab open…when you were a kid?" He was looking at McAbee as though he were an alien.

McAbee, of course, knew enough about the case to know exactly what Rufus was talking about. He decided to continue the dumbness effort. "So, for example, I wear glasses, he'd make fun of me?"

"Nah. That's simpleton stuff. That's for third graders who hop onto the short bus. He looked for hidden scabs. The kind people were very defensive about. Their being Puerto Rican, or Greek or…overweight like I am. Don't think for a second that I wasn't regularly abused. Oh, and poor Duke here, boy, did he come in for a ribbing." He patted Duke's head with still no effect evident.

"Sounds like he wasn't politically correct?"

He laughed loudly. Duke shifted positions. "He was tough. That's the point. He knew all the positions of all the groups in America. So if he ran into a nasty group or website he'd spew out the politically correct line."

"Give me an example."

"He got it on with the Right-to-Lifers, for example. He'd talk about the sacredness of a woman's right to choose. Oh, he'd lay it on. All the years of persecution, servitude demanded that the plight of women be remedied and that it should start with their rights to abortion. Fetuses don't exist as humans until they are born. They are vegetables, basically." He peered at McAbee. "I don't know how you feel about this issue. So, if I'm offending you too bad. He'd send it out to all those religious groups as coming from a Charter for Truth for Women or some such group. The Right-to-Lifers would go ballistic. He'd get more radical in response to them. In the meantime, some women's groups would join in support of him. Then he'd turn the tables on them and spew out Right-to-Life stuff. He loved to torment. I could sit here and laugh till I was cramping in my stomach. It was so funny. He'd see some poor SOB walking down the street and he'd instinctively pick up on a flaw about the poor bastard. I'm not trying to excuse him, but he was thoroughly funny." He laughed again. Duke paid no heed.

"He'd pick on you too? On Duke?" McAbee said, intent on hearing more about Regis.

"He'd slice us. But once you understood him you saw what he was about. He was a satirist pure and simple."

"Was he misanthropic?"

"No. No, not at all. He loved people. After all, without them, he'd have nothing."

"But he made enemies, didn't he Rufus?"

"Well…yeah I guess so. But look at it this way, you'd have to be crazy to take him serious."

"Not all these groups you're talking about are crazy. But they are thin-skinned. And he seems to have had great skill at getting them wound up." Rufus patted Duke's head, while he crossed his front legs but didn't respond to McAbee. "I have a hypothesis. One of these groups went over the edge and murdered him. That's my assumption. I also feel that they probably hung around this neighborhood, watching, following, casing, the whole thing. They probably found some kind of pattern and took advantage of it. You know it's not easy to do what they did to him."

"Why do you say that?" Rufus inquired.

"His murder was purposeful, planned and very coordinated. I also feel at least now, that it was a statement and message murder. But, the statement was so over the top, the way he was murdered, that the intended message was lost because of it. In other words, I have no way of understanding the message except for the obvious one."

"You mean like don't tread on me?"

"Yeah – but it's the me that's a mystery."

"You mean because he offended some super-sensitive bastard?"

"Yeah, yeah that's it, I think," McAbee said.

"You know what really got to Regis?"

"No. Tell me."

"Anyone who thought that he had some kind of monopoly on the truth. Anyone who would take a stand that stood against doubt."

"He was a sceptic?"

"In his spine."

"His satire was based on scepticism toward fixed or inflexible positions?"

"Yeah, now you're getting a hold on him. An understanding. His fool of a mother had no idea."

"She was one of them?"

"What does that mean?"

"She, Roberta, he saw her as being an authoritarian? An absolutist?"

"Oh. OK, yes. Exactly." He looked appreciatively at

McAbee. It was as if McAbee was casting some light on some things that Rufus only partially realized.

"And you Rufus? Were you alike? It sounds as though you and Regis saw the world in a relatively similar way?"

"It would be an apt statement. The difference was that Regis was technologically competent. He was a Beethoven when he got his fingers on those keys. That sir, I could never claim to match."

"So let's just say that some of the things I just said are true. Did you ever see any odd things around here? When you walked Duke for example?"

"Ah McAbee, I'm not the most observant man in Chicago, unfortunately."

McAbee chose to glance off of that self-admission by O'Hanlon. "Perhaps things will come to you. Did the Chicago PD interview you?"

"Well, sort of. They were in the building a few times. They all have a rotten attitude about them. They make it such that you don't want to help them. I didn't. I mean they asked some of the things that you are asking but I never got the feeling that they gave a damn. In fact, I had the feeling they'd be put out or suspicious if you gave them anything of use. So, to hell with them. But I'll put your mind at ease McAbee. If I think of anything I'll be in touch, I promise."

"Who lives upstairs?"

"Ah. Our actress Nancy Thorpe. Have you heard of her?"

"No."

"Well she's a bit big here in Chicago. Getting up there a bit now, probably in her forties. She's gone more than she's here."

"Who's the other?"

"Serge Pushkin, a writer."

"What does he write?"

"He's into science fiction. He's one strange son of a bitch, I'll tell you."

"Tell me," McAbee said with a smile.

"Well you don't ever see him in the light of day. I think that he's vampiric. At night, he races down the stairs like a hunted rat and he's out the door. Wham-bam kind of thing. When he comes back he's a creeper. You'd have to have advanced listening devices to hear him."

"From hunted rat to quiet church mouse?"

O'Hanlon laughed. "You know Regis would have liked you. One thing McAbee," he got up with effort, so did Duke, "what you don't know is that you probably would have loved Regis Chamberlin. I have to go now, a dental appointment." He removed a card from his wallet and handed it to McAbee who did likewise. "I have had some terrible dental problems and as you know you never want to piss off a dentist."

McAbee walked to the door with him. He asked "What was your line of work Rufus?"

Rufus looked back over his shoulder. So did Duke. Rufus said, "I'm retired now but when I worked I dealt in antique coins. Nice meeting you, sir. I'm sure that we'll meet again down the road."

McAbee walked through the apartment one more time. In the great room he sat on the sectional and gazed at the entertainment center that Regis had set up. He sat there for about a quarter of an hour. Finally, he picked up the shopping bag filled with some of Regis' materials and he left. He wasn't sure whether he liked Regis – but he was sure that he didn't dislike him.

CHAPTER IX

Roberta Chamberlin rang into his conversation with Augusta Satin in the small, low-keyed restaurant in the lobby of the Hyatt Hotel on Wacker Drive. McAbee looked at Augusta before answering and said, "It's Roberta. Hold on…Hello Roberta."

"Some bad news. Did you look at Regis' place today?"

"I…"

"I hope you did," she raced on.

"I did Roberta. I spent a long time there. Why?"

"Are you sure you didn't leave the doors open? What exactly did you do there?"

Her accusatory tone irked him. "Roberta! Stop! Tell me what happened and please stop the recriminations. I closed the door but didn't lock it. I left it as I found it."

There was a long pause. When she started up again there was a teary element in her voice. "You're right. Sorry. I'm just so aggrieved, so put out. It's one thing to have my son murdered and have all the powers that be sit on their hands. As if that's not enough; now they've ransacked his apartment. And that weird Rufus – he was beaten badly. And his dumb dog Duke they kicked him unmercifully.

They don't know if he'll make it. That miserable animal has had so many troubles."

"When did this happen?"

"I was called by the police ten minutes ago."

"I met Rufus and his dog, in fact, we spoke for a fair amount of time. This is very upsetting to me." He looked across the table at Augusta, pursed his lips and held his right hand outwards in a gesture of hopelessness. "Where is Rufus?"

"At Mercy downtown."

"I'll go see him. Then I'll go to the apartment. Will you be there?"

"Yes. I'm about to leave for it. I'll see you there." She disconnected.

McAbee explained the situation to Augusta as he hurriedly paid the tab. As they waited for McAbee's two-door Explorer Sport to be brought around Augusta said, "You were pretty upset about something else during that discussion. What was that about?"

"Ah. It's Roberta's way. She throws out accusations like she's Joe McCarthy. She'll take the quickest shortcut possible to a conclusion as long as the conclusion is accusatory and negative. I'm always on the verge of telling her to go to hell. Not a good way to have to deal with a client."

"Must have been hard for her kids."

"Somewhere in that tightly wound cord of causality lies an explanation for her son's behavior, I suppose. Tomorrow, I visit Regis' sister, I wonder what that will bring."

"The acorn doesn't lie far from the tree," Augusta said with an unusual fatalism.

"Here's the Explorer." He tipped the attendant; they drove hurriedly toward Mercy Hospital.

"Don't tell me – a parking place this close in the visitor's zone. Wow! How do you like that Augusta?" He quickly parked.

As they walked to the entrance she said, "Is there a patron saint for good parking?"

"Saint Valentine," he said with a touch of sarcasm.

"Touché," she laughed.

Rufus O'Hanlon was in intensive care in a semi-private room. A curtain separated him from a snoring male who sounded like a snowblower. O'Hanlon was awake, two tubes invaded his inner body pathways. The little color that he'd had in the late morning was now gone. It was this pallor that most surprised McAbee. It was set off by the two black and swollen eyes, a deep maroon gash on his left cheekbone and purplish bruises on his jaw and neck. They were colors that one didn't want to see on human flesh, especially a flesh that was almost as white as a sheet. O'Hanlon looked, and surely felt, forlorn. McAbee came forward as Augusta stayed in the background.

"Rufus – can you stand a visit?"

"Sure," he slurred, "I think you brought some bad luck to the place, McAbee."

"Looks like it. I'd like you to meet my associate – Augusta Satin," he reached his arm back for her to step forward out of the shadows.

"Hello," he said.

She nodded, "Hi, sorry about meeting you in this way."

"I'd like to hear what happened Rufus," McAbee added.

"You should know that I'm going in and out. They're

pumping some pretty heavy crap into me. All I have to do is press this button and the world begins to get fuzzy about two minutes later. So much so that even this vulgar chump next to me sounds like he's miles away. Regis would have a great time on that snore." He stopped and took a deep breath. He winced. McAbee figured that he must have been hit with a few stomach and rib shots too. "There were two of them. I heard you leave, it must have been about two hours later. I had just gotten back from the dentist. I thought it was you back again. Stupid, I opened my door. Oh! How's poor Duke? They both kicked him and there was no reason for it. Is he OK? The cops said they were taking him to the vet's? What do you know?"

"We're here because Roberta called. I haven't been to the vet. But I'll get there. She mentioned that Duke was at the vet being cared for. I don't know anything else, Rufus. As soon as I find out something definitive – I'll get the news back to you. Promise. Tell me about the two guys."

He was still dwelling on Duke, it seemed. His eyes welled in tears. "You know he's all I have."

McAbee touched Rufus lightly on the shoulder. He felt Augusta's hand come across his back. A consoler consoling a consoler consoling a consolee. McAbee felt a surge of energy from Augusta's touch. Nothing was said by anyone for well over a minute. Finally, McAbee said very gently, "Can you tell my anything about these two men? What they said? What they wanted?"

"If they aren't twins, they're brothers. I opened the door and I saw them. I asked them what they were doing. They got rough quickly. One of them grabbed me by the throat, hard. Poor Duke…," he sobbed and then came a flood of tears. He was wracked by grief. The consoling tandem went back into action. "Old Duke tried to put up a fight – they both kicked the old boy, I saw him try to crawl away. They kicked him one more time. One of them punched me. They wrecked his place piece by piece. They were so frustrated, they came and hit me again. Whatever they wanted, they didn't find it."

McAbee patted his shoulder. "It's OK, Rufus. Can you tell me about them?"

"Both thirty-fivish, black hair, long faces – long, long. Everything about them was long. Looked like Indians, American. Accented features. Darkish but white. Hateful eyes. They…"

A large, tough-looking nurse came to the room. "Excuse me! There is a 'No Visitation' sign on the door. You'll have to leave now."

Augusta went up to her, to distract her. "We didn't see any sign. Where is it nurse?"

McAbee knew that she was doing this so that he could get anything else from Rufus that was there. "Go ahead Rufus."

"They have your card. They probably know that you've been in the apartment. Who you are."

"I'll call security if you're not both out of here this instant," the nurse was now in an attack position. She seemed to be getting bigger all the time, the anger in her face apparent.

McAbee took her for real. He raised both of his arms in a surrender position and told O'Hanlon, "We'll be back Rufus. I'll also do whatever can be done for Duke. Don't you worry." He saw Rufus push his pain button for more medication.

As they were leaving Rufus yelled out, "McAbee, don't forget, they found your card. They know who you are."

When they got outside the room Augusta said, "The poor man – he doesn't look like he was a picture of health to begin with. I hope they didn't cause any permanent harm."

"I didn't tell you much about the dog. Very old, wobbly. It's hard to believe that he would or could hurt anyone. The two of them, Rufus and Duke, are quite the pair. You think that this is another example of my making things go bad?"

"Stop that Bertrand. Don't you think that kind of nonsense," she said sternly.

"Yeah, I know. I shouldn't talk that way, should I?"

"No mistah, you shouldn't," she said gently.

Her humor didn't cause him to stop wondering, however. He was ever aware of his proclivity to walk into cases and situations that seemed to turn ominous at his very point of entry. Those cases had piled up to such an extent that they now had acquired enough mass to send McAbee into occasional bouts of second-guessing. Case in point: Rufus and Duke were living a seemingly pleasant life until he entered their domain. Now they were both in their respective hospitals in pretty lousy shape.

"So they have your card Bertrand."

"Yes and I don't have theirs. That's what would be called a trade imbalance. I'll notify Pat in the morning to be alert for contacts from twins or brothers. In the meantime, Augusta, I'll be careful, promise. What do you think they were looking for?"

"If only I knew. It sounds as though Regis had

something. It wasn't PC connected either. Because they wrecked the house. Maybe it was a book, or a note, but it sounds like it was some tangible object, small, subject to hiding."

"Pretty good estimate," McAbee said.

"They wouldn't know that the cops took his PC. But maybe Rufus told them. We didn't exactly have a full and extensive interview did we?"

"Nope. Old tank commander nurse saw to that."

"Well, let's hope she's around if the twins come to visit Rufus. I guess that's the best way to look at it."

"You know Augusta, when I see people like that, and let's face it that nurse was a mean customer, I think about the way she was when she was fifteen, or twenty. She was probably nice to people. Then I wonder, she seemed to be about 45 or 50, what happened to her? What gave her that kind of hide? It has always puzzled me."

"Do you think that way about me, also?" she queried.

"Oh yes."

"And?"

"I think that you're the kind of person who only gets better. I have little doubt that you're a far superior person now than when you were 15 or 20. And if you ask me what I'm basing that on, I could not give you a good answer. I just know this." He looked over at Augusta, her face was non-committal.

She finally said, "Well you didn't know me then but I'll tell you now, you're right. You're dead right on that observation. I see they didn't tow you away. I was afraid that that parking place was too good to be true."

They got into the Explorer. "I'm going over to Regis' place. Now you'll have a chance to meet his mother."

"Can't wait," she said. "Oh, and by the way how about you?"

"You lost me."

"You know I didn't lose you one bit Bertrand. I don't think that's possible. So come clean. When you were 15 or 20 what was it like compared to what you are now. Are you better?"

"Wiser. Much wiser. Better? Yeah probably. More, now, of a free agent. The forces making a bid on my life in those years were fewer but intense and I was less a fortress in those days. Now…there are a lot more forces, but more dispersed and I'm more fortified. That's what I mean by being more of a free agent…does any of what I just said make sense?"

She touched his knee and said, "Yes, of course. But with all of these fortress analyses, I feel that I'm watching a Lord of the Rings movie. Are you trying to be Gandolf?"

He laughed, "No smart aleck. This isn't middle earth, either."

Roberta Chamberlin was sitting in the lounger in Regis' great room. She was staring into space as McAbee and Augusta came upon her. The lights throughout the room were dimmed pretty low.

"Roberta," he said just above a whisper.

"Yeah it's me Bertrand." She brought the foot rest down and got up. There was a muffled sigh from her. "And who is this with you?" She walked toward Bertrand and Augusta. When she drew near she said, "My, you are a tall woman," she held out her hand, "Roberta Chamberlin."

"Augusta Satin, I work cases with Bertrand, pleased to meet you, but I'm sorry about the circumstances."

Roberta shook her head despairingly, "I know, I know."

McAbee wandered around the room leaving Augusta with the work of consoling Roberta. He was struck with the thoroughness of the disaster caused by the twins – a word he was now using regularly to describe the two creeps who hurt Rufus O'Hanlon. The magnificent carpet that had covered a large portion of the floor had been rolled haphazardly and pulled to and fro across the room. It sat partially folded but at angles. It didn't appear to have been damaged, which could not be said for the sectional. They slit each part and removed much of the styrofoam stuffing. Most of it was strewn in the entertainment center area. The television appeared to be whole and undamaged. He turned back. The lounger where Roberta sat seemed to be without damage. He found that odd.

He went over to the three shelved bookcase. Many of the books had been tossed around the room but, he guessed, only after being shaken and inspected.

His eyes roamed to the bottom shelf, those books also had been tossed except for one volume of the Loeb series on Aristophanes. He picked it up and inspected it. Other than a few marginal notes from Regis he saw nothing unusual about the book. He looked back and saw that Roberta and Augusta were still chatting, Roberta seated on the lounger again while Augusta had rolled the office chair over toward her.

He left the room and crossed the hall into the kitchen/dining room area. The devastation was bad, but because Regis had been sparse with his furnishings, the mess had a natural limit to it. Pots and pans had been thrown around the kitchen, cabinets opened – contents askew, the dining room table was on its end as were three of the four chairs. He noticed a dark red stream across the floor – probably the blood of Rufus. The bedroom and bathroom had taken a like assault. His clothes, which Bertrand had inspected with great care in the morning, had been tossed all over the bedroom. He noticed that almost all of the pant pockets had been inside-outed. This suggested support for Augusta's hypothesis: that they were looking for some object or some small entity that could fit into a pants pocket.

He went back to the great room. The two women appeared to have connected, Bertrand felt a tinge of envy at this – it was a trait that he rarely noticed in men. He went over to them, "Excuse me, I'm going to go upstairs and see if either of those two are in. Are both of you OK?"

"We're doing fine," Roberta said to him as she turned her attention back to Augusta who before she turned back to Roberta gave a wide wink to Bertrand. He stood there for a few seconds distinctly feeling the way he felt when he had read an article in a recent *New York Times*. It was in the Science section of a Tuesday's paper, 'Are Males Really Necessary?' he smiled to himself over his silly tinge of jealousy.

He crouched under the taped areas and proceeded upstairs. Nancy Thorpe's place was over Regis' apartment. He knocked once softly, waited, again hard, waited, and again harder, very hard. He was about to leave for the other apartment when he heard a reply.

"Yesh. Who ish it? That you Weshley?"

He didn't know what to expect but he did know that

it was unlikely that a successful actress would speak with a lisp. But if she was drunk, that was another story. That was probably the right story. He heard a chain being drawn off the door, a double lock being disengaged and then the door opened wide. Her silken robe was peach colored and was barely tied. Half of each of her breasts were exposed but only for about two seconds before she moved both hands to each lapel and tightened the robe's coverage of her assets.

"Who the fuck are yoush? I thought yoush was Weshley." She squinted in a way that suggested that the vision of McAbee was a vile apparition. If she squinted long and hard enough he would disappear, perhaps.

"I'm representing the Chamberlin family. I'm Bertrand McAbee, I'm a private investigator."

"Well laddy da for yoush. Now couldja be good enough to go away?" She put her palm on the door and was about to close it.

McAbee returned the pressure. "Listen Regis' apartment was ransacked this afternoon and your neighbor Rufus was beaten up badly. I have to ask you some questions. It's important."

"Rufush? Oh no. And the doggie – Duke, Duke ish he OK?"

"No. He's in bad shape." He noticed that her bathrobe was open again, more breast, less awareness.

"I've been here all day, all the goddamn day. If things were going on, I didn't hear anything. By the way I'm drunker than pish. I'm on a toot Macaberry. Shorry, I can't help you." She peered at him closely and then said, "I'm going to puke. Closh the door when you're gone." She scampered off to her bathroom.

McAbee could hear the wretching noises coming from deep in the apartment. He grabbed the doorknob and shut her door, it was useless to persist.

He went across the hall and knocked at Serge Pushkin's door, again having to go from a series of soft knocks to some very hard ones.

He was pretty sure that he heard a noise come from this apartment but nothing came of it as no response was given to his efforts. He took out two of his cards and wrote identical messages on each of them. 'Please call ASAP. Rufus O'Hanlon is hurt badly and Regis' apartment has been ransacked.' He slid a card under each door and retreated downstairs.

Augusta and Roberta were still at it. He thought to himself, 'Wow. Maybe males really aren't needed.'

CHAPTER X

Even Barry Fisk was astounded at the number of hate sites that were laid on the abundant roads and paths of the world wide web. He quickly decided that any existing group or entity which stood for something that in almost any conceivable way could draw an opposition to its existence, that is, could raise the ire of some counter-force, would be nearly guaranteed to provoke an attack in the virtual world. On these roads of confusion a gifted and cagey traveler could find a world of infinite possibilities. Barry Fisk considered himself such a traveler. Regis Chamberlin, however, while gifted was not cagey. His whereabouts were discoverable. The web game, if you were going to play it, had one fundamental rule: never let your physical whereabouts be compromised. After all, virtual opposition could very easily become real opposition in the form of a noose. One could be at the end of a heavy rope tied around the cement supporting beams of the underpass to I-55 and Cicero Avenue. The virtual highway was peopled with murderers, pederasts, thieves, rapists, spies, terrorists, and assorted other nasties. Regis had let his satirical funny bone get in front of his common sense.

Regis had a very distinctive style of writing and he was

given to using a structure of entry that led with the word 'committee' or 'task force.' Thus, from the list supplied by Regis' mother and the much longer list faxed by Augusta, Barry easily found the sites that Regis had established for the purposes of drawing the mongers who would be attracted to his lead, for example, his Task Force to Disarm the Drunken Irish Catholics AKA IRA. Thus, any search entry made by a researcher or curiosity seeker that led with Task Force, Disarm, Drunken, Irish, Catholics, IRA could potentially get them engaged. If they narrowed their scope they could enter, 'Drunken Irish,' 'Disarm Catholics' and so on. One Regis mistake was to seek out financial contributors for some of the causes he espoused at each site. Was this some kind of effort to legitimize his site? Did he receive money? What did he do with it if he did? All of these questions needed an answer.

The content in each website was staggering in its quantity and its vitriol. Each one had a chat room that Barry wandered into as an observer. He was picking up chatter about Irish Catholics in Northern Ireland from people as far a field as South Africa, Peru, Iceland, China, and Canada. Many of the correspondents were without restraint as they hammered out their opinions in a no-holds-barred manner.

Barry Fisk stopped his work after awhile and reflected on himself. He knew that he was no angel. His mean-spiritedness, lack of patience, anger, and pettiness got the best of him in many situations. He found that it was best to avoid people because of his naturally contentious nature. So meanness was not alien to him. But he always felt that his meanness had some kind of intellectual center. In the blogs and chat rooms, however, he felt that he was in the center of a bankrupt culture that was fueled by sheer thoughtlessness, hatred, and ignorance. These cyber areas made him rethink some of his own actions, some of his personal pettiness; they brought him face-to-face with parts of his dark side.

But Regis Chamberlin reacted differently. Apparently he saw the whole affair as one of great farce. So, on the one hand, Barry felt personal embarrassment and discomfort at what he read while, on the other hand, Regis may have howled with laughter at the senseless dolts who fell into his coy trap.

He kept a record of the box numbers for each of the sites registered by Chamberlin. So, for example, he would engage the rhetoric of the Jewish Defense League except that he would advance their rhetoric to absurd levels. So if the JDL accused an author, e.g., of being an anti-Semite, Regis would jump onto this train, but he would also implicate the author's publishing company, his college, his professors and so on. The JDL would, of course, feel discomfort at the extremes that Regis would go to. He would also solicit funds on behalf of the JDL and its causes. These were to be sent to a post office box that he had registered in Chicago. Whether he ever received a nickel was unknown. What he could have done with a received nickel was also unknown. Barry knew of no way an organization could stop someone from soliciting funds for them as long as the solicitor did not claim to be a member or an official of the organization. Regis was very careful to make it clear that he was not a member of the Jewish Defense League, the Irish Republican Army, the Palestine Liberation Organization, the Communist Party of the United States, People for the Ethical Treatment of

Animals and a host of other organizations that fell to his satire and taunts.

Of course, when he would send his extreme words in supposed support of a PLO position over to a JDL chat room a flurry of vicious responses would follow. Fisk tracked what he could while imagining what had happened over the history of Regis' manipulations, in the face of the radicalism and abundantly rhetorical sub-cultures with whom he was entangling himself.

But Regis tinkered with some nasties. If he had gone after the Orange Growers Association or Travel Arizona he probably could have used those venues for years and come out unscathed. People just didn't give a damn. But old Regis went after people with mega-issues and mega-chips on their stressed shoulders.

He downloaded some comments aimed at Regis:

- "You will be hunted down like a filthy pig; we're on to you. Pig!" PLO Pal
- "Scum like you will meet a bitter end in your day." Moses of Moab
- "Death to the JDL and you, like the filthy Jews you represent, you will die." The Sheik of Tripoli
- "We will sit by no longer, your life is worthless and will be taken." A Bronx Jew
- "Stay out of Irish affairs or else," the Orange Vengeance
- "Collecting money for the Belfast establishment is a stake aimed at the heart of the majority of the Catholic population of Northern Ireland. Assassination is called for." The Shamrocker

- "IRA fundraising is a terrorist activity. Terrorism will come your way." Dean of Belfast
- "I know who you are. Death is nigh." Salamander for a Free Ireland
- "Skinning is my pleasure. Skinning PETA enemies is my passion. Skinning viruses like you is my adoration. You are warned." PETA Peter
- "A bunch of us work for the fur industry. I have children. You are attacking me and them. I will defend myself. Pennies will be poured down your throat." Fur Man
- "Commie sympathizer! The revolution is over but you're too stupid to realize it. Communism has probably murdered over 200 million people in its day. Think of it. And now bottom feeders like you come out and try to resurrect the infamy. Many stood by and let your likes destroy them through your organizing tactics. You can now erase that as an option. I will personally see to your death. I know who you are and where you are." Escapee from Estonia
- "Beat your chest you fool. You raise money to put a nail in our coffin? Capitalist pigs and vermin! Know that the revolution was subverted by Mao and Stalin. It has never happened but it will and you will be on the end of its spear. How dare you." A true Communist
- "Your likes have kept us down for centuries. You have taken our land, you have raped our women, you have torn the soul out of the American Indian. Now that we have our casinos and are tearing the

soul out of you white crap by hooking you on our slot machines you organize to take our licenses away. You violate our treaties which you now see as favoring us. You are a person to tear a heart from, to take a scalp from. I will do this." Indian Freedom

• "Defending the filthy and vile Indians is wrong. They have taken advantage of vague treaty language and short-sighted politicians. To have the gall to raise money for their legal defense is repulsive. I will not tolerate this. Death belongs in your house." Free Enterprise Jason

Barry Fisk printed off these and many others that caught his interest. In each instance, he was most concerned with the evident threats that were there but he was also looking for a quality of nastiness that he thought could transfer into action. He piled up all of the printouts and decided to take a rest. He wondered how McAbee would approach what he was beginning to feel was an almost impossible case. Suspects were everywhere – ubiquitous was the word. Yes, ubiquitous.

McAbee and Satin were back at the Hyatt by 11:45 p.m. As they walked through the lobby toward the elevators she said, "Hey quiet man. How about buying me a beer at the bar over there?" she pointed to a bar area about 150 feet to their left. He had hardly uttered a word during the drive home from Regis' place. That was a part of him she had come to know and respect. But she sometimes felt that it could go beyond what was good for him. This would lead her to test him such as she was doing at this moment. He was so self-absorbed that he didn't answer. She stopped and grabbed his arm gently. He looked at her as though she was a stranger, clearly surprised by her. "Hey Mistah – I asked you a question. More than that I propositioned you to make a purchase and what do I get? Silence. A deep freeze. Oh my, oh my – there was a day when I got full attention but now? A beer? Do I get a beer? After a full night of work? Mistah, mistah." She observed a variety of reactions in his demeanor. But almost without fail – her exaggerated use of the word 'Mistah' – with an elongation on the 'ah' almost always drew a laugh or at least a full smile from him. Oh! It worked again.

"I know, I know, Augusta. I'm being a recluse. Of course I'll buy you a beer and anything else you want…but you have to answer a question. Did you really ask me a question before, like you said that you did?"

Again, she took him by the arm and they started to walk toward the bar. She said, "I did but I was mumbling, the lobby's loud. I just wanted you to feel sorry for me is all."

He shook his head once. He was puzzled. "There's a seat over there. That OK?"

"Sure, sure this is great." They ordered, she a Michelob Light, he an O'Douls. Why he didn't drink alcohol she didn't know, but he never had a drink in her presence. "Learn anything over there?"

"Hard to say. The actress upstairs was drunk as hell. She first thought that I was Wesley. When I disappointed her on that score she tried to slam the door on me."

"Sounds like she didn't hear anything from downstairs, in that condition."

"Yes, she wasn't hearing anything. I'm pretty close to writing her off but she did give me a sideshow," he said coyly.

She knew she was supposed to bite. She did. "Side show? What does that mean?"

"Her abundant breasts kept trying to escape from behind her bathrobe."

She feigned surprise. "I'm really shocked, you bringing up this matter knowing full well that I'm a lady. You're a lucky man that I'm not given to blushing." He laughed. "What's so funny mistah? You making fun of my innocence?"

"Never my dear. Your innocence is widely known and beyond reproach. Plus, I don't know what all of this has to do with you. I'm talking about a flashing woman throwing a lot of flesh my way. I thought she had them covered but they popped out again. This, of course, earned me a dirty look from her. It was as if I had coaxed them out. Regardless, it's not relevant to the investigation. I think the whole show was meant for Wesley, anyway."

"I've heard that before."

"At the end of it all, she ran to her bathroom and vomited," he stated flatly.

She laughed. "You know Bertrand these things only happen to you. It's not the breasts, it's not the puking. It's the combination, only you," she said laughing her way through the words.

And he laughed too as the dark mood passed away from him. "My luck was better across the hall with the science fiction writer."

"What did you learn there?"

"He wasn't home."

"Caught me," she said laughing.

With a little more seriousness he said, "I think that you were right. The twins were looking for some object, something that they thought Regis had hidden. Something that could fit into a pants pocket."

"His clothes, turned out?"

"Yeah."

"Think they found it?"

"No. I think that something has unsettled them. Something is still out there. But they have my card via Rufus."

"Do you think that they think you might have this object?"

"Possible."

"Are you packing?"

"No," he said sheepishly.

This last admission didn't surprise Augusta. There was a running dispute between them about his lack of preparedness and disdain for weapons in general. She saw no benefit in reminding him of his folly. He would just dig in his heels deeper. "They sound like a pretty rough pair. Let's stay vigilant Bertrand. I *am* packing in case you were wondering."

He gazed at her for a moment. He said, "That's one of the many reasons I find you sexy. It's really reassuring to know that the person next to you can blow you away if you do something that irritates them, like not having a gun on me."

"Whoa! I didn't say anything. Don't you go throwing thoughts into my mind now," she said lightheartedly. He had her thoughts figured out all too well.

McAbee could shift a subject as quickly and deftly as a mercurial artist his art. "I'm going to call Pat tomorrow and put her on alert about the twins. It always bothers me that she's alone up there sometimes. I've made my share of enemies."

"Good point. I don't suppose you ever thought about arming her?"

"I have actually. She has pepper spray, at least. Also, she's done some karate but I think it's more of an exercise routine for her than a means of self-defense. She's pretty slight, but I wouldn't want to fool with her."

Augusta said, "She's irreplaceable."

"So what did you learn from Roberta?"

"The loss of her son has been overwhelming. She can barely sleep. She's enraged with the Chicago PD and she's not happy with her friends in the Daley admin. Toward the end, she confessed that her original impression of you as being an overly smart smartass had to be replaced. She never said it, but I think that she respects you a lot more than she did."

"Did she say that or is that your interpretation," he said with an earnestness that surprised her.

"That is a close approximation actually, my dear. I would never describe you in that way. I'd use much more endearing language," she said in a teasing way. She thought to herself that something had set him off. He seemed to be very pensive and self-absorbed, maybe insecure. She had seen it before but now he was centered in that place.

"What did you learn about Duke? I overheard her mention his name."

"Duke might be OK. He suffered some kidney damage and his leg is hurt but they think he might come out of it."

"Did you ask her about Regis?"

"Yeah but I didn't really get anything from her that you

didn't already tell me. She did know that Regis was prone to causing trouble. She had worried about him. She gets along with a daughter in Istanbul but the daughter you're going to see tomorrow…not so good. She's a very lonely woman, like many in her generation, defined by her husband. I imagine that his loss did some big damage to her. I think that when she throws her weight around part of it is due to her personal straits. Maybe as a way of reaffirming herself. The whole gang, the family, have very few positive ingredients. The negative energies are pretty intense and overwhelming." She looked over at Bertrand. He was staring at her. "What? What's the big stare?"

"I'm not used to your doing these kinds of profiling."

"Well, if you'd get more interesting clients like Roberta Chamberlin you might just get to listen to more of them," she said snappily.

He laughed, he paid the bill and they headed to the elevators. They were both roomed in the east tower on the eighth floor of the Hyatt, she in room 814, he in 822. He walked her to her room. "Let me know it's OK, then I'll leave."

"Hey Mistah, I'm the one who's packing." She opened her door, went in while he held the door open, she came back and said, "It's safe." She grabbed his arm and kissed him lightly on the cheek. "See you in the lobby at eight." He patted her lightly on the arm, turned and headed to his room.

CHAPTER XI

The noon to nine shift for this week suited her fine. It was a once every eight week event that enabled her to get a number of tasks done. She was still in disbelief at the amount of businesses that kept the traditional hours of nine to five thus negating their usage by hordes of people who were working during those times. Say what you want about Wal-Mart, Target, and shopping centers but they were attentive to this issue. Why couldn't the mom and pops open at noon and stay open until nine? It was inconvenient, in part, thus their continued slaughter in the marketplace.

She was about to leave her apartment to run some errands when the doorbell rang. No one was expected. She looked out the peephole and saw a 'one of those in his fifties somewhere,' he wore glasses, was balding, had a high forehead, and she had never seen him in her life. He was only about two feet from her and his speculative face couldn't see her. He rang again. She said, lowering the pitch of her voice, "Yes?"

"Are you Sybil Chamberlin?"

"Yes."

"I'm Bertrand McAbee, I'm a private investigator. I'm

looking into the death of your brother, Regis. Could you give me a bit of time?"

"Who sent you?"

"I'm working for your mother."

His voice was slightly high-pitched, a tenor, but casual, non-threatening. He wasn't coming across as a hard ass which would have doomed him immediately. He was holding up a card, identification. "Hold on." She released the double lock but kept the reinforced chain lock on and opened the door about three inches. "Hold up the identification near me." He held it in front of her eyes. "Iowa? What are you doing in Chicago? Is this legal?" She knew she was being bitchy, but his demeanor never changed. If anything, he seemed to be enjoying the whole thing.

"Yes and no. I'm a PI in Iowa. That gives me about as much status as I have in Illinois."

"Whatever the hell that means."

"Precisely. That's right on point. Exactly what I was saying. If you're looking for a police official, look out your window maybe there's a cop car in the area."

"I never met a PI but you sure don't sound like one. James Garner you're not," now she wondered what he'd do next, how he'd handle her bitchiness. He just stood there looking at her. "So? What exactly do you want me to do?"

"Allow me in to your apartment. Answer some questions. Send me on my way."

For reasons unclear to her she decided to do just that. He sat across from her. He wore a crisp pair of black pants, a camel sports coat, and a black collarless shirt. He was pretty sharp looking. He didn't have the look of a cop to him, or a PI, whatever the hell that was in the state of Iowa.

He looked closely at her. His eyes had a way of catching you. He said, "First, I want to give my condolences to you and your family."

"Yeah I know. It's tough on all of us. Now how can I help you?" She kept catching herself after she spoke. She couldn't fathom why she was being such a first class monster with this seemingly kind man.

"I'm trying to backtrack through the Chicago PD. I don't know how they came across to you but they didn't seem to make many fans in how they approached this case. I only have marginal access to their materials. I'm hopeful that we could do it over again, without prejudice."

"Have you always been a PI? You just don't fit the profile. Your name is Bertrand McAbee?"

"Yes."

"What do you go by?"

"Bertrand."

"OK Bertrand. I'll tell you what. I'll start from the beginning with you on one condition. Level with me. What did you do before you got into this racket?"

He laughed. "I was a college professor."

"Hah! Now you make more sense. What did you teach? Where?"

"A small liberal arts place in Davenport, Iowa, St. Anselms. My game – classics."

"No! Classics. Do you know I took a minor in them at Northwestern. Unbelievable! So tell me who's your favorite Greek, your favorite Roman. It's so nice, you can't believe it, so nice to hear that word classics again."

"I thought Nordstrom's had the classic look, classic clothes," he said teasingly.

"Come on. Enough with the corny jokes. Favorite Greek?"

"About a year ago I was doing a case that caused me to teach again. It enabled me to get in touch with Thucydides again. So let me mark him as my favorite Greek right now. But he's a tough man to read. It was a baptism of fire for me."

"Roman?" she demanded.

"Marcus Aurelius, at least at the top of a list, I suppose."

"He screwed the Roman Empire in supporting his rotten son."

"I know. But what he wrote was powerful and insightful. Just because he couldn't live out what he thought doesn't make him a hypocrite."

"Says who?"

"Me. He's in a long line of aspiration moralists. I don't think any of them died happy. Always some sense of incompletion."

"What about Socrates? He died pretty happy."

"Happy for the instance the situation provided him. Happy about his life in general? I doubt it. He had so many parts that he was working on."

"Hah! Nice distinction. So now I know that you're probably not lying to me about being a classics prof. So why a PI?"

"I needed a change and I had some good connections. Your father was a good friend of my brother who runs a pretty big operation out East. So this, so that, the end."

"Are you happy doing it?" She found him interesting. He was thoughtful and pretty unassuming.

"For the most part, yes. Sometimes not."

"This one of them?"

"No. This is a worthy case."

"Did you know my father?"

"No, your mother."

"Really. How?"

"She was adversarial to a client of mine some years ago. We slugged it out. We get along better now. You should get into the PI business."

"What? Why?"

"You like to ask questions," he said with a smile. He continued, "Were you and Regis close?"

"Not really. He and I were probably the closest. But that wasn't close. We're a big time dysfunctional crew. If you know mother you've already guessed it. Right?"

"I wouldn't tell you. So forget it."

"Hah! You're thinking it. But in answer to your question – we weren't close. Sorry."

"Your brother had scads of enemies. I think that's why the cops were throwing up their hands."

"I can understand that in a sense. I didn't know how deeply he crawled into the caves of miscreants. I can't explain why he did that to be frank with you."

"How did you find that out?"

"What?"

"That he was deeply engaged with miscreants – a good word."

"Nice, very nice, Professor. Look I'm kind of in a bind. Okay?"

"Sure. May I ask what that is?"

"Yes."

"OK. What's the bind Ms. Chamberlin?"

"Why should I trust you?"

"I have no answer to that. It doesn't help, apparently, that I work for your mother. You've just met me," he looked at his watch, "about 20 minutes ago. Trust is something that comes in years not minutes. On my side, I'm trying to find out who murdered your brother and I'll abide by whatever conditions you impose relative to what you say. If I can't work with those conditions I'll tell you so and that will be that. I can't really answer your question better than that."

"You're a very persuasive man, professor. I'm left to wonder whether you're Odysseus."

"You mean crafty and deceitful or smart and powerful?"

"Yes to the former. Your answer is cunning."

"You make it hard for a reasonably honest detective," he said. Then he sat back. His body language told her that he was done speaking.

She already knew what she was going to do. But she found herself energized by the discussion. The guy was interesting. He brought her back to her days at Northwestern, reminding her how much she missed that world. "Here's my dilemma professor. And understand this, if we can't reach an understanding, you need to disappear." He nodded his head in agreement. "Regis mailed me some CDs. I haven't totally gone through the first one yet. It's laden with information. It's a diary of sorts. It tells me more about his…er…dalliances than I ever wanted to know. The CDs were meant only for me as far as I can see. Mother would never get them and certainly not my sister in Istanbul. Those shrews, they're one of a kind."

"We are all aware of some of his activities."

"Like?"

"Playing off one side against another. Like a broker or

a referee at a duel that he himself arranged. The cops have that and I have some of what they have."

"I have a feeling that you only have a small percentage of what he sent me. Here's the problem for me. I don't want his memory tainted. In the wrong hands that's exactly what would happen. I did not disclose the existence of the CDs to the detective. I also don't need any crap about a failure to disclose evidence."

"These CDs," McAbee asked, "are they an accumulation of e-mails? Because I think that a lot of that could be ascertained."

"In part, yes, but it's more of a diary about the things he was into. He was like one of the Greek gods, causing mayhem for the stupid Greeks. Regis was like a god who thoroughly enjoyed bringing out the worst in human beings. He was an expert in reading the dark sides of people. I guess what I'm saying is this: Regis was mean. But he was my Regis, my mean brother. I don't want to look into a mirror and see traitor as my title. Do you get what I'm saying professor?"

"Sure I do. How about making me a copy or lending them to me. I'll look them over with a few very trusted associates. I won't do anything with them until I get back to you and you're in sync with it."

"And if I say no?"

"That's definitive. I'll leave."

"I'll get started. I'll burn copies for you. It won't take that long." She went into her study and began the process of creating duplicate CDs for McAbee. As that was proceeding she came back out to her living room. "You know he actually could be pretty funny, especially if you were in a dark mood."

McAbee told her about the events at his apartment along with the beatings of Rufus and his dog. "Was there anything else in the packet that he sent you?"

She showed him the letter that accompanied the disks. Then she said, "That's it."

"These twins were looking for something. Hard copy I think. A letter? A book? A piece of paper? I don't think they found it. Please be watchful and don't let strangers into your apartment."

"Yeah, right, like you," she said smiling. "Hold on." She went into her study. She had a copy of disk one. She loaded the second CD and went back to McAbee and sat across from him.

"Your brother had an interesting collection of books on one particular shelf."

"I can imagine."

"A number of Greeks and Romans and then upwards. Most of them satirists."

"Oh for sure. He was a debater in high school. His specialty was the use of the reductio ad absurdum. He loved to take an opponent's argument and bleed it to death by showing the stupidity that it fostered. If he got on a roll you couldn't stop him. Hold on." CD two was copied. She set up the third. When she came back she asked, "Do you think we'll ever find who murdered him?"

He thought for a bit and then responded, "We're going to need a break. Maybe the CDs will have something. I'm still not sure why he sent them to you."

"Same here. No call, no warning. Do you think he knew something?"

"Seems likely. But why didn't he call you?"

"Don't know." She went back to her study and set up the last CD for copying. "So don't you miss teaching?" she said as she re-entered the room.

"Yeah sometimes. But I keep up on the classics. I read them when I can."

"I wish I'd kept up. Nordstrom's is fun and all that, but I'm afraid it's not where my heart is."

"It's never too late."

"Well that's what you say. Once you get caught in this merry-go-round it's hard to get off." She went back to the study. All four CDs were now ready. McAbee stood, took them in his right hand and thanked her. He said that he'd be in touch. He left. She missed him. She hoped that he would come back soon.

Serge Pushkin sat at his kitchen table hunched over an electric typewriter with which he had an unsatisfying relationship. It had taken a massive effort 10 years ago on his editor's part to convince him to retire his manual Smith-Corona. For the past three years this same editor had hounded him to switch to a computer. He drew a line in the sand with her, she stopped her pestering at least for the past few months. But she'd come back to it.

He had a severe case of agoraphobia. He was taking 100 mgs of Xanax three times a day to deal with his anxiety attacks. On the advice of his psychiatrist, he performed many of his outside the house chores in the evening, making believe that he was invisible. If he could convince himself that he was so, he was relatively functional. Besides the terror he felt at being in public and toward technology, he also loathed noise. Serge was, in the words of his still separated wife, "one screwed up puppy." However, that judgment didn't stop her from handling all of his financial affairs, including royalties. He felt that she was probably stealing him blind but he said nothing. The last thing he wanted was some sort of intractable legal battle with her. He had enough money and he knew that his work in science fiction – under two different pseudonyms – was successful. He dreaded the idea of moving from his residence where he had been housed for the past 19 years.

When he heard that the crazy but good Regis had been murdered he could not write for five days. His mind shut down. He liked him because Regis accepted him for whom he was. What that meant is that Regis left him alone except for an occasional verbal jab.

The same could not be said for the slut across the hall who drank and screwed lavishly and who made too much noise doing both activities. He kept a wide berth of her and her 'artistic' friends. Once when he was leaving for his nighttime walk she and one of her drunken consorts opened her door and yelled "Boo!" at him as he scurried toward the steps. He thought that he would die on the spot from the fear those two caused in him.

Rufus O'Hanlon was still another story. When they met, he and that horrid-looking dog would just stare at him as though he was an ogre. When he passed O'Hanlon's door he would notice him gazing at him while keeping his door ajar. He was convinced that the dog and O'Hanlon conversed with each other. He had toyed with putting the pair of them into a novel that he was presently composing. They would meet an ugly end.

He went to his dining room window. It faced the street. He raised the blind about four inches, sat on a kitchen chair and looked out at the flood of daylight. His guilty secret gnawed at him, however. He knew what had happened downstairs yesterday. This fairly quiet house had become quite noisy. He had seen the two men, had heard Rufus groaning, and had heard the dog whine in terror. He had heard the dishes breaking in Regis' apartment directly beneath his place, had seen the two men leave, and had seen the ambulance remove Rufus.

He knew, however, that either the tall African American woman or the white guy with her would be back. He was sure that the guy was the one who knocked on his door last night. He thought he had heard a semblance of a conversation between him and the lush across the hall before the knocking on his own door. His name was McAbee according to the card he left.

To his shock, when he took up his position on the chair today he saw that same guy coming up the walkway. There was little doubt in his mind that he would be heading for his apartment. In less than a minute he heard the knock on his door. He looked around to make sure that is was impossible to know that he was there. He was relieved to confirm it. More knocking – louder and more insistent than the first time. He tiptoed from his kitchen toward the door; he wanted to make sure that the deadbolt was on. It was.

"Mister Pushkin. I'm a private investigator. I'm looking into the Chamberlin murder. It's important that I speak with you. Please open the door. I know that you're there."

Serge was petrified. How did this man know that he was there? Was he bluffing? Or had he been watching him? His breathing became labored, he pulled back from the door and went back toward the kitchen. He stood there. He could feel the man's presence on the other side of the door. He stayed completely still making every effort to contain his still uneven breathing.

"Mister Pushkin, I can't and won't leave here until you open the door and speak with me. I know that you're there. I am not a cop. I need some answers from you; it's very important. I heard you in there sir. Please be good enough to open the door. I mean you no harm. Just a few questions and I'll be gone. I am not a policeman."

The man's voice was mild enough and he was here when Regis' mother was in the house after the two attackers left the building and Rufus was taken away. He was in a bit of a dilemma. Maybe he'd open the door but then he'd know that he was hiding. Quite an embarrassment. Impulsively, he faked it, "Hello? Is someone knocking out there? Hello?"

"Mister Pushkin. I'm Bertrand McAbee. I'm a private investigator looking into the murder of your landlord Regis. Would you please give me a few minutes?"

"Oh. Yes. Sure. Just hold on, I need a minute." He stood there trying to compose himself. Maybe it would go OK. After a bit he threw the deadbolt and opened the door. Standing there was the man he had seen. The man backed away as if to give Serge space. "I'm Serge, McAbee, Bertrand – that's your name? You left a card?"

"Yes that's my name," he said pleasantly.

He was athletic, wore a pair of wire-rimmed glasses, and had a pair of gray eyes, maybe with a touch of blue. "Would you care to come in?"

"That would be great," he said gently.

Serge took him to his small dining room off of the kitchen. His layout was similar to that of Regis' except that he did not have an outer hallway. He figured that McAbee was taking all of this in, his being a PI and all. "You can sit there," he pointed to a chair. As they sat, he had instant regret. This McAbee could see that he had a chair situated in front of the window with a partially drawn blind. Great! He probably knew that he'd seen things. Shouldn't have let him in.

"Mister Pushkin I know that you're a writer. A busy man. I'm sorry to inconvenience you. Everyone is stymied about the death of Regis. The Chicago PD seems to have given up. His mother is beside herself. You've met Mrs. Chamberlin?"

"Yes. Yes once." He could feel that this PI knew a lot more than he was letting on. He'd have to be on guard. "Regis helped me with her. I'm a bit of a recluse. She's a bit…ah…outgoing. Different than me. Why do you ask?"

"I guess her pain is easier to understand, when you know her personally."

"Oh…I see, of course."

"I don't have access to the police files. So I'm kind of starting anew. Forgive me if I take you through some things that they probably already asked about."

"One detective came here. His name was Hennessey. A brassy man, Irish-brassy. Oh, are you Irish?"

"Yes, but long removed from the place. No offense taken. So this Hennessey was a bit pushy?"

"Quite so. But I didn't have anything to tell him. I think that if I did he didn't want to hear it anyway. It's like he was going through his paces." He saw McAbee staring at his open blinds. 'Boy,' he thought in anguish.

"I noticed that Regis had a good view of the street

from his dining room. Seems you do too. Do you look out sometimes?"

He'd been watching, he figured. "Oh yeah, once in a while I sit there. It gives me inspiration. But I never saw anything if that's what you're asking?"

"You mean the day that he was killed?"

"Yes, yes." He was sure that McAbee knew something.

"How about yesterday?"

"No, never," he announced too quickly. He reminded himself to slow down. McAbee would outfox him and catch him in a lie.

"Do you know about Rufus?"

"I knew they took him away in an ambulance."

"Did the cops come up?"

"Yes. I saw and heard nothing." McAbee looked at him oddly. His eyes rolled up and to his left as if he was weighing what Pushkin said. He then set them back on him – hard.

"Rufus talked about two men, mid-thirties. They caused a lot of hurt to Rufus, his dog, and did a lot of damage to Regis' apartment," he stopped and let the comment hang in the air. "What did you see and hear Mister Pushkin? It's pretty important. There's a good chance that they might be back." He stared hard at him, awaiting some kind of reply.

He could either lie now and then forever stay in that lie or tell the truth to this McAbee. He wavered back and forth. He looked at McAbee, who was now staring at the wall next to his window. He wasn't sure what was in store for him if he lied. He was in his reverie too long.

"Mister Pushkin just tell me what you saw and heard please."

McAbee was very conciliatory; he had to say that.

He decided to tell him the truth. "I did see the two men yesterday. I also saw them, I think, about a week or a week and a half ago," he stopped.

"Days ago? Where?"

"Across the street in a car."

"Kind of car?"

"Oh, I don't know. Black. Big."

"Did they see you?"

"Yes, but they wouldn't pay heed to me. Would they?"

"You saw them clearly and they saw you?"

"Yes."

"They saw you come into this building?"

"Yes…should I be worried?"

"I'm not sure but it's better for all of us that you're sharing this Mister Pushkin. How about yesterday?"

"Yes, the same pair. Dressed in pure black. A definition of a bad looking pair."

"Did you hear them downstairs?"

"I heard some dishes being broken and I heard Rufus' dog and I think Rufus himself. I should have called the cops. I thought that maybe it was a gambling thing. Rufus is an oddball. I thought they were enforcers."

"They're not. They were searching Regis' apartment for something. Did you think the dish noise came from Rufus' place?"

Serge knew that he'd be caught out by this guy. Now he felt uncomfortable. "I couldn't tell," he said lamely, hopeful that McAbee wouldn't persist.

"Tell me about the two men."

"Tall, dark. I thought them related somehow. Maybe brothers."

"How tall?"

"Well…over six feet for sure. In real good shape was my impression. I wouldn't want to fool with them. Do you think I should be careful? Do you think I'm in danger?"

"Be watchful. Don't be afraid to call the police. Here's another card. If you see them let me know, OK?"

"Oh, yes, I appreciate this."

"Had you ever seen this pair at any other time?"

"No. Just that night and then yesterday."

"The night you saw them. Was it the night Regis was murdered?"

"No. A few days before."

"Any other characteristic?"

"I think that they might have been Middle Eastern. But it's hard to say."

"Any facial hair, anything unusual?"

"No, clean-shaven, no glasses but they had a sinister quality to them, I'll tell you. Big shouldered. Like football players, one of them especially."

"Anything else, Mister Pushkin, about them?"

"No. Don't think so."

"Tell me a bit about Regis. What was he like?"

"He treated me OK. He bought the place about five or six years ago. We were all here, no one moves from here it seems. He got to know our habits. We're an odd lot, all of us. He accepted that. He was decent. He kept the rents pretty stable. He rarely bothered me even though I know he had a pretty edgy sense of humor."

"Did he ever seem scared?"

"No, but you have to realize that I hadn't spoken directly with him for probably two months. That's a nice part of living here. Even though I have to put up with Rufus and the she-cat across the hall."

The detective closed his notebook. He was not altogether unlike the others in the building, Pushkin thought. There was an odd sense to him. As he got up, Serge heard McAbee's knee crack but he didn't seem to notice.

"Now I have a question."

"Sure. What is it?" McAbee said.

"Will the murderers ever be caught?"

He turned, his gray eyes looked at Serge like high beamed headlights. "I think so. You know why?"

"No."

"They're too bold. They'll make a mistake." He moved toward the door. He turned again, "Don't forget Mister Pushkin: be alert."

"Will you report me to the cops?"

"No, of course not. I told you I mean you no harm. Goodbye."

He watched him walk down the path to the sidewalk. He turned left and eventually disappeared. Pushkin felt uneasy.

CHAPTER XII

"Can I help you sir?"

"Yeah. Please. I'm here to check on a dog that you have in your care. His owner is Rufus O'Hanlon, the dog's name is Duke."

"Oh yes. Let me see. Duke O'Hanlon, yes. May I ask? Are you Mister O'Hanlon?"

"No I'm not. He's in the hospital. I told him that I'd check on Duke."

"Please, stay here I'll be back in a minute. Doctor Nugent will want to speak with you," she left.

When Ellen Copeland came back the man was gone from the reception desk area. She looked out at the office and then she saw him in the far corner. He was petting a young beagle who was now lying on his back. The man was engaged in conversation with the beagle's owner whom she heard say, "He really likes you. He's a bit shy around people."

"Shy dogs like shy people," he smiled as he got up.

Copeland said, "Sir? Doctor Nugent will see you in a few minutes."

"OK, thanks," he responded.

Ellen thought that he had a nice way about him. She

noticed that the beagle's owner, a 35ish blonde, was eyeing him surreptiously. He didn't seem to notice as he sat down and picked up a magazine from a table that had a scattered collection of them.

She decided to go over to him. She liked his unprepossessing way. "Doctor Nugent had quite a time fixing Duke. He's a pretty fragile dog. We didn't know his age. Would you know that Mister?"

He looked toward her. He said, "My name is Bertrand McAbee. I don't know his age but I've seen him when he was unhurt. He's a pretty old guy, maybe 10 or 11. But I don't know." He looked at her chest and saw her badge, "Ms. Copeland, Ellen."

She smiled at him. If he'd show any interest she'd reciprocate. He loved dogs, that was a pre-condition for her. She continued, "The chart, I just noticed, says that his owner was in the hospital. Is he OK?"

"I spoke with him last night. I hope he'll make it out soon."

Doctor Nugent was a slim, energetic man with a widow's peak. He walked hurriedly and had a distracted air about him. He shook hands with McAbee abruptly and then escorted him into his office. McAbee was all too familiar with academic offices, many of them heaped high with books, student projects, exams, and other academic paraphernalia. Nugent's office was the practicing veterinarian's version of the same only now the office was filled with drug samples, scientific journals with coffee stains on their pages, dog biscuits, a microwave oven whose door stood wide open, its light bulb dimly lit a darkened corner of the place. Like a lot of faculty, Nugent was a hopeless slob.

"So you're a friend of this O'Hanlon?"

"I don't know about friend; I just met him yesterday."

"Oh?"

"His building was broken into and he ended up in the wrong place. He was beaten up pretty bad. I'm afraid that old Duke got some of the beating too," McAbee offered.

"And your business?"

"I'm a PI; that's how I know him. I'm on a case that indirectly concerns Mister O'Hanlon."

"Had you met the dog before?"

"Yes. He was present when I interviewed O'Hanlon."

"So, you realize this dog is not a youngster?"

"Yes. What are you getting at?"

"I'll put it bluntly to you. I was on the verge of putting him down. There's been some kidney damage, a few broken ribs and a leg fracture. I think he'll recover, but it's one of those cost-benefit things. We're at $950 and counting. I could have put him down for $75. Is this O'Hanlon good for it?"

"Dogs are a funny business Doctor. You just can't let them go easily. I'm sure that O'Hanlon wanted all of the care that you gave to his dog. I saw them together – they were quite a pair the two of them."

He jetted his hand through his hair. "Well the dog is ready to go. I'll release him to you but I need to get an OK from O'Hanlon. Do you have a phone number? Or we can keep him here."

"I don't think that Mister O'Hanlon will be out of the hospital for a few days. I'm staying downtown at the Hyatt. Dogs aren't welcome. So, how about keeping him here until O'Hanlon's condition clarifies."

"Is there any chance that this O'Hanlon might not make it?"

"Well, I guess so. We know that it's absolutely certain that none of us will make it."

"Let me explain. I don't want to get stuck with this bill. If something happened to O'Hanlon I'd have to take down the dog. Another cost to me. Nobody in their right mind would want this sorry animal. No offense meant, McAbee. But I'm running a business."

"Francis of Assisi you're not Doctor Nugent. I understand. To offset your concerns I'll write a check for $1,000. I'll deal with O'Hanlon on the matter."

Nugent sat back, a surprised look on his face. "Well, that would certainly put my mind at ease. I hope you understand."

"Of course I do," McAbee said evenly. Privately, he was running a tab on the twins. Besides the real costs incurred, the punitives would be immense.

"Please just pay at the desk," Nugent got up from his chair.

"Doctor, before I do, I'd like to see Duke."

After a slight hesitation Nugent said, "Sure, follow me!"

They went in the hallway and headed back into the building. He opened a door with two words printed in red on it, 'Private Hospital.' They went through the door. There were rows of cages lined up along the sides of a long narrow room. McAbee noticed on his left side some cats, seemingly all of them on that side of the room, while to his right he saw another row of cages for the dogs. The terribly sad eyes in the third cage caught his immediately. It was Duke. He recognized McAbee, making a feeble effort to rise, only to end up with a slow collapse back onto a blanket that served to soften his slow fall. Nugent opened the cage door and patted Duke's head with a gentleness that surprised McAbee.

"It's OK boy," Nugent said softly. He turned toward McAbee, "I'm going across the room, I want to check on one of the cats. It probably would be good for the dog if you spent a few minutes with him. He is on a mild sedative. So, between age, sedation, and those nasty injuries – don't expect much." He walked across the room.

Duke's doleful eyes, hard enough on the soul in normal times, in these times caused McAbee to feel terrible. He patted his head and spoke softly to him. As he was about to leave, the dog licked his hand. Nugent came and snapped the cage door shut. He looked at McAbee with concern. He said, "Are you OK?"

"Yeah. Yeah. Why do you ask?"

Nugent led them from the room and down the hall toward his office. When they got there he turned and patted McAbee on the shoulder, "Just pay Ellen at the desk…oh…I asked if you were okay because the sadness of that dog found a like soul in you. You wouldn't have made a good vet, sir." He turned and went into his office. His phone was ringing.

McAbee paid Ellen and left the clinic.

When he arrived back at the Hyatt in mid-afternoon there was a message from Augusta Satin on the inside phone system. "Bertrand, I thought you left your cell on at all times. I'm headed for the south side. Should be back by five. My cell is on in case you need to reach me." McAbee did not have fond thoughts about cell phones. He thought of them as just another example of invisible chains. Thus, it was an act of the will to put the phone on. For that particular quirk of character much grief was received. Augusta's voice had a tinge of anger and disappointment in it.

He called Barry Fisk who answered his phone with his customary rudeness. "Yeah?"

"Barry – Bertrand. I have four CDs. There were copied for me by Regis Chamberlin's sister, Sybil. I'm going to access the Hyatt's system with my laptop and send them on to you."

There was a long silence. Sarcastically, Barry asked, "Do you know how to do that?"

"Enough to get them down to you," McAbee said, peeved.

"Just zip them and then I'll unzip. If you have four CDs there's a lot of stuff."

"I think that they will give you a pretty good idea of how much of a termite Regis was."

"Great! Just want I need, a more complicated take on an already hyper-complicated guy."

"Do you have anything worth talking about yet?"

"Not really. I do think he had a death-wish. He was pulling the chain of a lot of bad people, bad groups."

"When I spoke to you about the twins I didn't have much. There's more. I visited Serge Pushkin who lives upstairs from Regis' apartment. So, now we have more. Confirmation. There's some kind of ethnicity involved in the picture. But I can't figure out just what."

"Foreigners?" he asked sharply.

"I don't want to say non-American, but it's sounding like it."

"Middle Eastern?"

"Perhaps."

"Hot dog! Our friend Regis had it in for the Islamic faith. Believe me. I dread to find any correspondence in the files that you're sending to me. I can only imagine what he wrote about Hamas, Hezbollah, al-Qaeda,…Wahabbis. Of course, he wouldn't pick on the run of the mill Moslem. He'd go right for the radical jugular."

"I'll send it along, zipped and all," McAbee disconnected.

A half hour later he had successfully sent on the information from the four CDs to Barry Fisk. He then started to track the adventures of Regis Chamberlin for himself.

The four CDs covered a seven-year period. There were neatly ordered with CD one covering the first two and a half years, CD two extending from the middle of the third year to the middle of the fifth, the third from the middle of the fifth to the end of the sixth. The last CD ended in the seventh year, a week shy of his murder date.

If he was putting together a case study that would be seeking to fathom the depths of Regis' mind, McAbee would begin at CD one and begin his tracking of the rising pathology that he was pretty sure would become self-evident in the Regis' CDs. But it wasn't a case study and pathology or no, Regis' actions were causative of his dire end. Thus he went after the fourth CD to catch the end of the matter. It was likely that in one of his riffs Regis had crossed some kind of line with an enemy who did not appreciate the banter. Maybe it would be discernible.

Augusta sat across from Big Brownie Bass. Roberta Chamberlin had pulled every conceivable string for a 15 minute interview with him. He was the power of the power on the south side of Chicago. An alderman representing the blackest of the black wards in Chicago he was considered to be the man who sat at the right hand of the Lord, that being Mayor Richard Daley himself. BBB was the monogram she saw on the neatly folded handkerchief that peeked out from the top pocket of his black cashmere sports coat. He was fiftyish with impeccable grooming. There was a studied casualness in his manner but she sensed under it a tautness, a watchfulness. His mustache was the only characteristic on his lithe body that struck her as odd. Beside him was a taller and stronger African American. She wouldn't be surprised to learn that he was a detective with the Chicago PD assigned to protect Bass. He stood away from the two of them.

Brownie Bass held out his hand. There was no warmth in his half-hearted shake. He pointed to a rear area in the busy café on the corner of 4600 South Michigan Avenue. "Let's go there Miss Satin."

Seated near the cash register, she had been waiting for him for about 15 minutes. She recognized him as he left the black Cadillac, having seen his picture many time in the *Chicago Tribune* and on WGN news. "This booth is OK," he commanded. They sat. The body guard sat across from them in another booth. He started looking at the small menu card.

Bass took her in, finally, seemingly for the first time. "So what's it like to live in a place like Rock Island?" he asked evenly.

"Not as bad as it might sound. There are a lot of us there."

"Yeah sure. That's why every time I see an ad for Rock

Island there's some dumb blonde fronting for it," he said with a sneer. "OK, I have less than 15 minutes. What is it that you want again?"

Great. He was going to break her ass because he had been muscled into the meeting by Roberta and her consorts in the mayor's office. He was looking for an excuse to call down the meeting. She was intent on not letting him do that. "Sorry about the pulling of strings. You're so high up in the game that there's no other way." The sneer left his face by a half. She went on. "A guy was murdered over on Cicero and I-55 about a week ago. He was the son of the woman who got me this meeting."

"Yeah I know, I know."

"The son was a bit of a screwball. He was into taunting."

"So? Who's taunting now?"

"He liked to pick on black groups. Nasty, digging. Knew how to hit the nerve."

"I know this too. I knew this stuff two years ago. Didn't know who it was but we knew this guy and we knew, from what he said, his context, that he was in Chicago. He picked up on me, too, the white piece of shit. He's a hate crimer as far as I'm concerned. Fuck him!" he looked at her with a stare that had fire and hatred in it.

"Roberta Chamberlin doesn't see it that way, I guess."

"You guess…? Well…you and she should guess again," he ended that comment with another glance at his watch.

She fought to control her temper. BBB wasn't listening. He was emoting. If she erupted now, he'd leave, and that would be the end of this and any future meeting. All of her charm was laid to waste by this tough bastard. "Mister Bass, I'm just trying to find his murderer. This wasn't just a shot to the head. It was ritualistic, a studied piece of work. A hate crime quadrupled."

His stare was full of scorn. "You know what I really hated about that guy? He peddled discord, he worked at trying to turn people against each other. This city, this country, has enough of that shit already sister, it doesn't need some fat freak stirring up the fire," again, a glance at his watch.

"Was he fat?" she asked disingenuously. It was a dangerous ploy she knew, but how did he know that Regis was fat?

"Hope you're not trying to be cute with me sister. Are you?" He was trying to stare a hole through her.

"No. I've never seen a picture of him. Was he fat?" She hoped that he didn't sense the lie.

He continued to stare at her. Finally, he said, "I made some calls on my way over. Among other things, I found out that he was a hugely fat maggot. But here's what I have to say to you. I'm going to come by you only once on this. Got it?"

"Sure."

"You're question is – are any brothers involved with this murder?"

"Right."

"My calls around the hood and this is off the record right?" he stopped talking and looked at her sternly. Augusta nodded. He then shook his head back and forth three times. There was no verbal comment. He got up and motioned to his minder. He left.

She had her 15 minutes with BBB. In the end, he gave her the answer she sought – a no. If she was wired, his answer was a non-answer. He was a shrewd species of a man. B.B. Bass would go quite far in Chicago politics. Whether he was up to Daley standards was another matter altogether.

CHAPTER XIII

Othman quietly sat upon the cushioned chair in the South Chicago Islamic Center. Ali eyed him from behind heavy maroon drapes. He had to admit that he both feared and admired Othman who, from observations lasting intermittently for over five minutes, did not appear to move one millimeter.

Othman had once told him that his heritage had been one of whole cloth going all the way back to the 800s. He saw himself as a prince, that he felt a royal lineage coursed through his bloodstream.

Ali rarely questioned or challenged Othman. He typically listened and nodded, assessing that he was one of those all too many who betook himself as being something much more than he truly was. God worked through instruments as they were useful to Him. And so Ali would use Othman.

He separated the drapes and quietly came through them into the carpeted room. Othman arose, turned to face him and bowed slightly. They grasped each other and separated in silence.

Ali motioned Othman to sit as he went to the side of

the room, picked up a chair, and placed it beside Othman. He sat, pointed up toward the ceiling, and then around the room in general. They both knew what that meant. Ali had reason to believe that the building was compromised by FBI listening devices. All the world had been changed since 9/11.

Ali whispered, "Your brother?"

Othman responded, "At home, studying."

Ali nodded. He looked around the room. He knew that if someone was behind the drapes where he had stood, he would be totally unaware that there were two people in this room, and if he was actually in the room would be unable to hear any words that passed between them. Othman's brother's name was Mohammed. He was far more remote and indecipherable than his brother, Othman.

Ali said, "He is well though?"

"Yes, Allah be praised."

Ali had prepared what he was going to say to Othman on numerous occasions. He did not want the brothers fleeing back to Jordan. On the other hand, he wanted them to be prepared for a possible police interrogation, although such was highly unlikely. Their unfamiliarity with the Chicago PD was a problem, but an ever bigger one was their total disdain for the entire American system of justice. These brothers saw it as being a sieve for avoiding responsibility, a system that invited lies and deception that were entirely justified when dealing with the infidel. Ali pretty much agreed with this assessment, but his knowledge was tempered by the realization that there were some very smart adversaries in that system that he detested. Ali also felt that he was not an arrogant man, but that was Othman's, and to a larger extent Mohammed's, greatest failing. If the police could ignite that arrogance, they might very well succeed in getting Othman or Mohammed to open up their hearts about their beliefs.

He leaned in still closer to Othman's ear, "You have not been approached or followed since the incident with him?"

Othman caught his eye in surprise. He said, "No. No … of course not."

"A Chicago detective came here. A black man. His name was Jones. He asked me if I knew a man named Regis Chamberlin. Of course, I told him, 'no'. He left, convinced, I believe. There is some pot of stew that we are in as a group, however. I want you to know this. I want you to be very careful. Do you know of anything that could implicate you in this matter?"

Othman remained motionless, presumably thinking. "His website was regularly approached by us. So, in that sense, yes. But many hundreds were active in his chat room. Of this, I have no fear if the police come. I read only. I did not engage in the chat room."

"Nothing more?"

The hesitation was too long, inordinate in a way. Finally, Othman said, "I sent a note to this fat man. I drew a knife, and I printed, 'You will die for your infidelity'. I did not sign it."

"Is there more?"

"He had tenants. One of them came near our car. I do not think that he could see in. It was dark. We were in preparation for our mission. There is nothing else."

"At the execution on Cicero and Interstate 55?"

"No. We had prepared it so that we could operate with great speed. Anwar and Hussein were with us. We brought the noose down from where we had stored it above the beam. Between us we had his head in the noose and pulled to a killing height within 45 seconds. We were not seen. They are both already in Cairo."

"The note?"

"Yes?"

"I believe that effort should be made to find it. I think that you should go to his apartment and search for it. This note was perhaps … excessive, my friend," Ali said trying to conceal his alarm.

Othman's head moved back a few inches as though his face had been slapped. Chastisement from Ali, no matter how indirect and non-threatening, was rare and when it came, it was felt deeply. "We will go then, as you say. If it is there, we will find it. We fear nothing. Allah is with us."

"Allah is indeed with us, but snares are all around us. Our enemies are legion. Care must be exercised. The devil assists them against our cause. You have done well, Othman. It is important that you remain safe for your future tasks. You have removed and sent to hell a great enemy of Mohammed. More will come, indeed. We must keep you out of harm." With this final comment, Ali arose as did Othman.

They looked at each other and pressed together. They separated and then bowed. Ali went back to his office elsewhere in the center while Othman left the building, went to the parking lot, and drove away in his black Lexus under the concerned and watchful eye of Ali.

Othman drove to his apartment on Harlem Avenue in River Forest. He was just one block from Concordia College. His brother Mohammed was napping. Othman let him be as he sat at the kitchen table. Ali, intentionally or unintentionally, had irritated him. He had the feeling that his good act was questioned. That, perhaps, he had been clumsy or stupid. It was only right that an adversary be told in advance of his impending murder, so that not only death but so also the premonition of it, would cause grief in the heart of the offender. But Ali was not pleased.

Mohammed awoke and entered the kitchen from his bedroom. His quick yawn was concealed behind his large hand. "Othman! I did not hear you come in. I am sleeping like an aged tree. How was your meeting with Ali? Do you have a new assignment?"

"Ah, yes and no. We must go back to this infidel's Chamberlin's house and recover our note foretelling his execution. Ali has been approached by the police, but not because of the note. But he has fear that this note is around and the police could perhaps use it to advance their investigation."

As usual, Mohammed said nothing. His look was grave and eventually it showed confusion. He asked, "We left no fingerprints anywhere upon that envelope or note. Does he think us fools?" He ended his remark with both fists coiled.

When Othman observed Mohammed's hands, he became alert. It was one sign that could foretell an explosion of Mohammed's uncontrollable temper, an event as rare as it was powerful. Gently and carefully he said, "No, it is not like that. These dogs need no help. There are so many scientific tests available to them. We would rather they have to guess at everything possible rather than being allowed onto the trail that led back to our faith."

Mohammed relaxed slightly. Othman reminded himself

not to go back to this matter unless it was explicitly raised by his brother who had come out of his nap very poorly.

His brother went to the bathroom. Othman remembered an incident in Amman, Jordan, some eight or nine years previous. It was near a McDonald's in the northern part of the city. He and Mohammed had been walking home from their mosque. As they went by this symbol of American corruption, they saw two young Jordanian women leaving it with two western men whose nationality was not clear. One man wore khakis, the other, jeans, but their Jordanian whores were dressed in tight shorts and halters. The whores were a disgrace to Jordan and to Islam.

Mohammed froze to a stop while Othman took his arm and attempted to urge him forward and away from any potential problems. Mohammed refused to move as the bitches and their keepers sauntered toward them. It was a meeting that only destiny could have arranged; it took that very spot, their unusual presence at that time and in that locale, and, of course, this audacious attack on Islam in the middle of an Arab country such as Jordan.

Perhaps it was their look of disdain toward Mohammed. Surely they knew what his inert body with eyes almost agog, Koran in hand, meant. But, alas, he too knew what their bold look and sneering smile meant. The two westerners saw trouble before the two bitches. They both reached out toward their lecherous vermin whores as Mohammed spoke, "You are a disgrace to our country and to our religion. How dare you show yourself in this manner!"

Othman stood in front of Mohammed now, face to face, as he grabbed both arms with his. "Please, Mohammed, we will go now. These scum are of no use to us. Please, come."

But the way he was positioned was his mistake. His back was to the four behind them. He turned back too late just as he saw one of the girls give an evil eye toward them, especially Mohammed.

One of the westerners, probably American or Canadian, said, "Ignore those two fuckers. They're from the middle ages. Keep moving." They, each, tried to forcefully advance the two defiant women away from the encounter.

As a further testament to destiny, the two westerners knew Arabic, just as Othman and Mohammed knew English. All was now in the open. The adversaries knew of each other's comments.

Mohammed's body shook for about five seconds before he easily broke free from Othman's not inconsiderable hold. He was around and by Othman's body as he lunged at the whores by grabbing the hair of one and narrowly missing the dodging other. He slung her to the ground as the westerners came forward. The khaki-pants fellow tried to kick the arm of Mohammed as he tossed the whore down. Mohammed grabbed the man's leg on its downward arc and sent him sprawling into the other jeaned man. Both westerners went down onto their knees as Othman failed to grab Mohammed.

People came out of the McDonald's and adjacent shops. They seemed to watch in a mixture of anguish and glee. Mohammed screamed, "Infidel!" as he threw a resounding punch to the jaw of the khakied one and then grabbed the rising jeaned one by a headlock. He ran forward to the curb and rammed his head into the back bumper of a Toyota pickup truck. Both North Americans knew how defeated they were as they held up their hands and yelled to him in Arabic, "Enough, enough," many times over.

By this time Othman was again trying to hold back Mohammed and, to his relief, he was assisted in this by three other Jordanian men. The westerners slowly walked away with their now chastened bitches. As Othman and Mohammed left the scene they heard the unmistakable sound of police cars rushing to the scene.

Although he already knew it in his heart, full knowledge came only after this incident. Mohammed was by far the physically stronger of the brothers. As long as they stayed together Othman would of necessity be the thinking one, the restraining one. He faulted himself now as he heard the toilet flush; it had been Mohammed's idea to insert the note under Chamberlin's door and he had been an all-too-willing accomplice in the unnecessary folly.

Ali was probably under the instruction of some master himself. It was not good to come under the negative gaze of that kind of man, he was sure.

Mohammed came back into the room and spoke, "When do we go back to this house?"

"If it is clear, we should do so immediately. Are you ready?"

"Allah is with us. Let us go!"

They walked toward Chamberlin's house, boldly and without the slightest hesitation. They were convinced that Allah was guiding them. They came into the entryway and went toward Chamberlin's apartment which had plastic yellow tape across the door with the words: 'Crime Scene – Authorized Personnel Only.' The unlocked door surprised them; they looked at each other with a slight smile. Another confirmation of their theological conviction. The apartment was as they remembered on that night of the assassination. Within a few minutes of their starting their search for the note, both were startled when they heard, "Yes, gentlemen, can I help you? Do you have permission to be in here?"

Othman quickly placed a restraining hand on Mohammed's arm. He said, "Sure we do." He walked toward the fat, sickly looking man with his ugly flattened-face brown dog and ridiculously obese body. They features in common, the two of them. The fat man now retreated slightly, aware that he had provoked trouble way beyond his expectations.

"Who are you?" demanded Othman.

"I'm a neighbor. What do you want here? This is a police scene. You have no business here." At this the filthy, stupid looking, dog growled. Two well-placed kicks by Mohammed sent the dog into a lying position as he gasped for breath amid a low gurgling whine.

The fat man was now fully cognizant of his dire straits as Mohammed grabbed him by the throat and Othman held one of his arms and landed four brutal punches on the over-sized pig of a man.

While the fat man was semi-conscious, they continued their search of the premises but they had no luck. Perhaps Regis Chamberlin had destroyed the note. That was as good a guess as any other.

Before they left they rummaged through the intruder's wallet who had now been half-dragged into the kitchen. His driver's license read, 'Rufus O'Hanlon,' his address was in the building. Othman saw a card in the bill section of the wallet. It read: 'ACJ Investigative Agency, Davenport, Iowa.'

Across the bottom was the name, 'Bertrand McAbee' along with a phone number and e-mail address. He placed the card in his pocket. At that moment something crossed over him, as a dark cloud? An omen? A sign? It was something that he would have to attend to after they were finished with their search and left the premises, but not before Mohammed took one of the dog's legs and gave it a vicious twist.

CHAPTER XIV

Rabbi Samuel Rubin was a dual-citizen of the United States and Israel. An only child, he was born into the home of two ardent secular Jews who had roots in Russia but had left that country in 1920, both of them in their early twenties. Samuel was born in 1940, his mother comparing the story of Sarah with her own late conception but all the while maintaining a distance from the theological nonsense of the Old Testament.

By the time Samuel was 11 he witnessed the black listing of his father by the infamous Senator from Wisconsin, Joseph McCarthy. The episode caused a fire in Samuel's heart, and the necessity for zeal and commitment on his part for the rest of his life. Before he was 13, his father was dead from a heart attack which Samuel felt arose from the organized terror-tactics used by the FBI. But his father's death created some unexpected consequences. One of these was his mother's drift back to religious Judaism. By the time he had entered New York University, his mother had already visited Israel twice and had become infatuated with the Israeli political star by the name of Golda Meier.

Samuel's mother finally left the United States for good

in 1963, the assassination of John Kennedy being a defining event. By 1965, she was a devoted Zionist and eventually became a department head in the super-secret and super-effective Israeli intelligence agency, the Mossad.

Samuel, in the meantime, after a number of personal odysseys in search of an absolute came under the influence of the orthodox radical Meier Kahane. It wasn't long before he began studies for the Rabbinate. All the while he was aware that while his mother was sympathetic but concerned about Kahane – his father would have been appalled by this turn of events to the heir of his family.

Now, in his sixties, Samuel Rubin was a well-known figure in both Israel and the United States. He had become a spokesman and a renowned figure in the settlement movement in the territories captured by the Israelis after their savage conflicts with their Arab enemies. His particular notoriety came with his pronounced opposition to the peace treaty signed by Anwar Sadat and Menachim Begin. Essentially, it led to the return of the Sinai to Egypt for nothing except a normalization of relations. Such nonsense demanded a resolve on the part of true Jews to guarantee that other captured lands stay in Israeli hands and eventually become part of the Israeli State.

Rubin was now a financial rainmaker for the settlement movement as he tapped into the wallets of sympathetic Jews especially in the United States and Canada. The experience of the settlers, the position-shifting of the Israeli governments, the Palestinian suicide squads, and a variety of other events led Rubin into a zone seen to be highly radicalized even by the current right-wing government of Israel.

Some of Rubin's comments and writings had found

their way into the Arab press. Some television-interview material had been aired on Al Jazeer. And although many of his friends would argue that he was not anti-Arab or anti-Palestinian, there were many in Israel itself who saw him as a leader of a radical fringe way over on the end of the spectrum of Israeli politics.

One op-ed piece in the *New York Times* argued that the likes of Rubin were the equivalent to the Arab countries as to what Bin Laden was to America. It concluded by pleading for the Israeli people to outrightly reject the poisonous positions of this 'Rabbi of Hate.' Three days later the letters to the editor section was alive with fury on both sides of the issue concerning Samuel Rubin. One fact stood out. He was a man of high negatives and high positives.

Samuel Rubin was aboard El Al Flight 007 from Tel Aviv to JFK in New York. Before he departed he had committed to a 30-day tour which demanded 45 speaking events, and at least 15 radio and 10 television appearances. He was a busy man.

He was also fully aware that his life was in constant danger. He did not underestimate his Jewish enemies on the left, assorted groups on the right, the Israeli government itself, the CIA and most particularly his countless number of Arab adversaries. Accordingly, an hour outside of JFK he called Moishe Blumenburg in Brooklyn. Blumenburg was a former New York City uniformed cop who bitterly left that arena after 10 years of thankless service. He and a partner incorporated and advertised themselves as specialists in personal security detail. For $15,000 plus expenses, he hired on as Rubin's personal escort throughout the one month tour.

Moishe answered his call while driving toward JFK.

"Rabbi, good afternoon."

"We're about an hour or so out."

"Yes, I'm aware. I'm heading there now. I can be outside customs or float around the airport perimeter in the vehicle. Which do you prefer?"

"Come in. There is cause for concern. More threats than normal. I've been warned, but what's new?"

"I'll be there."

"Shalom."

Blumenburg was indeed outside the customs area. He looked to Rubin as though he had put on 50 pounds since the last time, seven months ago. Not a good sign. The rabbi knew that his marriage had become troubled and that one of his sons had exhibited drug problems. But for his own safety, he felt secure. Blumenburg was tough and alert.

As they drove toward Brooklyn Heights Blumenburg came on as direct as ever, "So, Rabbi, tell me some of the concerns. Whatever was said to you I need to know. And, who said it?"

"Security in Tel Aviv. They said that they were picking up chatter. Too much awareness of my trip. Mostly in code, of course. But there was a transmission of data which corresponded to where I was at specific times. The specificity was more pronounced than usual. Like I was being watched, tracked."

"This is a problem. Have you alerted your host groups?"

"No, not yet. But I will as soon as I establish my presence. In the meantime, I will need you to be super-alert. They haven't taken to assassinations in other countries but just about everyone in Israel expects them to be forthcoming.

The war, Moishe, has only begun, I'm afraid. I've been telling this to them for years. No mercy for the scum is the answer, the only answer. The Israelis pull their punches, they hem and haw and they bow to the anti-Semites in Europe. Definitive aggression is the only answer."

"What will become of the settlements?"

"Ah! My heart breaks over this. The government has no idea of what they are in for if they persist in de-stabilizing our settlers. Someday peace may come to the holy land. But it will be long after my death and yours too, I'm afraid, my friend, Moishe."

When they reached the gated residence of Solomon Getz, where they would stay for the next seven days, the rabbi connected to the internet and called up his list of contact individuals involved with his tour stops. His email read,

> My Friends,
>
> I have arrived in the States in order to begin my tour. The trip itself was uneventful. I was met by Moishe Blumenburg whom most of you know from past trips. He will dedicate his considerable talent to my personal safety. I wish to underscore that there has been great concern shown by Israeli intelligence about my safety. I would ask all of you to be super-alert to any strange occurrences, events, inquiries, etc.
>
> Samuel

Ali received a call at 5:30 p.m. at the Islamic Center in Chicago. The message was as expected, terse. "It has come as expected. Peace." His cell went dead. He imagined one of those long rows of dominos. This call triggered the fall of the first one, which would then lead to the continuing fall of them until the very last one, the assassination of this vulgar and vicious rabbi, Samuel Rubin.

He immediately called Othman and asked him to be prepared to come to the Center tomorrow morning at 9:00 a.m. There was probably a new assignment for them. Othman's parting words were, "Praise be to Allah!"

That night Ali went to the home of his mentor and the source of his zeal. The word "peace" at the end of the message was the signal for such. His name was Faisal Ibrem. He was a real estate speculator in Chicago who had at his disposal incredible sums of money. He was a Saudi by origin but he had cultivated a number of American ways even to the extent of establishing personal relationships with Jews. He was a member of the Chicago Athletic Club, Rotary, and was a significant donor to Richard Daley's campaign war chest. Ali considered it an honor when he was approached by one of Faisal's associates, almost two years previous. "Would you be kind enough to meet with Faisal Ibrem? He has long admired your work in the Islamic community."

Ali's heart jumped for joy at such an opportunity. His first meeting took place in a suite at the Palmer House. His first hour there, however, was spent with two aides. In the span of that hour, it was made patently clear that every salient piece of information about Ali, his family in Jordan, his extended family, and his activities were known, and intimately so. His family was praised for its commitment to the ultra-conservative Wahhabi vision of Islam, which some infidels would say was reactionary and intolerant. Ali was no fool. While he considered the praise as genuine, he also knew that it was contexted, that his family could be marked for hostile action if, in any way, the potential contract that might be forthcoming was violated. The two aides left, entering another area of the suite. When they returned they said that a further meeting would occur. "Mister Ibrem is not available, at this time. This meeting is considered confidential, no one is to know."

He was, of course, disappointed; more so, as two weeks crawled by with no correspondence of any sort. Suddenly, a call came to him, "Can you be outside in ten minutes? We will pick you up." No identification was given. They knew that he knew; he knew that they knew.

The same pair drove Ali to the downtown Marriott. No conversation took place even as they entered the elevator that brought them to the top floor of the hotel. A muscular guard stood outside a door, three to the left of the elevator. Ali was hopeful that he would finally meet this important man.

The guard upon seeing Ali and the two aides silently opened the door and they went into an extremely large room. Behind an ornate desk sat Faisal Ibrem busily signing what appeared to be checks in a large leather-bound book of many pages.

Ali was brought to a chair in front of the desk as one of the aides pointed to it. Ali sat; the two aides went back to the door and exited the room. Faisal silently signed off on five more checks, never once looking at Ali. Finally, this elegantly dressed, perfectly groomed man of about 40 years looked at Ali. His deep voice was precise, very English.

"Sir, I have heard much of you. I am hopeful of a long and fruitful relationship secured by a common cause." There was a long pause before he continued. "Our common love of Islam is our standard in this land of outrage."

"Yes, yes it's right. Praise be to Allah," Ali said with humble enthusiasm.

"There will be things that will need to be done over time. I must ask from you that I receive your unquestioned support. If you can not give me this, you may leave and nothing will come of this meeting. You are free to go, sir. But if you stay, I want you to know that you have entered on to a road that will only end when either one of us, or both, die."

Ali said, "Let it be as you have said."

"A number of us have watched as America has been captured by a Jewish clique of financiers and capitalists. It is such now that these two, Jews and America, are joined at the hip. We also have money, but, we have not used it wisely. Some from my country go to London or Paris with an entourage of upwards to 30 or 40 as they spend a small fortune at five-star hotels for two, three months. The bills from this profligacy are in the millions. Do you ever hear of Jews who do such? These are millions that could go to our cause instead of leading to a stray path of vice and opulence. Contrary to what you might think, I live by an austere interpretation of our holy book."

"Of this I have no doubt," Ali said feebly.

"We are in a very careful process of selecting a core of fervent ones who will be placed in every major American area. Their job is to melt into the population; to parade as good red, white, and blue Americans and to await instructions for activities which have only one purpose – to break apart the relationship between Israel and the United States. I am the operational chief for this midwest area. There is one for the east coast, the west coast, and the south besides this area. America has been quartered, so to speak." He stopped and smiled. "It will be our job to have it drawn." Ali knew it was a joke and smiled. But the word 'drawn' did not impact him. "There was a group, a tribe really, in what is now northwest Syria, during the era of the crusades, known as the Assassins. Their history has been told by their enemies, the Caliphates and the Crusaders, of course. The assassins were said to be users of drugs, to have no principles, to be merciless and so on." He gazed languidly at Ali, as he went on with his commentary. "But if one reads closely between the lines of these lying commentaries and one-sided histories, we really see earnest followers of our faith who were prepared to die for their beliefs. Without using the term assassins, which is loaded with mis-interpretation, we are dedicated to like-enterprises with like-individuals. But we will not sacrifice ourselves unless such is the only way to accomplish our goals."

As Ali listened he was impressed with Faisal's earnestness and sincerity. The smoothness of his manners and voice stood in stark contrast to the mayhem he was espousing. "May I ask how this relates to 9/11?" He immediately realized that this was perhaps an overstep on his part, but it was too late.

"9/11 is done. It was bound by its own rules, self-contained. I know nothing of it and it is beyond me." He looked sharply at Ali as he continued, "It is not be ever be brought up again between us." His look was stern. Then, as an afterthought, he added, "That was an action against many innocent people – a broad paintbrush. We envision precision and exactitude. Quite different really."

"I see," Ali said while he thought that he did not see much at this point.

"Only you will know of me. No one whom you are told to direct will ever know of me. Call me X, if you wish. I envision you having a group of ten who will be assigned to you in Chicago. They will be as ones or twos. You will never meet with them as a group. They will never know of each other's identity. There will never be a written communication and all communications by equipment, faxes, cells, computers, will be in code and presented with studied innocence. You are to assume at all times that you are being watched and listened in on. When you meet with me you can speak freely as I keep all of my locations fully vetted." Faisal stopped and stared at Ali.

Ali said, "When do we start?"

"We have. You will hear when you need to hear." He reached into his desk drawer and withdrew a large manilla envelope. "This is for you. As they say in American football, it is a signing bonus." His other hand went below the desk. The two men who had brought him appeared.

Ali was ushered down to the lobby of the Marriott as the aides turned and went back to the elevator. Ali found an empty sector of the hotel lobby and sat. He opened the clasped envelope. There were many, many $100 bills. A hurried count had him surmising $50,000.

Ali vacated those thoughts of the past as he drove up to the gates of the Highland Park mansion of Faisal Ibrem. It was only his second meeting in the last two years that had spanned their relationship. This was the first time in the mansion. The other was just a scant month ago when the name of Regis Chamberlin was given along with mention of Rabbi Rubin. After the Chamberlin killing no communication came his way from Faisal.

The gate was opened by a guard, different from those who had been with him two years ago. He stopped the car after his entry through the gate. The guard came up to him as he opened the car window. "There is a parking area to the left, about 50 feet." He wondered why no identification was requested. As he drove forward, another vehicle came through the still opened gate. It did not stop as it sped by Ali's slowly moving car. The other vehicle had darkened windows but he felt that he saw the outline of the two men from the hotel meetings.

He approached the mansion with slow and measured steps, not quite sure of what would occur. He pushed a lit button at the mansion's doorway and waited. A tall Arab man in a galabiya opened the door and said, "Mister Ali, welcome to this house. Master Faisal is awaiting you in his study. Allow me to show you the way."

The servant moved gracefully and purposely toward an area about 25 feet from the entrance to the house. He knocked lightly, paused about two seconds and opened the door to the study. Without a word he turned sideways at the door and stretched his right arm outwards. Ali went into the darkened room that was bordered by shelves and shelves of books. Faisal was dressed in a galabiya dominated by dark maroon stitching. It appeared to be silk. He reached Ali and kissed him on both cheeks. He took Ali's arm and said in his low baritone voice, "Come and sit with me. I have tea for us." They both sat among the large pillows that filled the floor to the right side of the doorway.

After they both poured their tea and each sugared their beverage, Ali decided to say nothing until he could determine the nature of the meeting.

"My friend, Ali. You have done well. As we speak, a prolonged and in-depth analysis of the death of Regis Chamberlin is being prepared by a famed reporter at the *Chicago Tribune*. Chamberlin's death will eventually serve as a warning to those who malign us and curse Allah."

"Thank you, sir. My two men are very able and very zealous."

"Yes. But I do want to warn you. While the execution was masterful, there was risk. I know that there is scant traffic at that time of night but, perhaps, that being the case, what was happening could be noticed by any passer-by. Your men must be prepared for death, they must know this, if they fail."

"They do. The two brothers and the two who assisted in the hanging knew the cost of discovery. The two who helped the brothers have left the country."

"It is good. Are you prepared for our next mission?" Faisal said flatly.

"Yes. The rabbi has come to the sacrificial altar?"

"We have managed to download a full schedule for this man. It is in this envelope. Tell the brothers I want simplicity, not as they did with Chamberlin. He need not suffer first. He is a dreadful man. His zeal matches ours. He is guarded. But his death is essential."

"I have arranged a meeting with the brothers tomorrow."

"Be in a secure location. Your building must be vetted often, for I believe that it is compromised frequently."

Ali swallowed hard at this relevation but he held himself quiet and merely nodded his head.

"The police?" Faisal asked obliquely.

"They came to the center. A detective. He wanted to know what I knew or had heard about Regis Chamberlin."

"Yes?" Faisal prodded.

"I told him that I had an idea of his existence. He said that he had authored a number of tracts that were anti-Islamic. It was easy to say as I did, that this Chamberlin was one of many. He asked if I knew of anyone who would act against this hatred. I said that Mohammed preaches love and respect for others. He left."

Faisal stared through him for a number of seconds. Ali sat there. Finally Faisal said, "There is nothing else I need to know, my brother?"

Ali was at a crossroads. Should he inform him of the note that the two brothers had sent to Regis days before they murdered him? He decided that to do so would be unwise and unnecessary. Then he wavered, then he held fast. He would not tell Faisal of this foolish mistake. The important thing was to insure that it never happened again, that these impulsive brothers be held in check.

Faisal picked up a second manilla envelope and handed it across to Ali. "This is for your personal use. You are doing well. Are your men well?"

"Yes. But I don't see much of them."

"Their financial needs are met by another source. Your only concern is with operations, Ali. See only to their motivation and willingness to plunge the knife when called to do so." He arose. They kissed. Faisal opened the door of the study; the servant came. Ali was shown out. Ali was uneasy. Should he have told Faisal of the note to Chamberlin?

CHAPTER XV

Barry Fisk's unexpected and sporadic laughter sounded like a snarl. McAbee was being debriefed by him.

"I have read over the entire content of the four CDs. I read a lot McAbee, believe me. This bill is going to be enormous. There's some pretty funny stuff, like Leonard and Hiaasen. Their dismal views of life are really quite funny. But this guy Chamberlin, he is a master of all that is vicious," he laughed again in his snarly way. "He is A plus at what he does. If the family put out an edited copy of his stuff they'd have a best seller. Oh, and he managed to get all of these nasty groups biting and scratching each other. So funny." He looked at McAbee with a twisted smile.

McAbee could not remember a time when Fisk was so effusive, almost jubilant. "He was so good at it that he's dead," McAbee said, trying to rein in Fisk with the consequences of being so good at baiting edgy groups.

McAbee's somber mood didn't cross over to Barry who was still smiling at some memory of Chamberlin's transgressions. "I hope that you get a chance with this stuff."

"I have read a bit. I got the gist of him. Even listened to a few audios from his early wanderings. Seems like more of the same again and again. Find a group, find the counter-group and then have at them. It's a bit like a perverted piece of Hegelianism."

"Hegel! Hey Bertrand McAbee comes out of the classics and storms into the nineteenth century for a brief reposte. I'm impressed."

"It's Hegel with a twisted sense of the dialectical method. Pre-thesis of the thesis. Maybe just a prolonged teasing of the dialectic, I suppose."

Fisk looked surprised. The smile came off his face as he was forced to come off his prattling about how clever Chamberlin was. "OK, OK," he said, "so you want a suspect or a suspect group. Right?"

"Right," McAbee said flatly.

"The detective, Hennessey. He had it right. It's a case on a never-ending platform. So, OK, here's what I did. Because of Augusta's work, I've taken down all of the black groups out there. This is what it's going to be like methodologically. It's like chopping off avenues in a large city until we can get it down to a manageable number. Your brother has been in touch with the Mossad. They gave him, admittedly off the record, a 90% assurance that no Jewish group was engaged with the killing of Chamberlin."

McAbee interrupted him, "I know that we're just eliminating pieces that might, again, show up. But I'm following you."

Fisk looked back at the file that was spread across the desk in McAbee's office. "I first studied the work he did with the various political special interest groups like PETA, Doctors Without Borders and a bunch of other scabs that he liked to pick. That's where I started."

"And?"

"I didn't see most of them as suspect. PETA can be violent like burning down labs, raiding mink forms, being a general pain in the ass. But I could never see them doing a ritual execution. And that's my assessment of the murder. It's not in their history, at least. Murder is for murderers. Past behavior is the best predictor of future behavior. He ran a website about the mafia."

"As far as I know the mafia and the FBI have not verbally duked it out in a public forum, nor could they be drawn into one like Chamberlin ran," McAbee said with a light touch.

If Fisk was paying any heed to McAbee, it wasn't apparent. He was on a run and as such the rule was for McAbee to keep his mouth shut. Furthermore, Bertrand was expected to laud the extraordinary genius of Fisk. Fisk continued his analysis, "He pursued the following categories, one – ethnics, two – races, three – gender, four – sexual orientation, five – religions, six – political groups, and seven – assorted individuals that he ran across. There are miscellany and there are targets who fit more than one category, for example, Islam and radical politics, or Catholicism and abortion rights and so on. But he always zeroed in on extremists whether in behavior or ideology."

"Moderation has no place?"

"Yes. You could say that. If it was possible to radicalize a moderate, he'd be up to it, but he definitely steered pretty clear of down-the-middle types. He was more interested in the five percent on the extreme ends of any continuum. He wasn't interested in just a Catholic, he wanted one who was pre-Vatican II or a feminist Catholic who was into killing every fat prelate in that swamp of a religion."

"Whoa – sounds like you'd be one of those five percent from that last comment." McAbee was aware of Fisk's anti-Catholicism.

Fisk thought for a bit and then responded, "You're right. You caught me. I got a big kick out of his tauntings. When you get a chance get the pieces that went out there between the Cattleman's Association and PETA," he laughed meanly.

"At this point all I hear is your repeating of Detective Hennessey – problems all the way around."

"OK, OK. Back to point. It's one thing for a rancher to say that if he catches a PETA freak on his land he'll roast the son of a bitch with a huge spit up his ass. But reaching the end point of a ritual murder, is something else. It's the crossing of that huge divide that has to be the focus. But there is one group in that belief circle that I feel must be a candidate. Regis went after them with a particular venom. The Animal Liberation Front. The FBI has called them a terrorist organization. I feel that they need a close look."

"Yes. A very supportable proposition. But I worry about Moynihan's comment that suggests that America keeps defining itself by lowering the line. In this case, meaning that it's easier to see more and more groups crossing this lowered line," McAbee said.

Fisk moved restlessly in his seat. "Well, OK, taking that into account as I did without even thinking of the metaphysics behind what you just said, I think that I have some supportable findings. I've eliminated some. First, I'm deleting races. Even without Augusta getting an assurance on black groups, Chamberlin was overall pretty light in the black area. Oh, he couldn't let it go, of course, but he spun a heavier web elsewhere. If it was 60 years ago, I'd say that the Ku Klux Klan would be a candidate, in fact they were ritual murderers. Maybe some of the rioters in black LA, too. But I just don't see ritual murder coming out of that lake of mud." He stopped while McAbee silently acknowledged his statement with a head nod.

Fisk continued, "But let me keep up on this angle, who else can be eliminated? Sexual orientation. There's just nothing in that category. Oh, the exchanges are a riot. But violence of this sort? No. Just not supportable. Same thing on gender. Not there. You with me?"

"You're doing OK. Very defensible."

Fisk was visibly pleased, his legs wiggled back and forth. "Now it gets a little touchier. He picked on a number of individuals. This is where he frequently abandoned this technique of setting one group against another. He just pretty much assailed someone on the basis of a physical, ideological or emotional handicap. There are plenty of disturbed people in these categories. It was very risky for Chamberlin to do this. One of them could just stab him or shoot him. A very problematical piece of territory. What makes me conclude against individuals is the ritualistic aspect of the murder. It took at least four to six men, the police say, to pull off that kind of lynching. While it's possible for an offended individual to collect a group, of course, I doubt it. Maybe a beating – but a murder? I don't think so, at least ritualistic. I'm on a bit thinner ice here, but you want a narrowing and that's what you're going to get," he said, almost truculently.

"I understand, I understand," McAbee said. "So, you're down to ethnics, religious, and political groups where I'm assuming you're placing the Animal Liberation Front, to this point your only viable suspect."

"Yes. Good. That's it. But can you guess how many suspect groups that keeps alive?"

"No – don't even want to touch it," McAbee said lightly.

"33! And that's fortunate. If he had a chance to do this for 20 or 30 years God knows what we'd be dealing with." McAbee nodded his head in agreement. "But the categories, of course, aren't pure. For example, a gay group can also be a political group or a racial group. The categories have a porous quality to them. Just when I think that I have put one to sleep it morphs into another. Just so you know. This isn't science."

"I know Barry," McAbee said re-assuringly.

"I categorized 33 entities within these three categories, ethnic, political, religious. Did you know that he had a small success pitting American Danes against American Swedes?! Are they going to do a ritualistic killing assuming that they even made an effort to find just who was behind this hate-spinning? No, is my answer. Just staying on the ethnics I have three that I lingered on – Italians, Jews, Irish. But your brother Bill got some assurance about Jews. That helps too when I go over to religion. Also, the Jews don't have a history of ritual murder – they just send a cruise missile down your throat. The Italians – they'd ritualize – but only when and if the mafia engages. However, they don't proclaim. They seem to me to be too busy pimping, scamming, and drugging to care about their identity. After all look what Hollywood does to them regularly. But they don't do anything. A few bullets in the heads of some producers and writers would change such liberties. So, I'm taking them off the board. Now – the Irish, that's different. When Hennessey spoke with Augusta, he mentioned a meeting that he had with some guy on the south side of Chicago. He got a possible name from him. The Irish, apparently, took umbrage especially when Regis crossed from Irish into Catholics and Protestants and Northern Ireland. I'd put them on my short list. There are other ethnics – total 13, but the Irish are the ones I'm interested in. They have done ritualistic murders, they speak in code and they knew about Regis."

"You really have taken a scalpel to this."

Barry went on, probably not hearing McAbee's complimentary comment. "Now to religion. Here's where we get into serious shows of distemper. It's the hardest area."

"Maybe that's because ritual is virtually definitional to it and you've made ritual an important piece of your analysis."

Fisk thought about the comment. "Yeah, maybe that's it. Good."

McAbee felt that for the first time Fisk had really heard him during this encounter. He chose to add nothing further.

Fisk said, "He worked hard on 10 religious groups. Because of your brother, the Jews are out, as I said before. That helps, but even so, I'm disinclined to suspect Jews because I think that they're so used to crap from haters that they wouldn't know where to begin if they were going to retaliate. I hardly think they'd begin with an oddball like Regis. To them, his kind is a dime a dozen, I would think. All the groups he went after – Mormons, Whiskeypalians, Catholics – I don't see it."

"Whiskeypalians?"

"Ha! That was his term for Episcopalians. He argued that they sat around all day in country clubs boozing, ordaining queers, pissing their useless lives away. Great stuff!"

"I'll bet," McAbee wasn't in the mood. He was realizing

all the more that Regis and Barry were kindred souls with the former working out his hate through humor and the latter with just plain nastiness and misanthropy. Perhaps Regis was having an uplifting effect on the dour Fisk.

"But here's the deal Bertrand. It comes out at you like a ton of bricks. Islamic radicalism! Assassination and ritual and, if so chosen, code. Come up three big, ripe cherries on the slot machine of probability. Not Sioux or Apaches these twins – but how about Arabs. Big meaty al-Qaeda-types. How's that?" He sat back, his legs going in rapid movement.

"How heavy was Chamberlin's hand in Islam?"

"Islam, Arab, politics – the whole pie. Regis had a field day with it. He drew in hate toward them and vice versa. It was like a doomsday scenario out there – missiles flying in and out. You can't imagine Bertrand, how hot it got in that field. Incineration's the word, sheer burn-down. Regis flourished in this environment, cultivated it. I think of all the affected groups this was the one he enjoyed churning the most, simply because of all the motion that has spun off of 9/11. Had to be Nirvana for Regis, the mother-lode. Whatever term comes to mind."

"Let's just say that it comes down to some radical groups out of Islam. Sure, Regis worked up some hate-mongers. So they decide to kill him. Getting a group together would not be hard, let's say. There is a touch of ritual to the murder, I'll give you that. Tell me more about this though. What about a proclamation? What good does it do to murder him in such a public fashion and yet remain silent about why and who? Taking a risk like they did and for it not to have a payoff of publicity for their cause doesn't make good sense to me," Bertrand said speculatively.

Barry was undaunted in his firm response. "Ah, ha. The people they wanted to know knew. That would have to be it, if my hypothesis has any merit."

"So far none of the three of your prospects has proclaimed?"

"I haven't given up. But perhaps the proclamation will come in time and with other murders. I'm working diligently on getting their measure. But you're right. Nothing's out there that I can get my hands on. If you think that I'm done you don't know me. But you do know me and you know that I'm not done." Fisk's legs kicked out as in a form of defiance.

"Is this it?" McAbee asked.

"Whatever do you mean?"

"You've worked it down to three groups?"

"More or less. Remember your challenge. Whittle it down to the bone." He withdrew a disk from his bag and slid it across the table.

"What's this?"

"I know you're busy. So I've taken all of the Irish material, all the animal lib stuff, and all of the Islam material and packed it into this," he pointed to the disk that was now in McAbee's right hand. "You owe it to yourself to experience as much of it as you can. Perhaps you'll see why I argue the way I do."

McAbee said, "Your reasoning is pretty solid Barry. Don't think for a second that I'm dismissing it. I'm just surprised that you cut so deep. But let's put a magnifying glass on them and see what happens. I'm assuming that you have a second and third tier?"

"Oh yeah. Five in the second tier and seven in the third. Do you want to know how many in the fourth?"

"Sure, why not?"

"18!"

"OK. OK. I got the message," McAbee smiled.

Fisk reached into his bag and brought out a report which he pushed across the table. "The lists and the rest are all in here along with my bill. I expect a quick turnaround, of course on this bill."

"Have I ever let you down?" McAbee said lightly.

"No, but there's always a first time. Especially since you continue to keep that red-headed vixen in your employ. You know she does nothing for you. A very bad impression."

"Forget it Barry. Let it be. She's not going anywhere."

"OK, OK. You've been told. That's all I'll say."

A continuation of the ongoing and intense war being waged between these two good souls, Barry and Pat, he reflected. McAbee chose not to delve into the dynamics of what caused it. But he was convinced that Barry was the primary source of the conflict. His qualms about being paid were also without merit. McAbee not only saw to it that he was paid almost immediately but over the years had financed huge computer equipment outlays for Barry Fisk. So, while Barry billed at a very modest rate, his additional rewards from McAbee were extraordinary. But, Barry had to be difficult or he wouldn't be Barry. He saw Barry Fisk out and into the outer office. Pat eyed him with a pronounced squint. Barry left without even catching her eye.

When Bertrand turned back from the door he went to Pat's desk, "He was particularly difficult I take it?"

"Someday I'm going to tie him up and toss him into a garbage pail," she said, while shaking her head back and forth.

He handed her Barry's bill. "Will you turn this over immediately?"

"Of course, what's new? Sir Barry gets the red carpet. Oh," she was looking at the unopened envelope "I see you didn't even look at the bill."

"No Pat. He's quite honest and he's essential to my success. Pay it and thanks for putting up with his eccentricities."

CHAPTER XVI

The CD that Barry gave McAbee isolated Regis' efforts relevant to the three likely sectors that he had fingered: Islam, the Irish, and animal liberationists. The material was prolific and it was obvious that Regis found particular pleasure in persistently returning to these groups. Regis knew when and how to hit people and did it with abandon, like a cat teasing the mouse it was about to kill.

While there was good reason to see him as a mere crank, there was equally good reason to see him as a rabid hyena in need of being put out of his misery. His continuous and prolonged efforts at badgering groups not known for their forbearance apparently cost him his life.

He read Hennessey's notation about his meeting with Mickey Mullins. In Hennessey's view, it was the only lead that they found. He never had the time nor the desire, from Augusta's view, to tease out all of the possible groups. She felt that Hennessey, although competent, was overwhelmed by the possibles, the lack of resources, his personal animus toward Roberta Chamberlin and the dirty tricks that she resorted to get him thrown off the case. But Fisk was impressed with the amount of information Augusta had secured from the detective.

McAbee considered the findings of Barry Fisk to be worthy, although Fisk may have cut too close to the bone and, in effect, may have cut some likely suspects. McAbee was also very aware that Regis excised some individuals who could easily go off the deep end. He wasn't quite as convinced as Barry that such individuals couldn't mount a vigilante group to pull off the murder.

Pat came to his door and said, "Jack Scholz is here."

"OK, send him in."

Scholz, ever the precisionist in his grooming, posture and bearing came into the office as McAbee rose from his desk and with a sweeping hand gesture indicated that they would meet on the side of the office with the small round table. After they sat, Jack said, "I've been waiting for a call on this Chamberlin matter. Anything happening?"

Bertrand recounted the events that had transpired. Scholz sat impassively. He concluded his comments with a question for Scholz, "What do you think?"

Jack remained silent for awhile. Then he said, "I respect Fisk's ability as a researcher, a ferret," he paused before adding, "but as you know that's where it ends. That said I think that there's a good chance that he has it right. But now you have to send in the troops Bertrand. From listening to all of this, it sounds like the Irish connection is tops. Hennessey the cop had a bite on this Doyle character. The Irish police could care less about a crime in Chicago. Their interview with Doyle was inconclusive. I have some connections in Ireland, both pieces of the cursed isle. I could arrange a more serious chat with him using some of my pals over there."

"A what?" Bertrand asked skeptically.

"A chat with a purpose, Bertrand. That's the way of the jungle that we are in. After all, he was outed by Mullins. Of course, with the Irish, that in itself may merely mean that they're trying to compromise the sorry bastard for their own purposes and it not having anything to do with Regis. There are some tough tribes there and they know the art of the double and triple cross all too well."

McAbee had never heard Scholz talk about the Irish before and he was unaware of any involvement Scholz had there. The U.S. Marines or whatever had no affair over there as far as McAbee was aware. But with Scholz you never knew. There was more than just the Marine in his background. "I didn't know that you had any business with the Irish, Jack?"

Scholz shrugged before saying, "Oh, I was over in Belfast for just a bit of time as an observer. A team of us. Just watching some of the tactics used by the Brits," he said evasively and with a hand dismissal.

"That's the North. But what do you know about the Republic of Ireland? That's where Doyle is?" McAbee said with purposeful persistence. After all, it was rare for Scholz to give much of a glimpse at his past.

"I went aground there for a bit," he said obliquely.

"Why? The British weren't controlling crowds there?" McAbee took a certain pleasure in chasing Scholz who was noticeably uncomfortable now that McAbee had a talon into his tough hide.

"A long story and classified. In fact, I've already told you too much. Let it be said that Doyle could be conveniently disappeared for awhile and questioned carefully enough to categorically remove him from the list or to solve the case in one quick shot," he said with quiet ardor and on a clearly formal note that was meant to end any further discussion about his activities in Ireland.

McAbee noticed the oxymoron of 'observer Scholz.' He wondered what kind of dirty tricks he actually passed on to the British. Assuredly, he would never find out from the tight-lipped Scholz. As Bertrand looked at this man in front of him, he could hear the warning voice of Augusta telling him that Jack was morally corrosive. He knew that his soul was in a war zone on this issue. But try as he may to follow the advice of Augusta, he found that the tough cases more easily resolved with the intercession of Scholz and his shock troops. As to Paddy Doyle and his innocence? Well, this could be determined if Scholz was used. And if Doyle was innocent? What about that? McAbee felt that if Doyle hung with the likes of Mullins, he had done some bad things and although innocent on this matter the punishment inflicted by Scholz's people could be due for past offenses that had escaped detection. That logic would send Augusta through the wall; he had only voiced this theory once to know that he should never go there again with her. "Hennessey, the first detective in the case, had an address in Cork. It must have been valid since the Irish PD got back to Hennessey that he had been questioned but to no avail. How long would it take you to get to him?"

"I have a man in Waterford, on the East coast of the Republic. He's retired from the SEALS. He'd do what's necessary in a matter of hours, if asked. He has boys there to help. As you know I don't scrimp in manpower. There'd probably be three used to tuck him into a van, or a house in the country. It wouldn't take long to get the truth. It'll take money, of course. But you said there was a bottomless wallet?"

"Yes," McAbee said somberly as he felt himself crossing over the River Styx into hell.

"If he's still at the address that Hennessey was given I'd say that in two days, assuming my former associate William Dineen is available, that the matter could be taken care of. My question is this? What if he's guilty? Do you want him… erased?" He gave a steady look at McAbee.

"No!" McAbee said too loudly for the context of the discussion. "Jack what are you saying?"

"Well, you'd have no way to get him back to the States and little chance to work up a criminal case against him?"

"And?"

"Well, what's the reason for finding him guilty and then setting him loose?" he said with a genuinely puzzled look on his face.

"Don't go there Jack. I'm not crossing that line. You know damn well that I have problems going into the zones that we go into. But assassinations are another story altogether."

"Bertrand, it's your say. We'll do what you want. But to be honest with you, half steps are just that. Wasn't there some philosopher in ancient Greece who spun paradoxes? Surely you know him?"

"Zeno of Elea. Sure. Very astute of you Jack. He tried to protect his mentor Parmenides who denied motion and change. He posed a series of logical puzzles that would leave defenders of motion and change in discomfort. So he used, for example, the hare and the turtle. If the turtle made the lead in a race the hare could never catch him because no matter how many times the hare halved the distance there was an infinity of halving that could never allow the hare to catch the turtle. Cute pieces of logic, at the end of it all."

"Well that may be. But here's my point: you either go the whole way or you will never reach a satisfactory end. Half stops never work with bastards. I guess this Zeno would say you'd never catch this mean-spirited turtle," his smile was twisted.

"My point is the same Jack. Your logic makes sense but only in the context of its cuteness."

"Bertrand, it's your call. If you want to eliminate a possible, I just gave you the ticket. If we can get rid of this, we're down to two. If he's guilty, you have the answer. What you do with it is up to you. But I suggest that because we have a specific man we pursue it. Of Barry's three leads, it's the easiest one to ascertain."

Bertrand thought for a bit. Then, he said, "OK. Give this Dineen the details and set him loose on Doyle. No permanent damage; no killing. Give me the answer and then we'll see what's best to do."

"That it?"

"Yes, that's it. If Doyle is innocent, we focus on the other two. If he's guilty, I've got to think about it."

Jack arose from his chair and said pointedly, "I know that my world is hard for you. But you have to admit, it works."

"Yes, Jack. And perhaps that's what is most frightening about it."

Scholz left. Bertrand went to his desk and just stared out into space for a long, long time. He had just hired the services of a brutal man, not for the first time and surely, not for the last time.

It was good to hear from Jack again. It had been over a year from the last job that had taken him across the Irish Sea to England and then into the Channel for a quick piece of work in a Paris hotel. Scholz paid well and didn't have the curse of over-thinking things. Speed and simplicity were his forte.

A reminder of their days came to him during Jack's call when they would be singled out for missions by a variety of acronymed governmental agencies who made it clear that if they were apprehended they were on their own. Dineen and Scholz had teamed on three specific missions that quickly came to mind. In fact, all three flooded his head with memories the minute he heard the quiet voice of Scholz ask, "Is this a good time to talk William?"

The first mission was Beirut during the interminable civil war and fairly soon after the Marine tragedy at the Holiday Inn. Early '84. They were to hunt out a Shiite cleric who had disappeared into southern Lebanon around Sidon, a coastal city about 25 miles south of Beirut. It was to be a torture/murder thing. It went well. Some solid information was secured and it was with pleasure that the sneaky bastard was dispatched.

The second mission was in Athens, early 90s. The Greek government was playing footsie with their local radical terrorist group. Jack had a name given to him by the CIA as a good will gesture by the Russians. The assassin and his girlfriend were involved in the murder of a CIA officer in Athens. But even under the most extreme torture, his team could not break either of them into giving names. Maybe they didn't know any. They murdered both of them, anyway, as their guilt was affirmed.

By the mid 90s, they were both looking at retirement. Could they take on one more job? For old times sake? They did. It took them into eastern Turkey. A Kurdish thing. The mission took them across northern Iraq and ultimately into Iran. They found the Kurd in question. He gave them the name they wanted, willingly. After they got out the name, the man was passed on to the Turkish secret police, or so they were told. On their retirement eve, they were told that a ring of terrorists had been nabbed over in Istanbul. Thanks. The Kurd had spilled his guts.

Scholz went to the midwest, Iowa. Dineen went back to his birth area in Waterford, a dual citizen. He lived by himself, out of choice. He knew that he wasn't fit for domestication regardless of how willing the woman appeared to accept his ways. His marriages and affairs had all ended up in the trash, including his relationship with two daughters and a son. He lusted for the occasional odd jobs that came his way via Scholz and three others of like character.

He fished a bit, did ham radio, hung out on the computer, rolled his own cigarettes, jogged 30-40 miles a week, and did weights. His retirement benefits were good, his investments solid and his health excellent. He was 55, and more often than he'd ever admit, he seriously contemplated blowing his head off on top of one of Waterford's cliffs. More than anything, he missed the bestowed sense of purpose that the U.S. government gave to him, the camaraderie of like-minded men, and the adrenaline-laden missions that came his way. Simply put, Dineen liked to be in the center of murder, mayhem, and punishing bad people.

He was careful to conceal his eagerness when Jack called.

"Jack, old friend, good to hear your voice."

"Yours too William. I'm on a job for a PI I do occasional work for. There's a guy over there that needs a meeting."

"Ah. Down here in the Republic?"

"Yes."

The phrase 'needs a meeting' was code for ass kicking. Dineen could feel his blood flow catching the head winds of action. "Glad to help Jack. Been a bit slow here."

"There's always a place for you in the midwest."

"Yes, I know that. But there's something about being here that tugs me along."

"On a flight tonight, there will be a letter for you explaining what we're after. Aer Lingus, lands in Shannon tomorrow at 10 a.m. Flight 124 from O'Hare. The letter has all of the details. I would think that you might need two besides yourself. I need a quick resolution for my runner, but with updates."

"The boys will be easy to come by Jack. When I get the letter I'll be in touch."

"Take care," Scholz hung up.

The oblique communication was quite clear to Dineen. He would make the three hours drive this evening to Shannon and spend the night there. Aer Lingus would produce the letter with an ID from him in the morning. In the meantime, he was on the phone, a call to Dublin, and a call to Belfast. The two men assented immediately and would be in the Fire & Water Pub at 11 a.m. tomorrow in Shannon. No questions were asked. They all understood. The three of them were SEALS, retired. The two he called were probably dealing with the same restlessness as William Dineen, including the contemplated bullet to the head. The call to violence was an itch that could never be scratched to satisfaction.

Briefly, as if swatting away a fly, he wondered who the sorry bastard was who had come into the crosshairs of Jack Scholz. It was a fate he wouldn't wish on any but his very worst enemies. Stopping in the midst of a 'meeting' was not one of Jack's virtues, Dineen remembered. It had to be Jack's employer who wanted 'updates.' As he looked around his cottage he said to Skipper his dog, "Updates, Skipper! Now that's a new one. And from Jack Scholz of all people. The world is going crazy my dear dog."

CHAPTER XVII

Moishe Blumenburg and Rabbi Samuel Rubin landed at O'Hare Airport by way of a United Flight from Logan Airport in Boston. So far, all was well on the tour which was now about two-thirds done. Blumenburg had picked up nothing on his all too alert mental radar, although he was still upset that the rabbi's organization had posted such an explicit schedule of appearances. It was too easy for the bad guys. And the rabbi? An obsessive-compulsive if there ever was one. If the schedule read that he'd appear at 11 a.m. on Tuesday this rabbi would show up at that precise time or break his neck trying. It was a virtue and a vice. For a would-be assassin, it was a golden opportunity.

They took the hotel bus into the Loop area. They were to stay in the Marriott on Michigan Avenue. After they received their key cards, they took the elevator to the ninth floor. Their rooms were beside each other, a connecting door assured quick joint access. It was a requirement insisted upon by Moishe in every hotel where they stayed.

Moishe knocked at the connecting door and it was opened by the rabbi who silently went back to unpacking his suitcase. Their stay in Chicago would last for three nights.

"Everything OK, rabbi?"

"Yes. I need some down time, a nap. My meeting in Skokie is at 7:30 tonight. Let's see," he looked at his watch, "it's 4:35 now. I will have a light dinner in this room. I'll call room service. I'll be careful Moishe, relax. We have very good friends in Chicago."

"It just takes one enemy," Moishe said plaintively.

"Yes I know, I know. Why don't you attend to things and take a walk. If we are in the rental car by seven we'll be fine. I need some time to prepare and some rest of course. I won't open the door, I'll double lock it, chain it and stay alert. How about coming by at 6:50 so that we can be in the car by seven. Make sure that the rental is modest. I don't need a limo," he smiled wryly.

"As you say. I'll be knocking at the connecting door at 6:50 sharp. Humor me rabbi, lock it now when I leave. After all, they wouldn't know which room you're in – just another foil."

"Yes, yes." He patted Moishe's back and led him out of his room and across the threshold to Moishe's room. After the door closed, Moishe waited for the click of the safety lock. 30 seconds later he heard it. He was quite sure that this subtle rabbi had a message expressed by the delay.

Moishe left his room and headed for the management offices on the mezzanine floor of the hotel. He knocked at the door marked security and then entered a large room. A secretary was coming out of an interior office and walking towards her desk, which straddled three closed doors.

"Hi. Can I help you sir?"

"Yes. I'm Moishe Blumenburg, I have a meeting scheduled with Bob Conlon."

"Hold on a minute please." She knocked on the central door of the three and entered. About 20 seconds later she appeared before Moishe and said, "Yes. Mr. Conlon said for you to come in." She pointed to Conlon's half-opened door.

Conlon, white haired, and with a tight, thin mouth, was just finishing a phone call. He waved at Moishe and pointed to a chair in front of his desk. Moishe knew Conlon from two previous stays at the Marriott when he also had overseen the hotel protection for the rabbi. He struck Moishe as a competent and no-nonsense man. Small talk was not his gift. Conlon hung up. He stood, almost erect, and extended his firm right hand. "Moishe, good to see you again."

"Thanks Bob. Everything OK?"

"Yeah, thanks. You?"

"Well, there are good days and there are bad days," he said lightly.

Conlon smiled and said, "Rooms OK?"

"Yeah."

"Got you on our radar. Our ninth floor is given full attention, as you know. Is there anything I need to know?"

"Not really. His schedule is out there in public space for all to see. Worries me, of course. The rabbi is attentive but not totally so. You know what that's like. He's been such a high profile target for so long that after awhile he lets his guard down a bit."

"There are five cameras on that end of the ninth floor and the monitors are watched. You'll be alerted ASAP if we sense anything funny, Moishe. I assume you've got a full slate of appearances. Watch the garage. I always consider it to be our weakest point. Think about dropping him off at the front door and I'll have a man there to bring him to the lobby until you park the car. Give us a heads up about 10 minutes from here. Here's the phone number. Give them this code number 771. But please ask the rabbi to be cooperative. Two years ago, he got a bit uppity with one of my men."

Moishe held his hand outward and smiled, "I know, I know. He can be a bit of an ass sore. I'll talk with him." Moishe got up, "I really do appreciate your help and concern."

"That's our job. We don't want either one of you getting hurt."

Moishe left and went to the lobby where he arranged for a modest sedan from Avis. He was on Michigan Avenue at 5:30. It was time for a walk.

The French national Juliette Simeon had worked at Marriott International for 11 years. She had come to the United States almost four years previous in a transfer that had brought her to Salt Lake City. All of her assumptions about Americans had been borne out – they were either drug infected morons who sat mesmerized in front of a television screen watching steroidal athletes or they were puritanical money-grubbing, religious creeps assured of a ticket to heaven. What would be on the extreme in other countries was the normal in this polluted and dangerous enemy to world order. Somehow, this deranged country had to be reined in. The only hope that she saw was in the comparative rag tag gang of revolutionaries coming out of Islam. Covertly, she started to attend lectures about this religion in a store front on the south end of Salt Lake City.

When she was transferred to Detroit as the associate manager of the Marriott, she found that Islam was much more than a store front phenomenon as it had appeared in self-righteous Salt Lake City. It was, rather, a dominating and pervasive religion in Michigan. Tentatively, she began to attend some prayer sessions in several mosques. While attending one of these, she met and fell in love with a Lebanese Moslem – Raheim Azakar. After a considerable amount of time, she found out that he had been imprisoned for three years by the Israelis at the notorious Khiam Prison in the south of Lebanon, which at that time was occupied by the Israelis. At the point of his arrest by the Israelis he was not a member of their target group, the Hezbollah. He was subjected to vicious treatment before being released suddenly and without comment. But he had been transformed by the false imprisonment.

Shortly thereafter he was brought to America by his sponsoring brother who was now a successful restaurant owner in Detroit. His brother, a political and religious moderate, was not aware of what had happened inside the mind of his brother who now had a burning desire for revenge. Few knew of this, but Juliette did. Juliette sometimes came to see the world as he did.

Their situation became strained, but didn't break, when Juliette was transferred to Chicago from Detroit. They vowed to sustain the relationship over the 275 miles of interstate and to their joy their relationship deepened. Even after his three short cell phone calls that day announcing his intention to show up at her apartment in the Wrigleyville area of Chicago; his appearance brought gladness to her heart. She rang him through to her upstairs apartment in a five story building four blocks from Wrigley Field, the home of the fabled baseball team the Chicago Cubs. Her smile froze on her face as Raheim's forefinger rested across his lips as his eyes seemed to be even more intent than normal.

"What's wrong?" she asked in a half whisper.

His hand motioned her into the apartment. They went forward to her sofa and sat. She became uneasy, almost frightened.

He spoke solemnly, "Juliette, a favor has been asked of me. That favor can only be fulfilled by my asking a favor of you. It is not a desirable thing. I am saddened to come here, but I must do so. I believe that you can stay out of any loop of responsibility and your favor will be unseen except by myself, the eyes of Allah, and one other. If this were not so, I would not come here on this errand. The favor will die in my heart. Your name will never be revealed by me or the other. Of this, I give my fullest promise." He stopped and looked intently into her eyes before continuing. "While I was in Khiam Prison there were two guards among the many who were most vicious. They strutted around the yard, they beat us at will and they helped blacken my heart against Zionist dogs. One day, I went into the office of the most vicious of them, his name was Elias. On his desk was a book. It was entitled, *The True Zionist Israel*. It was authored by a rabbi named Samuel Rubin. With his metal stick in his hand he arose from his seat and came behind me. He hit me across my neck, very hard. He said, "You will talk before you ever leave here you Arab bastard." I said nothing. I never did. I screamed, yes, I cried, yes, but I never spoke to them. He smashed my ear. He came to my side and picked up the book by this rabbi. "Look at this, pig! Remember it. It is the map of how we Jews will rise and reclaim what is ours." He hit me five more times. I never spoke. I ended up on my knees but I never spoke to the man. They dragged me out and threw me back into the cell with the others. But I never forgot the book and the author. When I became free I acquired the book and read it, four times. I know that there are good Jews, reasonable people. They do not think like this rabbi. They reject him. I have no interest in these types. But this man? I do have interest in. I feel that his type brought about Khiam. This Elias was one of his disciples and that the stick that he used was an instrument of the rabbi. My feelings about this matter are known by few; I have told a bit to you. But I found out about him, that he is alive, that he raises money, that he rants and raves to his fellow Jew radicals." He paused.

Juliette listened carefully to him, noting the increasing intensity in his voice and the lines of anger that marked his face. All this while she wondered where his logic was taking him and what the matter had to do with her.

"Long ago, we found out that all our communications – computer, paper, fax, telephone – all of it was being monitored. In fact, we all assume that anything done in these media will be intercepted by American or Israeli intelligence. They are the same aren't they?" He looked at her for agreement.

She gave him a small nod, not wishing to interfere with his stream of thought. She wasn't in full agreement with what he said, however.

"So we speak in these media, if we must, by code. So, if I say 'the air is good' it may signify that a spotted surveillance is no longer visible. The watchers, of course, are never quite sure and given the paranoidal nature of the business that they're in, their guesses cause them havoc. We prefer oral communication in safe places – at ballparks, public areas, where there are distractions and much noise. We have grown up together. We know what a small gesture says. The uplifted pinkie, the beard stroke, the silent whisper. They can't beat those methods. They know this in their hearts. And they also know that dedication and secrecy is the Islamic dagger suspended above their hearts."

She had heard this radical side of Raheim, the extreme comments, the intense emotion. But there was a new sliver now. A sliver with a sharp edge that she realized would somehow find its way into her. "It is secure here, Raheim?"

"Yes, I believe so."

What led him to that conclusion she didn't know. How could he be so sure, given his theories?

He removed from his satchel a metal meter of sorts. He put his finger to his mouth once more as he started to roam around the small apartment. When he came back from his wanderings he said, "I make sure the place is clean. Now comes the hard part but before I cross it, do you love me?"

"Yes," she said noticing the slight pull in her voice. Her love was by no means unconditional. She was still French, after all.

He leaned forward, only inches from her face. "This rabbi. This Jew holy man is a terrorist. I know this. The Jews are systematically killing our people, excusing it as justifiable because of 9/11. So, leaders in Hamas, Hezbollah, genuine organizations trying to help the people, have been murdered with the use of American bombs and American permission. The Americans sell them smart bombs to make them even more effective murderers. And it is said that the Israelis are not terrorists. They're fighting for freedom. Only Arabs are terrorists. It's definitional. You do see this?"

"Yes, yes, of course, I do."

"The time has come to take the battle out of the West Bank, out of Israel, out of southern Lebanon and onto the world stage where it belongs. Peace will only come when the whole world is engaged. When everyone on this planet is aware of the issues. And…that no Jew is safe in his bed anywhere, anytime."

"I don't quite see where you are headed Raheim."

He took her right hand and held it firmly. "This vile Rabbi Samuel Rubin must die at the hands of the brotherhood."

The idea of an assassination was abhorrent to her, even if such a murder was directed at this prominent right-wing Israeli. She said nothing, knowing that another shoe was about to drop. She gave Raheim a small nod of understanding.

"This vicious assassin has decided to make a pilgrimage to America to raise money for his sordid enterprise. He is so bold, so sure of himself that the Zionist pig even publicizes his appearances before his damned kind. We have his schedule and we know his whereabouts while in America. He is a man who knows no limits. I think their word is 'chutzpah'." He shook his head in disdain. "I have been called," he said mysteriously.

Her head snapped back, away from him. She was aghast. "No, no. You are not a murderer, an assassin."

He looked down at his hands quietly before looking back at her. He said, "No. I'm not that. Neither are you. But I have been called by a power to which I am indebted. A man, a guide." He stopped, seemingly aware of her edginess as she was sure that she projected.

"He is to be at your hotel for some nights. His removal is a certainty. I come to you for help, for information, for aid."

He asked her this in such a bold manner; she was unsure of how to respond. Memories of her mother's comments forced their way into her head. "Stay away from Arabs," "Watch their politics," "They think of women as being chattel." But she also loved this man who sat near her with pleading eyes. "Raheim, what could I possibly do? I'm not violent. You have told me again and again, that I need not be violent to become a Moslem. But now you ask me to participate in such an act."

"No, no. Not participate. Nor would I. I am not violent either." He held his hands up so as to stop her train of thought.

"Perhaps in the world of Islam this is the case. But in my Catholic upbringing this would implicate me, even as we speak of the death of this man, rotten as he might be. I can not do this, I can not participate. How could you come to me about this?" She made effort to get up as tears came to her eyes. He tried to hold her by grabbing her arms, she pulled away and ran toward her door. She had to get away from him. He was only here to have her participate in a murder. She turned the handle of her apartment door. She felt the belt around her neck and the sharp and persistent pull. In less than 30 seconds she would be dead.

When Raheim realized that her body was lifeless and her beautiful face was left in a state of anguish and shock he knew instantly that his life was forever cursed. He knelt beside her and vainly tried to whisper her back to life. He crawled over to her couch and sat their occasionally looking at her body. The twin emotions of anger and despair preyed on him as sobs came forth from deep in his heart. She had done nothing to deserve what he did. Forty-five minutes later he ran from the apartment to his car and fled the scene.

CHAPTER XVIII

"What do you have on the Animal Liberation Front, Earth Now, and PETA?" Bertrand asked as he pictured his brother Bill mentally processing the question.

"Why do you want to know?"

"I'm going after three groups as possibilities in the Regis Chamberlin matter. An Irish possibility is being run as we speak. The Islamic stuff is a true Pandora's box as you can imagine. I've decided to keep that one out of the equation until I can take the Irish and the animalists off the table."

"Where's your gut pointing you?"

"Not prepared to answer that one yet."

"Bertrand! You're not in mushy-headed academia now where you can sit around arguing for five years about what to teach in the second week of some goofy and irrelevant course!" Bill said acerbically.

Bertrand held himself under control. Bill was in a dark mood, itching for a fight. He, on the other hand, was trying to solve a problem about the eco-movement, two different battle fields. He decided to drift back to the issue. "So, do you have any operations on the ground?"

"Well, I don't know. Let me sit around and think about it," still romping in sarcasm.

So, Bertrand was going to have to go through the battlefield with him. "Hey Bill, what's wrong with you? I'm asking you a pretty simple question. What the hell is with the attitude?"

Bill, a man of unpredictable responses, snorted a laugh. "Just warming up for a meeting I'm having this afternoon with a Dean from Yale who happens to have two qualities, he's smart and he's, in equal strength, as indecisive as anyone I've ever met. I have decided to come after him full bore."

"So I'm a test case?"

"Yeah, that's about it. So, what would you say if you were this Dean?"

"I'd tell you to go straight to hell. Don't mistake due consideration, an academic quality, for character weakness. I think you'll find that you'll be gored by him. OK, so now that we've had spring training on academia, will you kindly answer my question?"

"It's a complex question. I'll do it by numbers. Range it out 1 – 10, with one being mildly concerned about eco-animalism matters and 10 consumed by it. One of the Hollywood goofs who buys a hybrid, a Prius let's say, is making a profound statement. About as profound as their phoniness. I'd put them at about a one or two. There's some acting out. But it's legal and ultimately, who cares?"

"OK, I see your point," Bertrand said, noting that his arch-conservative and distrusting brother was on one of his rhetorical and bellicose horses.

"The fives are getting close to the line. They're the types who will 911 the highway patrol, which, by the way, is busily scraping a body out of a burning vehicle, to report that someone doesn't have their kid in a seat belt or a tissue has flown out of some car window. They're legal, but they're a pain in the ass. It's when you get beyond five that they begin to cross over. This is what you're looking for."

"The tens?"

"Yeah – nine and 10. They'll do anything to protect the environment and/or animals. They spike trees, break into labs, smear blood on fur and all the other things they can do in order to disrupt this world as we know it."

"How about murdering Regis?"

"That's a tough one. I know of no act of murder by them as happened to Regis Chamberlin. Some of the spiked trees have caused death, some trucks carrying clear cut have had their brake lines compromised, thus causing death, but these kind of attacks have been indirect as in disruption first and if death occurs well, so be it. The Regis murder is in a class by itself. I don't know of any incident like this. A month ago, somewhere in northern Minnesota, a sable farmer had his sables let loose. He died of a heart attack. What would you put that to? Murder? What?"

"Good question. I'd answer yes in a roundabout way. But it's not a primary intention."

"Right. Now if they had put a bullet into his brain they'd have moved to a different level. Why are you picking on this scab?"

"Regis was playing them hard, to the hilt, while also playing with the enemies of these movements."

"What about those enemies?"

"No. Nothing there. Had some strenuous material thrown at Regis, however, by the eco-types."

"Threats?"

"Yes, very much so. A few quotes, 'Humans can be spiked too,' 'A dead skunk is better than a live piece of trash like you,' 'We will find you.' How's that for a start?"

"Who's signing off on this?"

"Names like 'Eco Jim,' 'PETA PETE,' 'Tree Hugging Verna, 'Viva Animals'. For a movement with no record of deliberate and sheer murder, they sure do talk a tough game."

"Some of us have pooled on this. There are questions out there. But I'll warn you in advance. Some of the real crazies are so decentralized and paranoidal that there's no way to break into them without a huge stroke of luck. They're loners to the extreme. They only work solo. And they'd be unlikely to even touch a computer key if they felt some need to communicate with Chamberlin. Their whole game is untraceability. They would see the Unabomber as an extroverted, publicity-hungry fool. Hold on. Let me make a call."

Bertrand felt the silence, then the quick da…da…da… and the pick up of a phone. It was answered on the fifth da by a youngish-sounding woman, "Weather?"

"This is Bill Mack."

"And?"

"The weather is clear."

"Good morning Bill."

"My brother is on the line with me."

"Hi," she said.

"Hi," Bertrand responded.

Bill picked up the flow. "My brother is investigating a murder. It was violent and it probably needed a cohort of at least four individuals to pull it off. No credit has been taken and it happened about a week and a half ago. What do you think?"

She was quicker in responding than Bertrand had thought she'd be. "No. It's not in their M.O. Can't see it. Give me the dope, though. I'll keep an eye."

Bertrand dictated a brief summary of Regis' doings and some details around his murder.

She said, "Whoa. The more I hear, the more I'd have to say it's way off the meter. Nothing close has come our way and we have a number of thermometers up the collective asses of these screwballs."

Bill laughed, bade her goodbye, and disconnected her. "That's Lizzie. Tough babe from Fargo. If anyone has a take on these characters she does. So where does that leave you?"

"The Irish thing is going down today sometime. I think it's a longshot but there are points of merit to its consideration. But if it falls through then I go to Islamic radicalism."

"I'll tell you this right now Bertrand. You might as well get in line when it comes to radical Islam. It's a goddam porcupine and some of the best minds in the world are working it. It has thousands of quills, thousands. Keep me informed. By the way, are you still using that Scholz guy?"

"Yeah. He's driving the Irish piece of the investigation. Why do you ask?"

"He came into my radar a month ago. That's all for now," he said mysteriously.

"Are you going to tell me anymore?"

"No. It's not important. If it ever becomes so, you'll be the first to know. Gotta go," he hung up.

Bertrand was pretty confident now that the eco-types

could be removed from consideration. As to Scholz, he wondered whether it was a positive or negative radar event. Bertrand had always figured that part of what drove Jack Scholz to work with him as zealously as he did was for a possible hookup with Bill's agency. Jack Scholz and Bertrand were, after all, significantly different from each other. Jack Scholz and Bill, on the other hand, were philosophy-wise at least, identical twins.

"I'm looking for a packet, my dear, which was aboard the flight from Chicago, 124," Dineen said thinking that if this female Aer Lingus booking agent was Irish, then Ireland had become eastern European while no one was looking.

"Your name, please?"

"Dineen, William. And where would you hail from my dear?" She shot a suspicious look at him. He continued, "You don't look Irish at all."

"Your point being?"

Dineen, if such was possible, wanted to break her neck then and there. Instead, he smiled and said in a low voice, "Get me the fucking packet dear. We'll do business only from this moment."

Her head snapped back as if she had been slapped. She gave him a fearfully suspicious peek and said, "Ah. I'll be back."

Within about two minutes, she came back with an 11 by 14 inch sealed envelope to which was attached a signing card. "You have to sign on this line."

He did so. She tore off the signature card attached to the envelope and handed the envelope to him without even looking at him. He noted her name 'Alana' and strode off hoping that somewhere in the future, she'd come into his crosshairs.

He drove to the Fire & Water Pub. He was early. He read the terse contents of the packet. He awaited his two mates. It seemed a simple enough job assuming that Paddy Doyle had an understanding about torture.

The three of them were in Cork by about 2:30 p.m. and after discreet inquiries were at Paddy's door by 3:45. He lived in a shabby six-plex a few blocks from the city center. They didn't want any noise as the building construction looked as though it could magnify a dropped pin to a sound like a thunderclap. When they arrived at the apartment, Dineen slowly turned the doorknob. To his joy, the door opened. He turned toward the other two and saw that their eyebrows rose in relief as he pushed open the door. He motioned the pair forward with a flick of his fingers. They withdrew their magnums and rushed forward into the small studio apartment. He watched as they stood over Paddy Doyle who was coming out of a deep sleep, pulling his arm away from an overweight redhead whose eyes were agog with alarm.

"Shut up the two of you and you'll live," one of Dineen's pair growled.

Dineen came forward. He spoke to the woman who was now as pale as a cottonball. "Cover yourself you fat whore and if you make a sound it'll be your last. Our business is not with you. You're in the wrong place at the wrong time."

She pulled the sheet over her body and arose to a sitting position, hiding her nakedness as well as she could. Dineen wanted to laugh at her and slap her on her fat ass. He wouldn't, of course, it wasn't professional. He pointed to one of his men. He was to guard her. The other would help him key on Doyle who was looking at the whole scene with a practiced eye. He'd been around the block, Dineen noted. He nodded his head toward his man guarding the redhead, wanting him to take her away from the scene as far as he could in this cramped apartment.

"Don't give us the eye Doyle. This is for real."

"Shit on the two of you," he snapped back at Dineen. He brought a pillow up against the backboard and placed his hands behind his head, dismissive of the threat and unabashed about his nudity.

Dineen had seen many types under similar circumstances. He had had his share of Doyles, poker players. Perhaps he had a strong hand and would cause Dineen to play many of his nastiest cards. But for everyone like that there was the other, full of the brag and the bluff who would talk at the first show of force.

While his man kept his magnum pointed at Doyle, Dineen sat parallel to Doyle's outstretched knees angling himself for maximum torque, his back to him. "I'm going to ask you some questions. If you don't answer to my satisfaction, it will be a hard day for both of us, sir. Do you understand?"

Doyle grunted non-committally.

"What do you know about Regis Chamberlin?"

"Never heard of him," he answered too quickly.

"Once more – Regis Chamberlin," Dineen said quietly.

"Shit on you!"

"Mickey Mullins?"

"Ditto. Fuck the pair of you," he said, picking up confidence.

"If this was baseball, they'd said that you struck out on three pitches."

"If this was baseball they'd say that you were a minor leaguer. Now why don't you put your toys away and leave me alone with my woman, you queer bastards," his face red with indignation.

Dineen waved his arm across to his man and motioned him to put his weapon aside as he pointed to a black valise which had been placed by the only window of the dingy apartment. Dineen in one final motion leaned far to his right and downwards and then clasping his hands came up, across and down with his left elbow crashing into Doyle's testicles with as much velocity as this muscular and violence-knowing man could deliver.

Doyle screamed at the top of his voice which Dineen quickly cut off with a hard downward fist-smash and then held his hand over the mouth of Doyle who was now doubling in pain. From a side glance he saw that Doyle's fat redhead was puking into the kitchen sink loaded with unwashed dishes. He hoped that he wouldn't have to stay here for too long. It was such a dirty business, but how he loved it, thrived on it.

They tied Doyle's protesting hands to the backboard posts. His waist was cinched with rope which they attached by knots to his spread apart legs. Doyle tugged unsuccessfully at the professionally done knottings.

Dineen said to the redhead's guard, "Bring her over and tie her to a kitchen chair. We want it to be that the last ones they see are each other's ugly and stupid faces." The sobbing woman was tied to the chair in less than a minute.

"Now, I think that we are properly prepared to conduct

business wouldn't you say men?" Both of his men nodded their assent somberly.

Dineen spoke softly to the redhead. "Dear, how long have you known your man here?" He pointed vaguely in the direction of Doyle.

She looked at him in terror and mumbled something that was incomprehensible.

"You won't be coming to harm if you do two things. One, speak up and two, be honest." He took out a nine inch knife that was attached just above the ankle of his left leg. "Otherwise," holding the knife as if measuring and assessing its heft, "I'll cut your face into tiny pieces. And I don't have the time for you to think it over. If you say yes, we talk. If you don't, I start cutting on you. Answer me!"

"Yes I'll talk. Whatever you need to know," she said quickly amid sobs.

"You heard my question. Answer me."

"I grew up with Paddy. We've been on and off."

"This is your vision of being on, I take it."

"Yes," she said hesitantly.

"I want you to tell Paddy to cooperate with us. To stop his belligerent ways." He looked back at Doyle whose eyes were closed.

Quickly and fervently she called out shrilly to him, "Paddy, for Christ's sake, tell them what they want to hear."

Dineen held up a restraining hand toward her. She had said enough. Another minute of that whine might cause Paddy to have a stroke. "So what's it to be Paddy?" His men were now placing prongs into the two electrical outlets near the bed. Dineen saw Doyle catch a quick look at the apparatuses on the other end of the cords.

"What the fuck do you want with me man?" He said with a touch of fear in his voice.

There was enough of a plead to tell Dineen that he'd get to the truth quickly. "I'm going to try again. I know a lot already. If you lie to me you won't be fucking your girlfriend here for some time." He placed the point of the knife under Doyle's limp penis and flicked it up in the air.

"Jesus Christ! Tell me what you want."

"Mickey Mullins," Dineen said quietly.

"A Chicago man. He raises money for the cause."

"The cause?"

"The IRA. He's a watcher. He knows a lot of people. A contact man for the midwest in the USA."

"He told us about you. That's how we know of you. Good old Mullins," he said tauntingly.

"There's nothing to tell for Christ's sake."

"You left Chicago the night after a murder. We all think that you did it."

"That's just bullshit. I don't kill. If he told you that I killed someone he's screwing around with you."

"Regis Chamberlin."

"Regis Chamberlin! A goddamned screwball. What can I say? There was some talk to get the bastard. But nothing ever happened. You said he was murdered. If anyone in my crowd was going to get him, it would be for a talking to, not for murdering. Maybe a slapping around. Give me a break. No one in our group would murder him. If Mullins is saying otherwise, it's to cover up his own misdeeds. This Chamberlin," he was now into full plead, "was a nothing. A crank. It would feel good to kick his ass a bit. But that's the end of it." He was looking closely at Dineen who was now carefully weighing what he had just heard.

"Why did you leave Chicago?"

"Ran up some credit cards. You know the score. Time to get out for awhile."

Suddenly, Dineen arose and signaled his men to disconnect the equipment. As they were doing so he stared at Doyle. "I believe that you're telling the truth. If it comes out that you lied to me I will make it my life's mission to hunt you down and chop off your genitalia." He turned toward the redhead, "As for you, this is a private matter. If the police get involved or anything adverse occurs your face will get you into a circus-freak show. Pleasure doing business with you." They left the apartment.

CHAPTER XIX

The conversation with Dineen was over in less than a minute. Scholz, and virtually all of his contacts, assumed that someone was listening in somewhere. Legal wiretaps by the government constitute probably less than 10 percent of the wiretaps that were going down at any one time in America. He replayed the conversation in his mind.

"Jack. It's me," Dineen said.

"Yes?"

"I took a look at that horse. He's clean-legged. Slight interest in a light workout. Not by him, maybe others like him. But nothing serious. I'd say it was a buy on my part. 15 would do it. No reason to go any further into the matter. I'm heading home unless you tell me otherwise."

"Thanks. Get me a post number and I'll wire it over."

The horse was Paddy Doyle and his clean leggedness meant that he wasn't involved. However, some of Paddy's friends might have wanted to rough up Regis but not kill him. Dineen was confident, so much so, that he was heading home. The number, 15 = $15,000, was simply the amount of money Dineen needed to pay off himself and his men.

A listener would have a hard time deciphering such an oblique message.

Scholz dialed Bertrand for a meeting. He didn't like doing business with McAbee on the telephone. McAbee was not good at coding. He always wanted details, thus compromising any effort at obliqueness.

They met at the levee in downtown Davenport, close to lock and dam 15 on the Mississippi River. It was a beautiful day in mid-October. Scholz liked to meet here because there was a steady noise coming from the lock and dam systems and also because he loved the Mississippi backdrop with Rock Island, Illinois, about a half mile across from where he stood. As he looked east, he saw the Government Bridge which joined the U.S. Government's Rock Island Arsenal and the City of Rock Island in a Y construction of sorts. As he looked west he saw the Centennial Bridge, the primary span linking the cities of Davenport and Rock Island. He saw McAbee walking across the railroad tracks toward him. McAbee's walk was very open, a wasting of motion. Scholz shook his head slightly and raised his eyes upwards for a second, as if pleading for deliverance. The simple fact was that McAbee had no business in the field of cloak and dagger. He was just too abstract, too hesitant, always looking under unnecessary rocks when an answer was so clear.

His brother Bill set him up in the business. Perhaps he saw something that Jack didn't see. He was coming up to his truck and Jack got out.

"Jack," Bertrand said convivially.

"Hello Bertrand. Got some news for you."

"OK."

They started to walk. "We found Paddy Doyle over in Ireland."

"And?" Bertrand asked hesitantly.

Scholz thought to himself that it was a here we go again scenario. Bertrand knew full well that using Jack meant using force and torture. But he was in his usual denial. "My men talked with him." He stopped.

Bertrand said, "Talked?"

"I don't know the details surrounding the conversation."

"Go ahead," he said stoically.

Scholz wanted to grab him by his lapels and shake him. "The man I used is very good, experienced, capable. He said that there's nothing there. Paddy Doyle is innocent, at least in relation to Regis Chamberlin. Of course, he's the type of guy who has done plenty of bad things, so however this information was gotten, I'm sure that some past sin was being attended to."

"What does that kind of thinking get us?" But Bertrand thought of Augusta.

"It relieves guilt for people who might be inclined in that direction – like yourself." Scholz wanted to pull the last sentence back. He was being more direct than usual with Bertrand. On several occasions he had seen some dark center in McAbee. A center that would act like a black hole, obliterating everything that came toward it. Specifically, he would just shut down as if deciding that the person no longer existed. He would enact no further contact, a psychological murder of sorts. If it happened it would take place under these kinds of circumstances. When he was pushed too far or when someone had encroached upon him beyond what was allowable. There was no objective way to define or measure it. It was a Bertrand-thing.

After a few seconds Bertrand responded, "So. I guess that I have you to thank for my clear conscience. You do have to admit that you're an interesting specimen for purporting to ease people's consciences." McAbee said without rancor and pretty evenly.

It was a comment that Scholz knew was loaded with shrapnel. At this point it was best to retreat by changing the topic. "Where do you want to go from here?"

McAbee probably saw this as a peace offering since he thankfully dropped the matter. "My brother's people tell me that the eco-types are most likely clean. The Irish are coming in clean; we have even, in our endearing way, caused some justified punishment for a poor Irish soul for past wrongs." He looked hard at Scholz indicating that he did not forget his forwardness. "So it looks as though Islamic radicalism is our next target. And I'll tell you right now it's the one hive that I didn't want to get near."

"You don't have much, but you do have something."

"I have an ID on two guys whose skin was tanned and/or dark, naturally. I know that they came back as if to look for something and whatever it is, it's still out there, presumably. I know that Regis worked his tawdry malevolence on Islam. He kept playing Russian roulette and maybe finally he caught a loaded chamber. So let's assume it is they. The 'they' is the problem. The U.S. Government has been hunting for Bin Laden with thousands of soldiers and billions of dollars. And, it knows who Bin Laden is. I take it that there are thousands of cells all over the world dreaming of killing Americans. Regis was eligible to a fault. Thus? It looks to me as though we have thousands of suspects. We also have the CIA, the FBI, state agencies and God knows how many others morbidly fixated on them. And here comes the ACJ Agency. I guess that some would say that we were on an idiot's mission, no disrespect meant to any of you working with me. It's huge, thousands of acres of forest out there and we're looking for one tree."

"Sounds like you've made up your mind. Time to bail out?"

"No. It's time to really think carefully before going into the forest. If I rush into the forest I'll be lost before I know it. Then, I'll bail but it will be because of incompetency. It may come to a bail out, but I don't want it to be because I was stupid."

Scholz listened carefully. It was not like McAbee to share his inner thoughts with him. Those thoughts betrayed a man who thought too much and acted too little. You might get lost in a forest but if you bring along a good buzz saw a lot of equalizing could take place. "So, what are you suggesting?"

"I'm going to go back to his home. I think that there might be something there."

"How is that old guy with the dog?"

"Rufus O'Hanlon and Duke. They're back home again. Rufus is ailing, but getting better. The dog is a bit better too."

"Police done?"

"Yeah. The apartment is available. Roberta will leave it be until I give her an OK."

"How is she behaving?"

"Impatient as always. I'll report to her that we're down

to radical Islam. Who knows? Maybe she'll call me off when she hears my conclusion," Bertrand said.

"What about the sci-fi guy upstairs?"

"Serge Pushkin won't answer his phone. He's a jittery soul. I don't think he has anything further for us. But there is something else that strikes me."

"What's that?"

"Brazenness. Those two men seemed to think that they could do as they wanted whenever they wanted. To me that's odd. It's almost as though they thought that they were immune. That they were under some banner of protection. When I see that, I think of religious zealotry."

"Maybe they're just stupid," Jack said.

"Sometimes the traits are from the same weaver. But you know the old Greek formula for all of this. Hubris invites nemesis. We've seen the hubris. Nemesis is probably not far behind."

Jack shrugged. His world and Bertrand McAbee's world were extremely different. As Bertrand started to walk away a stray thought came hard at him. He fought it off successfully. A tribute to his mental control. The thought? It was that maybe Bertrand McAbee wasn't as ill-fitted to the profession as Jack thought. He got into his truck and drove away, the thought banished.

Othman and his brother Mohammed were not surprised at the rabbi's insolence. A man so hated and so vicious toward the Islamic cause probably saw himself as invincible. Who else would put on the internet a full schedule of events for 30 days? Only a fool and one who was damned. Unfortunately, his assassination would take extra boldness, given a failed effort between a confederate and a stupid French whore who worked in the hotel. A murder had resulted as the confederate left for the Middle East, according to Ali.

Othman was in the lobby of the hotel when the rabbi returned from a talk that he had given in Skokie. He saw him walk across the lobby in his black suit and tie, white shirt and yarmulke. His beard was black and white speckled. He wore thick glasses. He was escorted by a young, blonde, athletic-looking man who did not seem to be overly concerned with his apparent responsibility to guard the Israeli dog. They both sat in the lobby until a third man joined them. He was a more serious man. Portly, athletic, and watchful, he seemed to ignore the young man. Soon, he and the rabbi entered an elevator. The lobby was about 90 percent empty. It was 11:15 p.m. Othman followed at a distance noting that the elevator stopped at the ninth floor. He concluded that the system to be used was for the rabbi to be joined by hotel security while his bodyguard parked the vehicle. Then the bodyguard and the rabbi would proceed to their rooms. The bodyguard was obviously armed, given the rather large bulge under his left armpit. It did not look as though the hotel guard was armed and even if so, he did not look like serious manpower. Othman noticed that he had gone to the front desk and was flirting with the night clerk. The point of vulnerability would be in the exchange when the rabbi was dropped off at the entrance to the hotel and the bodyguard parked the vehicle. The shooting would be easy, but the escape would be more difficult. It would have to be tomorrow night after the rabbi spoke at a synagogue in Evanston. The weather was predicted to be one of heavy rain and fog. These were good conditions for an escape.

The bodyguard would appear in the lobby only to find that his charge had been delivered into hell. The blonde fool the hotel supplied would also have to die.

This process was flawed, of course. It would have been preferred to have gotten access to the rooms via the French bitch but she proved to be uncommitted to the cause. Apparently the unknown confederate had been warned, but he was in love. He should have known what everyone among us knows, we are different and ultimately incomprehensible to a western mentality.

As they drove back from Evanston, Rabbi Samuel Rubin noticed that Moishe was unusually quiet. "So Moishe? Why so quiet?"

"The driving is terrible. I'm concentrating on the road rabbi."

"That's all?"

"Well, I'll be truthful with you. Those three who sat in the back of the hall. The three who identified themselves as sociologists from Northwestern." He stopped as if that was all that needed to be said.

"Yes, Moishe? Your point?"

"Why didn't you have me escort them out. They're the worst kind of Jew. Self-haters. They didn't come to support you. They came to beat you down. You're trying to raise money for your cause. They were out to defeat you. Why did you put up with them?"

"Because of that. They are Jews. I can not as a teacher run from them. Yes, they are misled. They wish to trust the Palestinians. They wish us to ride in busses with them. They are appeasers. If they came to Israel they would, of course, take private cabs. Their minds are diseased and contradictory. But I repeat, I am a teacher. They were not supported by the congregation. The pledges were enormous. If I had acted viciously or with force, I feel that I would have played into their hands. After all, their contention was that I'm violent. Now, if they had physically attacked me it would be a different story. You see my point?" The rabbi looked over at Moishe who was studying the road intently. He saw the slightest knit of his eyebrows as a response to what he had just said.

After awhile, Moishe finally said, "It's their rectitude, their academic insolence that bothers me. Do you know what I mean?"

"Of course I do. And no argument of mine will change them. I am a man of religion and they are an oxymoron, secular Jews. Do you know what that means? That means that they are atheists! Hah! And they want to tell us how to run our land."

Moishe didn't respond. The rabbi noticed that both the rain and the fog had worsened. He was beginning to make out the shadowy presence of downtown as they came under the post office that spread across 290, the Eisenhower Expressway. "We'll be at the hotel in about 10 minutes. I'll call through." Moishe used his cell adroitly. "Yes, hello also. I'm about 10 minutes from you. I have the rabbi." There was a delay of a few seconds. He continued, "Good. Last night worked well. Keep your eyes open, please. It's a mean night." He disconnected. He said, "You heard rabbi. Like last night. Stay near their man please."

"Of course, of course."

To himself, the rabbi thought that if someone is gutsy enough and has enough firepower they would get you regardless of all the precautions that are taken, especially in the circumstances that he found himself in a country such as America.

Moishe pulled up in front of the Marriott. The same young man who met him last night was waiting. He had an umbrella. His name was Everett. The rabbi slid out of the car and placed himself under the open umbrella.

"Good evening Rabbi Rubin."

"Hello Everett. Is this typical weather?"

Everett laughed. "No, no. It's not usually this bad."

The rabbi walked with him to the rotating doorway. He pushed forward as he saw from the corner of his eye Everett trying to close his umbrella and follow him in the next opening. As he entered the lobby he was about to turn and await Everett who was just coming forward. A tall, dark man came at them. His eyes were black, his look intense. The rabbi looked at Everett who was still busying himself with his umbrella. As he turned back toward the advancing figure, less than 10 feet away, he saw the gun. He felt two brutal jolts in his chest that rocked him back a few steps. The last thing he heard was a scream from Everett as he felt searing pains flash through his entire body.

CHAPTER XX

McAbee had no immediate reason to connect the murder of Rabbi Rubin and a hotel security agent to any cases with which he was currently involved. He was surprised when he read the *Chicago Tribune*, by the boldness of the attacks, however. The downtown Marriott, where he had stayed several times, was square in the middle of heavily-traveled Michigan Avenue. Even given that the night was dominated by fog and mist, the assassination was most assuredly a planned event. It was highly unlikely that the murderer relied on the adverse weather which surely enabled him to escape. Two witnesses gave somewhat similar identifications. The man was tall, Caucasian, but dark of skin. The escape car was black, large, and expensive-looking. As he was about to turn the page he stopped and reflected. While there were a number of dissimilarities to the Regis Chamberlin case some elements had the feel of recognition, especially the brazenness.

On page seven another article came by his attention. A French national, Juliette Simeon, was found strangled to death in her apartment in the near north side. She had been dead for probably three days, the police estimated. It was the last line of the relatively small piece that made him sit up a bit as he absent-mindedly petted Scorpio's head. "Ms. Simeon was employed by the downtown Marriott, she had been in the United States for several years in various positions with the company."

He was pretty sure that the Chicago PD would be struck by the possible tie-in of the two murders but, on the other hand, maybe not. He phoned Fisk.

"Barry, this is Bertrand."

"Yes?" he said in high grouch.

"I have an odd coincidence that I'd like you to run down. Thorough, very thorough. Just in case."

"I'm listening."

Bertrand ran through the names and events for him. He pointed out that the most striking detail that he had found was the reckless quality of the rabbi's assassin and that he matched, yes – admittedly so did 20% of Chicago, the description of one of those seen by Serge Pushkin and Rufus O'Hanlon.

When McAbee had finished his comments, Barry said, "I think that you're pushing on this. But, I'll concede that there's a very slight chance, slight."

"The big item with the French woman is this. Does she have any connection with Islam. If there is something there, then perhaps we've got something."

"Well this rabbi murder is a big deal. Everyone has been fearful that the next chain of occurrences would involve the murders of Jews outside of Israel. For example, if the Israelis now murdered someone of renown among the Palestinians, I don't think there's any doubt that the Middle East mess would explode around the world. And…maybe this is the beginning."

"You have a good point."

"I hate to say it, but maybe it will be resolved when the killing becomes so intolerable that it forces both sides to sit down to finally resolve the matter. The number of innocent people who die in the process will be staggering. I'll get on this right now, but don't get your hopes up Bertrand. This is really a long shot."

McAbee drove to the bike path that spanned Davenport and Bettendorf. He was to meet his running partner Judy Pappas for a 10 mile run. Scorpio was expectant as McAbee reached for his doorknob.

"No Scorpio, not today." He patted him on the head as the dog sat in front of the door with his saddest of looks in his large and intense black eyes. He felt guilty but he had noticed that the last time he had taken the dog on a run he seemed to be favoring his right front leg. Scorpio relented, finally, at Bertrand's urging, and allowed Bertrand to pass through the doorway. By the time Bertrand was pulling away from his condo, Scorpio was upstairs in a bedroom window casting a long look through the room's curtains at the departing McAbee. His look was depressed or was that Bertrand's guilt kicking in?

Judy Pappas was all too familiar with Bertrand's mercurial qualities. She had seen him ebullient and extraordinarily outgoing and extroverted. This was typically a function of his being fully engaged with the run, absent physical aches, with a mind cleared of clutter, and his being accompanied by his dog Scorpio. Such wasn't often the case as he had an aging dog who could no longer hold up to 10 mile runs, however slow they might be. Complicating the formula was McAbee's case load which seemed to increase geometrically with his exposure in an issue of the *AARP Magazine* which featured him relative to successful career shifts. She knew that he had accepted their doing a story about him until he had second thoughts. Unfortunately, it was too late to withdraw and the story went ahead. It generated other stories that made it as far as *The Wall Street Journal*.

She knew that he craved simplicity and order. Conditions like he was experiencing were breaking him down. He didn't tell her this, nor would he. He was private to a fault. She was sure that his view of the world was affected by some of his Roman and Greek classics. Probably the stoics more than anything. She had done some reading on them and she thought she had a better hold on him as a consequence of her study.

She saw his Ford Explorer Sport off in the distance on Jersey Ridge Road. He hurriedly came east from there onto George Washington Boulevard, turned into a driveway, backed out and parked facing west.

He bolted out of the SUV saying, "Judy, Judy, I'm late, I know. Sorry. Have you been here long?"

"Nah, a minute or two." In fact she had been waiting for him for at least 10 minutes. She noticed that he was disorganized and fidgeting as he busied himself with his gear from the back of his vehicle. She was in no particular hurry today. She came up to him as he was cinching his water belt around his waist. "Bertrand, I'm in no hurry today. So, don't rush on my account."

"I appreciate that. I've got a case that is lurching its way into the badlands."

She knew that he had been out in South Dakota a few years back. He had considered the ravine area of the badlands with its serrated rock formations the worst terrain that he had ever seen. He had said that explorers who happened into that area must have been bewildered by such an impossible landscape. So, now he had a case that squared with his musings about that trip. They walked to their starting line – a scrupulously laid-out point from which they would begin a 10 mile run, typical for their training schedule. They had reasoned that 10 miles was a solid platform from where they could proceed into marathon training. She looked over at him as he was hitting his Polar watch dials that would give him the run-time and a measure of his heartbeat which was relayed to the watch from a band that he cinched near his heart.

He looked at her and said, "Ready?"

"Let's." It was their custom to do the first leg of their run, usually about 50 minutes, talking to each other about what each was up to. At Middle Park in Bettendorf they would stop, drink Gatorade, and then listen to some tape or radio station for the rest of the exercise. She led off by talking about a new restaurant that she had tried in Moline, Illinois. It had been a disappointment and she detailed her complaints. She wasn't sure whether or not he was listening. She tested, "Have you ever heard of the place?"

"No. And from what you said, I hope I won't hear of it again," he said lightly.

Well, he was listening. She decided to try to draw him

out about his case. Usually he didn't speak of these except in the most general of terms. "So you have a tough case?"

"Judy, it throws me right into the middle of all this terrorism craze. I don't know where the damn thing will take me." He stopped abruptly. Then he added, "I'll be spending more time in Chicago."

She knew from past experiences that was about as much as she'd find out from him. They, she primarily, chatted about other matters, her progress toward her doctorate in statistics from the University of Iowa, movies that she had seen and the like. She didn't have to be told that he was engrossed with a case that seemed to have burned into his personality. He was pretty much into shut-down mode.

About three miles into their run she was delighted to see up ahead, along the Duck Creek part of the run in Bettendorf, a woman whom they had befriended who would be regularly walking two greyhound dogs. Her name was Skip and the dogs were called Sybil and Roo. They were adopted by Skip after their racing days ended at the dog tracks that dotted Iowa and Wisconsin. McAbee had a childlike quality that would come to the fore when he saw them.

He yelled, "Sybil, Roo!" They jumped forward as the smiling Skip held their straining leashes. "Judy, we're in luck. They're out," he said with the first sign of enthusiasm that she had seen today from him.

Both dogs were female. Sybil was the larger of the two, dark tan with black striping throughout. She was forthcoming and friendly. Roo was gray and somewhat withdrawn. Roo would have to think things over before she would give herself to being petted. But McAbee had recently taken to including Milk Bones in his waist bag and the dogs gave him extra attention as he withdrew a baggie and took out four medium-sized treats. Joyously, the dogs took them. Sybil had both of hers eaten in a matter of seconds. Roo was gentle and chewed hers into mini-bites, all the while being fussed over by Bertrand and Judy as they spoke with Skip. Sybil tried to get a third one before Roo was finished with her first. McAbee laughed but protected the treat until Roo finally took it. It was the only time in the entire 10 mile run that Bertrand was able to forget himself and his musings. Disappointingly, he declined their usual coffee meeting at the local Panera Bread Company. He had a meeting.

His last comment to her was, "Judy, I'm sorry I've been such a slug. I don't know when I'll be able to do this again. I might be in Chicago for a bunch of days. I'll call."

"You did well my brother. That it's Allah's work is manifest from the protection that they received. They are bold and yet you and they are untraced. A sign from Allah. When I heard of the execution, I was gladdened of heart. I have spoken with my contacts. Your bank account in Riyadh has grown significantly."

Ali bowed in recognition of the generosity of Faisal. He said, "It is as if Othman and Mohammed have shields of invisibility. They are under the protection of Allah's angels."

Faisal sat quietly for some time before speaking. "We must, of course, be careful. Not all of our adversaries are monkeys, stupid dogs. Some of them are watchful, ambitious, mean."

"The brothers have been warned to be vigilant. That eyes and ears are everywhere. They have become better. Of course, their fearlessness has produced the filthy rabbi's assassination. There are very few who could have done what they did, with such professionalism and efficiency."

Faisal stroked his bearded chin, but said nothing. Ali sensed a strain in the environment. His other meetings with him had been held in studied friendliness. Now he sensed a tautness in Faisal's silences. Were they to a purpose aimed at him?

"So my brother tell me again, as I am unclear. Othman, our would-be prince, and his brother went back to this Chamberlin's apartment. You said that they forgot something? But they didn't. They found it in their car. But they were seen by some fat old man and an absurd dog. Am I right?"

"Yes," Ali became apprehensive and guarded. It seemed that Faisal had a piece of information, knew something beyond what Ali had told him.

"That something?"

"A note. Not delivered. A warning to this Chamberlin."

"Where is this note?"

"Destroyed."

"I am puzzled Ali. How would they not know if they had delivered a note? How is that possible?"

"They are men of great passion. Their emotions sometimes run ahead of them."

"Did you authorize that they go back to this house?"

"Yes."

After another lengthy silence Faisal said, "I am gravely concerned. It is one thing to attribute success to Allah but carelessness is not well regarded by me. Was there not great risk? Was it not a crime scene?"

"Yes. Yes indeed. But I saw it as necessary. I did not wish

to bother you. It was on my authorization." He felt the sweat within his armpits.

"This old man that they beat? Can he not identify? Are you not confusing blessings with luck?"

"I see Allah's hand in it all. Just as we lost the agency of our brother with the French whore – we still managed the murder of this Jew rabbi."

Faisal sat back at that comment and rubbed his chin and beard. "You said to me that a business card was recovered," he referred to an index card with minute Arabic writing that was lying on the side of his desk. "ACJ. Bertrand McAbee?"

"Yes. That's the name I believe. We did not associate it with Regis Chamberlin. It was found in the fat man's wallet. I think of it as an incidental, unassociated."

"Is that right?"

"Yes," Ali said with an unflinched finality.

"This name of McAbee means nothing to you?"

"No," Ali said tentatively. He was becoming convinced that there was a bomb in the conversation. His chest was sweating.

"This name of McAbee? You would have no reason to know of it. I do, however. I was not familiar with the given name, Bertrand. But there is a William McAbee agency in New York City. It has caused us much damage over the years. It is highly associated with Israeli interests. His agency is a dangerous and vicious force. They have made effort to penetrate us." He looked piercingly at Ali. "When you gave me the name of this Bertrand, I did checks, hoping that there was a coincidence in it all. There isn't. They are brothers. Somehow a McAbee is engaged with this case. Whether it reaches to his brother William is unknown.

What is known is that there is too much coincidence. I have placed on this Bertrand a tail. He lives on the eastern border in the state of Iowa. I called you because he has arrived in Chicago, presumably again. He is on to something, I fear. I am greatly concerned. Our intention is to send fear to our adversaries. We have gotten to a good start with Chamberlin and the rabbi. After two more very public executions we will announce ourselves. But now I see and hear the name McAbee. These are dangerous people. I must know something. This note of the brothers? Was it found? Are they telling you the truth? Or is it still in the apartment? I must know the truth Ali. Find out."

"I will, I will, of course. But they said they found it," he lied.

"In the meantime it may be necessary to send a shock to the McAbee family. This Bertrand, unlike his brother, runs on a public bike path without any protection. He is a bit of a fool, I think. Perhaps he doesn't see far enough ahead. Othman and Mohammed may have to strike again. In contrast, his brother William travels with an armed escort. We have had him in our sights for years. There have been efforts but to no avail. But recently we almost succeeded. But we await our opportunity. Someday…Allah willing." He looked down and away, something still awaiting articulation. "It is important, of course, that Othman and Mohammed be kept in total darkness concerning my identity. You, also, must show great caution. Visit with them only in extremes. The nature of our cells demands strenuous vigilance. The William McAbee Agency will resort to torture and murder. This Bertrand seems a gentler sort, but we don't know. We do know that there's violence and mayhem in their DNA.

You, of course, must be prepared to dispense of the two, Mohammed and Othman, if such must be. I don't want them taken by these privateers. The FBI we can handle, the fools are bound by rules. But," he looked menacingly at Ali, "you must be prepared to either leave the country immediately, if such is feasible, or die."

Ali knew that his brow was wet with perspiration and he knew that Faisal saw. He answered with as much enthusiasm as he could muster, "It is as you say. My loyalty is complete."

"That is good. You have been in touch with the French woman's murderer since the rabbi's fall?"

"No. But it could not have been easy, even though she was an infidel at heart, for him to murder her."

Faisal sat quietly, constantly stroking his beard. He said, ominously, "No contact?"

"No. I am awaiting a call from him. Is something wrong with him?"

"No. There is nothing wrong with him. His action against the woman was reckless. He exposed himself as a warrior to this woman who was a sex toy for him. Is it not a mistake to have two murders attaching to the downtown Marriott within a few days of each other?" His eyes flashed in anger as he left his question in the air.

Ali said, "I saw it all, looking back, as a sign of Allah's blessing, despite the obstacles," he said in semi-plead.

"The man was a fool. Careless! He has paid the price. It is not Allah who protects our, your, good fortune. I am alarmed with some matters, Ali. We are endangering our first great effort."

Ali thought that he knew the answer but he had to know with certainty. "He? Paid the price?"

"He was executed. He is buried in the woods of the upper peninsula of Michigan."

Ali protested, "But he was only trying to assist. I thought he had left the country."

"Such assistance is not desirable. He was a fool. He acted out of haste. He left a trail, don't you see? It is good that you never knew his name; just his cell number."

Ali weighed all that was said. He didn't know what to conclude. Was he in danger? Had Faisal lost faith in him? And this McAbee? Why did the name so anger, or was it intimidate, Faisal? And lastly, were Othman and Mohammed dangerous fools rather than the blessed of Allah? He needed to be free of the threatening presence of Faisal. Then, perhaps, he could sort out his affairs. He was very much discouraged given that he had come to the meeting with great optimism and confidence. Matters were askew. "In the name of Allah I will see to things so that your trust in me will be restored in full." He took the hand of Faisal and kissed it in obeisance.

Faisal sat calmly but looked into Ali's soul. He said, "Don't come again until you are called. Allah indeed sees all. I see most. You may leave."

Ali, unknowingly, drove through three stop signs and one red light on his way home. He was now possessed of great fear.

CHAPTER XXI

Rufus O'Hanlon had just sat down. He was going to watch CNN's Headline News. The buzzer outside of his apartment sounded, just once. It was short also, he especially appreciated that. Duke raised his head slowly and then eyed Rufus. It had come to this, nowadays. Rufus allowed a mournful 'ah.' He reached down, found his cane and arose slowly and painfully. Ever since the beating, it seemed, most of reality had sped up while his reaction time had become more and more lethargic. The buzzer was pushed once more, quickly. When he reached the door he looked out through the one-way. It was McAbee. Without hesitation he said, "Hold on," threw the deadbolt, slid the chain free and then opened the door. "Please, please come in," he was happy to see him if for no other reason than McAbee's kindness during his hospital stay. The tab that he had picked up for Duke was above and beyond any courtesy that he had ever been paid.

He recalled their last meeting. McAbee was a confusing sort. He seemed cold and analytical at one moment and warm and caring at the next. There was mercury in his nature. Duke limped his way out to the hallway and looked up at McAbee with his doleful eyes. McAbee went through joy to concern in a second. He bent down, extended his right hand in front of Duke's snout, determined that he had passed sniff test dogs use and then crouched. He petted the boxer for a good twenty seconds. The half-inch protuberance that stood for the dog's tail twitched slightly.

He arose and looked Rufus in the eye. He said, "Rufus it's so good to see you. I was horrified at what happened to you." He touched Rufus' arm lightly. "How are you doing? Am I intruding?"

"No, no. I was just settling down to the news. I'm glad that you came. I wanted to say some things to you. Please come into my living room. I'm still a bit shaky." He looked down at Duke and said, "And so's the big guy."

After they were seated, Duke laid down close to McAbee's chair.

Rufus said, "I wanted to thank you for what you did. I am on a fixed income and while I could have paid for Duke, it would have hurt. So on behalf of both of us, thanks. I guess that I don't expect private detectives to be doing things like that. I've read enough mysteries to have an image of a hard…ass for all of you."

"I don't feel responsible for what happened to you, Rufus. I think that it would have happened regardless. You walked into a bad scene. But that doesn't mean that I could close my eyes to the affront. I'm happy that I could help. And I'm really glad that you and Duke are on the way back. Tell me how the two of you are faring?"

Rufus went into some detail about his pains and aches, his medicines, and the overall prognosis – which was good if he'd begin to conquer his weight problem, his high blood pressure, and his type two diabetes. McAbee was a good listener, empathetic. Yet ironically, he appeared to listen just a bit more closely when Rufus detailed Duke's situation. This was a curious man by any standard. He, again, wondered how he had gotten into his line of business. He still figured that the novels that he read more accurately portrayed the occupation than did this man, who, when Rufus had pretty much said everything that he wanted to say, bent down and stroked Duke. Rufus finished by saying, "So how is the investigation going? Progress?"

"One foot forward, one sideways. At least nothing backwards. There is a model in physics that was transferred to management theory relative to how things get done. It's called the punctuated equilibrium model. Ever hear of it?"

"Sounds familiar but I don't know, if I ever did."

"In essence – progress is made in chunks. Usually things start up and move well at a beginning and then they can sit for a long time, until something happens, usually some kind of time-demand and then they move again and then there's a long pause before another huge movement. I find that many of my cases can be fitted to this model. Some things have happened, for instance, what you walked into, that advance the situation. Then there's an equilibrium-torpor and then something occurs out of the ordinary and bang there's more movement. Movement creates the possibilities. There was a movement a few days ago. It might advance the cause. But I guess that I'd still like to backtrack with you."

O'Hanlon noticed that all during his oration McAbee's eyes wandered all around the room. They would occasionally find those of Rufus, settle on him and then roam away again. He reminded him of some professor in a college, focused yet diffuse at the same time. Each time he thought that McAbee would wander somewhere in space he would come zooming back with a relentless intensity.

Rufus said, in the midst of the long McAbee pause, "As I'm sure you know, they were looking for something. There's no doubt about that. I'm pretty sure that they never found it."

"Yes. I'm very interested in your take on this."

"It had to be small. They were tearing through books and drawers, inspecting. I saw one of them put his hand into socks up to the toe. I was thinking a coin or a key or a piece of paper. Small is the impression."

"And they?"

"Tall, arrogant bastards. Almost all of the talking came from one. The other was sullen and I think the more dangerous. There was something about him that scared the bejesus out of me. He was the one who first kicked poor Duke. Then he beat him."

"And neither said much?"

"Lots of pointing and dirty looks. Broken English. Indians/Middle East, maybe."

"Indians?"

"Either kind – from India or America."

"American Indians are pretty much beyond broken English, I'd guess," McAbee said speculating.

"Yes, I guess."

"Can you think of any specific comment?"

Rufus thought. "You know, yes, at least this comes to mind. When the sullen one, I should say more sullen, as they both were, I think that I heard him say, "Filthy dogs."

McAbee said, "Why does that strike you? Seems appropriate if one is going to kick a dog, right?"

"No, that's it. That's why it struck me and now comes back to me. I think that one would say filthy dog. There was only one dog, Duke. It was like he was condemning all dogs. The whole species."

"You think that while the kick was aimed at Duke it was aimed at a broad number. Like not just at Duke, but all dogs?"

"Yes, yes that's it. But now that I think of it – I guess that it's not a big deal."

McAbee went into himself for a moment. He finally responded, "Well I don't know. It's significant. It struck you – it was out of the ordinary. Subliminal importance is frequently more important than anything else you have. If I tell you that the two of them were Arabs would you reject that assertion for any reason?"

Without hesitation, he said, "No. Can't say I would. Is that what you think?"

"Yeah. But it's very tentative. I'm beginning to get a few pieces that connect together. But Ptolemy did the same thing about the geocentric theory and he was all wet." McAbee chuckled ironically.

Rufus concluded that the man dialogued within himself. He'd be easy to under-rate. He wondered how much of an actor operated in this man? The more he thought about it the more his head ached. He wished that he would not have to deal with elusive people during his convalescence.

McAbee asked, "Rufus, tell me about Regis? I know what his mother saw, his sister saw, but not you, at this distance from his death."

"He was a loner pure and simple. Eccentric as hell. He lived in his own world. He liked me and he'd tolerate me and Duke up to a point."

"Girlfriends?"

"Not that I ever saw."

"Gay?"

"I don't think so."

"Visitors?"

"No, other than his mother and that sister, what's her name?"

"Sybil?"

"Yes that's it. They seemed to be OK with each other."

"I met Sybil. She had some materials. We're looking them over. They were from Regis. Among other things he feared for his life, it seems. Does that surprise you?"

"No, he was on edge that last week. He didn't say anything but I could tell."

"How so?"

"Regis was, at heart, a very observant guy. He needed to see people at their ugliest and meanest. Maybe that made him feel better about things in his own life. I'm not a psychologist. But you have to realize that I really liked him. Eccentricities and all I was a fan. Not many things make me laugh – he could. He was so, so funny." He noticed that McAbee just sat, listening carefully.

After a bit, McAbee asked, "But he gave you no hint of what he feared? Nothing unusual?"

"No. Well…there was one thing. Odd, but not all that inconsistent with his character. About five or six days before he was murdered he bought a walking stick. God knows where. He showed it to me and he said something to the effect that with it he would slay the heathen lords or something like that. He loved to speak in the grander tones."

"So you'd draw from that that he was scared."

"Oh no, no. There's more. I teased him. I said that his stick would be good for clunking one person, not a horde," Rufus chuckled involuntarily, "and then he pulls the top from what's a scabbard and voila – a sword with a pretty sharp point. He backed away from me and he made the sign of Zorro, all the while laughing. Duke barked at him, it was such an unusual behavior from Regis."

"So he had a sword?"

"Yes. It looked like a cane. It was all metal, steel probably. But at the top was a circular part, probably about four or five inches in diameter. There was a release button on the side of the shaft. When he pressed the button, the shaft separated from the sword. He was so proud of it."

"Why didn't he have a gun if he was scared?"

Rufus laughed quietly. "You don't understand him McAbee. He wasn't the type. He was of another age."

"You're making him sound like Don Quixote, fighting windmills."

"But…that's it. Precisely! He was at battle with the world. And humor was his weapon until he took up something like a sword. But in a way the sword had an element of craziness to it. Don Quixote? Never thought of it that way. But it's a good image, a good comparison. Regis was one of a kind. And the sad part of it all is this. He was kind, generous, and basically non-malevolent. There was a bit of autism to him, if I have that right. If they told me that he was autistic as a youth and with my understanding of that condition I would not be surprised."

McAbee's eyes were now wandering at great speed. A beacon in search of some target, some kind of fit. His eyes now alit on Rufus. He said, "Rufus, I hear you detailing a tragic figure. A guy who didn't see his humor causing damage. Another question. He showed you this sword-piece. But did he ever call out any group or person to you?"

"No. Emphatically no."

"Was he truly scared?"

"Well, in a manner of speaking. He lived in a different kind of world than we do. He was a terribly vulnerable man-child, McAbee. And you know I've never articulated these things before. I think your questioning has caused me to further my understanding of my feelings around Regis. And you know what McAbee?"

"No…?"

"It makes me even sadder. Who's the idiot who said understanding makes you free? All of the things that we just talked about have made me miserable. Understanding shackles more than it frees." He looked at McAbee whose eyes had a look of puzzlement to them along with a heavy melancholy.

After a long hesitation McAbee broke into the silence that stood between them. "This walking stick and sword – where is it? I don't remember seeing it."

"He kept it near him. Probably in his hallway closet. I don't know, I haven't looked for it."

"I'd like to check it out." He arose. "I'm going to go over to his apartment and look around again. Perhaps there's still some kind of clue over there. I'd be surprised if it's still there…but nonetheless."

"Regis was crafty McAbee. Remember that. He was crafty in the way that a child is crafty."

McAbee bent down and patted Duke. Then he said, "You take care. I'll be back again, I'm sure."

The apartment was nowhere near a crime scene anymore. The yellow tape had been removed and the place had obviously been tended to by some diligent cleaners. He was pretty sure that Roberta Chamberlin had masterminded this latest cleanup. He would have liked to have been consulted but all told, Roberta had managed to keep her dark side under considerable restraint. He would not raise it as an issue.

McAbee prowled the apartment with his eyes and did an occasional feel on an object that waded into his presence. Nothing out of the ordinary struck him. He then went to the hallway closet. Behind some coats he saw what Rufus had referred to, a walking stick, about a yard long on the inside edge of the closet. He withdrew it. It was as Rufus had described except for a point not mentioned – it was heavy, a solid eight to ten pounds. It looked light, however. There was a good chance that Rufus had never felt its heft. The instrument was not cheap. He was quite sure that given enough torque the stick, sheathed, could do serious damage. More so, if he grabbed it by the pointed end and swung the piece so that the rounded top part led an attack, it would be like a small battering ram. He pressed the release button at the end of the shaft and the sword lifted out of the casing. It had at least half of the weight of the whole unified piece. It was very sharp to McAbee's touch.

He swung it around and was impressed by the balance of the piece. He sheathed it, but to his surprise it did not fall true into the shaft. He pushed it with some force and only then heard the awaited click. He pressed the release button and withdrew the sword again. He looked down into the empty shaft and saw a crumpled piece of material. He turned the shaft upside down and tapped it against the floor a few times. Whatever was in the shaft had now dislodged slightly. He tapped it again a few times; there was further dislodgement. He then inserted the sword about two thirds of the way into the shaft and maneuvered the sword so as to snare the material. He could now see that it was a piece of paper. Further tappings and manipulations with the sword finally dislodged the paper from the shaft. He picked out what was a piece of paper from the open end of the shaft. When he spread it out on the foyer table and read it, he knew what the twins had been after.

CHAPTER XXII

Bertrand had another brother. His name was Jack. He was a celebrated antique dealer in New York City. Their relationship had a strained quality due to Bertrand's misguided attempt years ago to get Jack and his Belgian wife Marta involved in a case. They were almost killed. Never again would either one of them look upon him as a harmless PI out in the midwest. Marta, especially, was leery of him.

Whatever the cause, he figured that he had evened the score with a huge windfall that came out of a case that tracked all the way back to World War I and a missing toy. It was, however, not without a slight misgiving that he called Jack for some advice relative to what he found at the bottom of the casing that housed a sword.

"Good morning – Jack McAbee."

"Jack? This is Bertrand."

There was a long delay before Jack responded. "Is this a social call or business?"

"Both."

"Well, let's get the social part done first. Marta and I are both well. How about you?"

"Fine." Bertrand figured that either he or Jack were

left at the door by gypsies. Jack was a precisionist of the highest order. He was known in the antique world as being impeccably honest and a man with an acerbic tongue. He loved to flush out frauds and fake pieces. He was to the antique world what his brother Bill was to the world of crooks. Maybe Bertrand was the gypsy gift, after all, in the family. He overheard a low voice. "It's Bertrand." He pictured Marta making throat slitting signs. "Are we ready for business now?"

Jack said, "Shoot, what's up?"

"I'm on a case out here. The details are unimportant. I have a piece of paper with a threatening message. I'm interested in a take on something in the message."

"I'm listening."

"Beside the words, there is a free-hand drawing of a knife. The drawing is very precise. The knife in question is highly unusual. I've never seen the type. I assume that either you or Marta might know or that you would know of someone who could give me a lead. I'd like to fax a copy to you. If that doesn't work I'll take a scan of it and send it by e-mail."

"Marta is the expert on knives. Hold on, let me explain to her." There was a delay of about a minute. "OK. She'll take a look at a fax. If that doesn't work, or even if it does, she still might want to see a scan. When can you send it?"

"Give me your fax number. It'll be there in less than a minute. I'll call back in five minutes. How's that? I have one right where I am now."

The number was given and in exactly five minutes from the sending of the fax from Regis' machine he called.

Marta answered, "Bertrand. Hello. First off, does this

have consequences? Am I going to have to watch for my life?"

"How did you know it was me?"

"Caller I.D. Now, please, answer my question. Is there danger in the transmission of the fax?"

"No, of course not."

"Well, you have a record that is not exactly trouble free. I need to know."

"The answer is no. Now, can you help me?"

"Yes. I won't need a scan for this. This knife shape is Arab through and through. Are you familiar with the phrase Damascus steel?"

"Yes."

"There was no better. World famous. Now I don't know if this is a copy of a true piece of Damascus steel. Not important. What is important is that the shape of this knife, with its sharp curved point and wide belly, is a classic copy of Arab knife-making and specifically a frequent kind of knife for Damascus steel usage. If you gave the fax to a hundred experts in the field, they would all tell you the same thing. If he drew it free hand he's a good artist, great eye. Whatever the case, he's quite familiar with this kind of knife because of the sense of detail. The way it was used was to pierce the neck under an ear and then the knife's shape would lead you to a clean throat slitting as you withdrew it."

"What about all of the knives from Germany, Texas, and so on?"

"No. What are you saying to me? You wanted my opinion and now you question me?"

"No offense meant Marta. A simple question."

"For such a simple question I give you a simple answer.

It's an Arab model. Whoever drew it is probably an Arab. But that's an inference. The knife itself is a pure Arab model. I know knives. Is that all?"

"Yeah. Thanks. Is Jack there?"

"He's with a customer."

"Tell him I said goodbye."

"I will." She hung up.

Bertrand shrugged as the phrase 'kinship piety' flashed across his mind. But more critically, he was now even more convinced that he had walked in on a terrorist's party of some sort just as did Regis.

He called his brother Bill. He reflected that there was a lot of family stuff going on this particular day, fully aware of the quicksand that could entrap him if he were not careful in these affairs. Surprisingly, he got right through. He updated Bill right through to his last call to Jack and Marta. Bill, most unusually, said nothing, as Bertrand recounted his suspicions, hunches, and theories. When he finished Bill said, "I can see how you got to Z in your speculations. But you had to go through a number of letters to do so. But I'll give you the benefit of the doubt and agree that you've probably got a group of angry Arabs. I'll even concede, for the sake of argument, that you have an organized cell that is probably not finished with its work, if they will ever be, outside of their being exterminated. Ironically, if your case is accurate and true, this cell will be harder to smash than before 9/11. I know that's counter-intuitive but, unfortunately, it's true. Never again will there be big fat clues hanging off of branches as there were for our FBI and CIA. Any existent cells now are wrapped in extraordinary secrecy given our post 9/11 efforts. So, only a big break will catch you any fish."

"Are you saying that I've gone as far as I can?"

"No. Listen brother Bertrand, I'd love to see you come at this in your own way. I'm afraid that I've lost some faith in our organizations. Maybe you, with your unorthodox ways and odd cadre of characters can pull the rug out from these murderers. But…you do need some reserves and help. I brought you into this case and I'll try to help you. I'll call in some favors and see what the FBI and CIA might have. This piece about the rabbi is really pretty interesting. Are you going to pursue it?"

"Yes, although he's my concern only by way of Regis. I might be able to open up something off of it. Whether it's connected to Regis is problematic. But I do find it an oddity that I can't shake off. I smell a connection," Bertrand said.

"The rabbi was not looked at kindly by lots of Israelis. He had a lot of enemies right there. In his own way he was as radical and irascible as some of the Islamicists that he spewed against."

"But you wouldn't be shocked if the assassination came out of a radical Arab group?"

"No. I wouldn't either if it came out of Mossad or some fringe Jewish group. All I'm saying is that it's an interesting theory to associate Regis and the rabbi. But be careful about going too far with it."

"OK. Well, whatever you can find out for me would be a help. I'll keep you informed."

"Wait, wait. Before you hang up, damn it, be armed Bertrand. Whoever this is is a dangerous player. Let's just say that there is a connection between the two. Both of the murders were bold and over the top. They don't seem to know fear. This really concerns me. They'd blow you away in a second."

"Gotcha. I'll be watchful, promise."

Immediately after his conversation with Bertrand, Bill called a direct number into Israel. It would be about seven p.m. there and typically Isaac Linowitz would be working. He was, much to Bill's relief. After an exchange of pleasantries Isaac asked, "So Bill, you are not calling me for idle chatter. What do you need?"

"Chicago, few days ago. Rabbi Samuel Rubin assassinated in the downtown Marriott. My brother is running an investigation that might be crossing nearby. What can you tell me?"

"No tears shed here. He was in bed with the nastiest of the settlers. He was thick with them. He had lots of money sources and shook them down regularly. The money found its way into dangerous places and into the hands of dangerous people. If you're asking who did it, we don't know. Honestly. But we are concerned. If the bastards in Hamas or Hezbollah start straying off the board by killing our people in foreign lands, they will be shocked at what we're prepared to do in a return volley."

"When you say you don't know that's not the same as saying you don't suspect. What's your best guess?"

"Something out of Islam. Something from this part of the world. Rubin had a top notch bodyguard and the hotel security was pretty OK, I guess. The one who did it acted with impunity. As if he wouldn't be caught. We did everything we could do with the security tape. We got tall and dark. The rest is a blur and it's over in an instant. I don't understand, Bill, why these fools if they're going to go to the trouble of having security cameras and all of the other features, they stint by using crappy black and white tapes that yield pretty worthless material," Linowitz said loudly.

"Do you have any likely groups over here?"

"Is the sky blue my friend?"

"Come on Isaac. Midwest?"

"Bill. In Detroit alone – there are about 40 at the last count. Chicago 22, St. Louis 12, Minneapolis 14, Indianapolis 10. I can go on."

"Hating Jews from killing them? Big difference and it has to affect your numbers."

"Sure it does. Now show me how to do that. When you study them, there's little difference. Do some of them merely talk big? Sure. But do some of them talk big and would they act big if they had the chance? Yes."

"You're too clever to leave me with that answer Isaac."

"OK already. I'm getting there," he laughed.

Bill could picture him in his mind. He knew that the Mossad higher-ups called him Arafat behind his back. They thought that he not only looked a bit like the deceased Arafat, but that he could do an uncanny imitation of him. When he was in the mood he had a great sense of humor. "Are you testing my intelligence Isaac?" Bill asked lightly.

"Hah! If you had good intelligence you wouldn't be calling me about this. We do know something. At least we're touching some part of the elephant. Chicago. There is something there, we think. Not like the others. A dark hole with money and discipline. We see it and then we don't. It's a feeling that we get."

"Who gets it? You, one of your men? How deep is this?

What I'm saying is how much of this is conjecture and how much is real?"

"Bill!? What am I to say? It's like string theory in physics. It's there and it's not there. Is it some fraud meant to throw us off track? Maybe. But I doubt it. Now while we're leveling with each other how did your brother get engaged with this phantom? And? Who is your brother? We think that one of you is enough."

Bill gave him a brief survey of the situation beginning with the Regis Chamberlin murder and ending with Bertrand's conjecture of a tie-in between Regis and the rabbi.

At the end of it Isaac said, "Thin, but we've gone on thinner material, believe me. Let us say that we call this organization 'the spirits' in keeping with their mysterious nature. They mean harm and perhaps this is the kind of harm that they will do. You've brought up the name Regis Chamberlin before, when you called. The rabbi and Chamberlin are very unalike, but in a way they both have a lightening rod quality. How is your brother going to proceed? What kind of support does he have?"

"Support? Bare bones. Proceed? He'll proceed nicely if I can give him some information. Like names, addresses. But this is not my brother's forte. He's an academic dealing with a second career. He doesn't usually carry a gun. But he's smart and he's lucky."

"Bill! Get him away from this. Smart? We're smart, your CIA and FBI are smart. Smart! So what? All the smarts in the world and what happens? 9/11! And luck? Are you serious? Luck – schlock! Get him out of this."

"Isaac! It's his case. Did I mention that he's a bulldog?

Do you think that if I called him and told him to back off that he would?"

"I don't know. Would he?"

"Not a chance. So – here's the question. What can you give me?"

"I am embarrassed to say very little. But there you have it, little is better than nothing. There is one person that we're keeping an electronic eye on. He has come up in a few sweeps, but there's nothing hard. We've given his name over to the FBI. He's now on one of their lists. Their lists are endless, as you know. His name is Ali. He oversees an Islamic center in Chicago. He's too cagey – do you know what I mean?" He didn't pause for an answer. "He speaks sometimes in a code. His English is fine, his words are clear and then all of a sudden there is a sentence full of clouds. Words are not used in a proper context or his typical way of speaking has changed. Like some pre-arranged signal, five sentences in you will find the coded message."

"How did you get his name?"

"We have some software. It ferrets out language anomalies. We use it on virtually all inter-Arab communications that come our way."

"English?"

"Yes…But we're busily working on Arabic. Wait until we get that up and going. You want addresses and phone numbers for Ali?"

"Whatever you can give to me."

Isaac gave what he had. He concluded, "Bill, my dear friend, let me be clear on this, everything is circumstantial about this man and even about a potential cell. But, on the other hand, they smell bad. Really bad. Your brother?

Tell him that it's a tough game out there. Backup, backup, backup! Also, I expect that you'll share with us whatever you come by?"

"Goes without saying Isaac. Peace!"

"Peace – hah!" He disconnected.

Bill's return call about an hour later found Bertrand on his p.c. Virtually the entire content of his call to Isaac in Israel was repeated back to Bertrand. It was Bill's assumption that Bertrand would latch his computer whiz, Barry Fisk, onto Ali as soon as the call came to an end. After all warnings had been re-asserted, he hung up.

Barry Fisk was alerted and Jack Scholz was queried about getting observers in place. To Bertrand this was the way to go; the only way he could see that had some hope.

CHAPTER XXIII

Barry Fisk spent hours working the name Juliette Simeon. He managed to crash into the personnel files of Marriott. She was what she was, he concluded. College-educated, she had pretty much committed herself to the hospitality industry having secured an internship with Marriott during her college years. Her language skills were strong, besides French and German, she was virtually fluent in Italian, English, and Japanese. There was passable Spanish and Portuguese. She was marked as someone of high potential by the hotel giant. But there was nothing in the file that caused him to see any connection with Regis Chamberlin or the rabbi, the current pet theory of Bertrand – 'Mr. Intuit to a Quick Conclusion' McAbee. Well, he thought, as long as he pays, the hoops will be jumped through.

He tracked her life to Utah, then Michigan and Illinois. He wondered nastily how she fared in that cosmopolitan bastion of Salt Lake City. He checked all public files, never finding anything that generated her name. Finally, he found his way into the Salt Lake City Public Library. To his mild surprise, she took out a card. Three months before her transfer to Detroit she borrowed five books dealing with the

Moslem religion. He sat up sharply with this finding. That didn't exactly fit his profile of this woman whom he recalled had listed her religion as Roman Catholic. Of course, most of the French probably did that out of some sort of historical sentiment. She had kept all five books for the allotted three weeks, and she then renewed two of them for another three weeks.

Detroit, what was Marriott thinking? Salt Lake City and Detroit? She showed no interest in the public library of Detroit. She did, however, write out some checks to the Red Crescent, the Islamic equivalent to the Red Cross. That was a surprise. Perhaps it had something to do with Iraq and her being French.

Later, he found that more checks, modest but noteworthy, were given to a mosque in Dearborn. He went into the website of that mosque to search out a membership list. He had to get through some walls but he found a listing, she wasn't on it. He was about to exit when he saw a guest list. He exclaimed loudly, "Jesus Christ." It read, Juliette Simeon guest of Raheim Azakar. It didn't say when and how often but there was some kind of crossover with this pair.

Raheim Azakar now came front and center. Just as with Juliette, it took a considerable amount of time to ferret out information concerning him. But it eventually came out of this ethereal world he so loved.

Raheim was a Lebanese who had come to America under the sponsorship of a brother in Detroit. He had graduated from Wayne State with a degree in mechanical engineering. He had worked for the Ford Motor Company before he left to become a member of an Arabian Kingdom Associates firm that had multiple engineering and consulting contracts in Arab countries. He was unsuccessful at accessing the personnel files of this firm. Grumpily, he wondered whether they even had files, given that they were Arabs.

Raheim was not a silent witness of Islam. His name showed up on a number of lists in the Detroit area, probably the largest Moslem population concentration in America. He was publicly recognized as a voice for the community. However, his cachet with the media eroded significantly when he made some provocative anti-American statements about 9/11. Specifically, he repeated the canard that the world trade center buildings were devoid of Jews on that dark day because they not only knew of the plot but had engineered it.

He complained, after a few weeks, that his life had been threatened and that America was not truly a place where free speech was permitted. He went so far as to compare America with the Khiam prison in southern Lebanon where he claimed to have been tortured by the Israelis. Several months later, it seemed, even the mosques had kept their distance as his name passed into oblivion. His work continued with the engineering firm, however, as his name was still active on the list of Arabian Kingdom Associates.

Barry was unsuccessful at securing a phone number for the man, although he was able to get at his credit records. Raheim was not an avid user of credit, his Mastercard being used primarily to purchase gas. Other than the mosque reference to him and Juliette, nothing connected the pair. He found an address in his credit file but still no phone number, his best chance at establishing a connection of some sort between him and Juliette.

He worked his way back through Juliette's records but to no avail. Eventually, he decided to make a few calls.

"Hello," the voice said carefully.

"Mister Azakar? My name is William Pharma. I'm with the Department of Immigration and Naturalization. I'm calling about your brother Raheim."

"Yes?"

There was tangible element of fear in the man's voice. "There seems to be a snag of some sort. We are unable to reach him. I will need a current phone number and also your testimony that he is adhering to the laws of the United States."

"Yes. Oh yes Mister Pharma. He is a good man. He has a cell phone, I know." He gave the number to Barry.

"When was the last time that you spoke with him, sir?"

"It's been a week. This is unusual. We speak, normally, three or four times a week. But he is fine, I'm sure."

Barry decided to push more than he normally would. "Our records indicate that he has been involved with a French national, Juliette Simeon. She is currently under investigation. Can you tell us anything about their situation?"

There was a long pause. "Oh no. They are no longer seeing each other. When she moved to Chicago, he ended things with her. I am sure that he is no longer involved with her," his voice was now in high treble.

"He is still employed by Arabian Kingdom Associates?"

"Yes, yes."

"Can you refer to me a name there? Please don't be alarmed Mister Azakar. This is just normal background checking."

With the next response came more confidence. "Mister Hasek. He is a friend."

"Well good. Thank you for your cooperation. This level of assistance really helps us, sir, and ultimately your brother. Good day." Barry disconnected before any response was given to him. There was a surge of pride in him. Up to two years ago, he refused to even attempt phone masquerading. It was McAbee, in fact, who had pushed him on this point. He told Barry that his failure to persist in his inquiries via telephone was a weakness. They both knew that Barry's only defense was his disinclination to engage in personal contact with his prey. It was one thing to strip someone via the impersonal lash of the web but to actually have to exchange words was another story altogether. Barry knew that McAbee had him good and hard. After all, Barry had used a similar argument against countless foes in his failed academic career where he had been attacked behind the scenes by people who hid behind confidentiality. He had compared it with American pilots who bombed the hell out of North Vietnamese peasants from the safety of 30,000 feet.

When McAbee had used the polemic that his use of the telephone could give him even more of an edge up on his adversaries, Barry decided to explore his latent acting talents. To his wonderment, he found the phone to be a useful and sometimes perfidious instrument of pleasure. From tentative trials to now secure and frequent uses, he added it to his prohibitive arsenal of discovery.

Mister Hasak was not as easy as Mister Azakar. His attitude was one of skepticism toward Barry and his alleged job at Immigration and Naturalization. "I will only remark that the man works here and that his papers are in order. I know nothing of his personal relationships outside of work. Our records indicate that he has missed the last three days of work. This is very unusual. He has not called. If you do succeed in catching up with him please let us know. Me. Me, personally, let me know or tell him to call immediately. He is on an important project for us."

Barry's call to the cell number given to him by his brother came up empty. Raheim's phone was turned off. He did not leave a message. After an hour he finally broke into Raheim's phone records at Verizon. Was there still a connection between him and Juliette? His short legs started kicking under his desk when he discovered that Raheim had called Juliette three times on the day that she had been murdered. This was a big deal. He looked closely at the other numbers in the bill profile of Verizon. It seemed that his work would never end. McAbee's bill was soaring. And he still had the Ali name in front of him. He wondered what that would bring forth when he finally got around to it.

He stood about 5'7" at the most, probably not more than 130 pounds. His black hair was closely cut at both top and sides. He had a neatly trimmed mustache that covered his upper lip to the end of his mouth. He wore a small pair of glasses surrounded by a tiny wire frame that just barely covered his eyes. The man's features were compact, tight. Every movement seemed studied, precise. His name was Simon, his sobriquet, the weeper. He was an Egyptian Coptic Christian. His eyes were expressionless, almost dead. His actions had made him a suspicious figure around the world: wanted for questioning by over 35 national police agencies. Many others also wanted him, needing the services of a professional assassin who had truly learned the art of disappearing. It was an unconfirmed whisper that both he and his victims cried at their executions.

He traveled with ease and impunity because while his actions were known, he wasn't. His presence was knowable but he was unknown. It was said of him by those who know that his trade was protected by God since he had never been arrested anywhere nor as far as could be told had he ever failed in a mission.

Faisal was one of those who knew what was to be known. His approach was made to an intermediary in Aleppo, Syria, who in turn messaged to Tripoli in Libya. He had no sense of how many more contacts were used but he was convinced that there was a chain and if any one piece showed any stress the connections would end only to undergo a rebirth with a different order of things.

Faisal spoke to him. "I have in place a group. There is a commitment to excellence by this group and all within it. We intend to create havoc by precision and public assassinations thereby instilling fear into the American's overlords." Simon sat and looked unmoved. He was said to care little for explanations. Faisal was ready to confirm that. "Just as you have put together a carefully woven organization, I also am doing the same. I am not as advanced as you. But I will get there. A problem has arisen that must be eradicated. That is why I have called you. Your work must be carried out in a way that points to a transgression, that incites fear in the others, but which ultimately creates discipline…of the type with which you are familiar."

"Your wish, my command," he said with a gentleness that surprised Faisal.

"There are three, maybe a fourth – a meddler, not one of us."

Simon nodded understanding.

"These are the addresses, there are the names," Faisal pointed at the written lines on the paper.

"Tell me of these."

Faisal described the three men. Two of them he had never personally met. One he knew because he had recruited him. He saw no reason to mention the recent demise of Raheim. It was outside the purview of Simon. The reasons for that murder, would, however, be promoted after Simon had performed his services.

"I will need you to procure weapons and explosives for me. Here is a list of what I will need. I will need a driver who is as silent as the sands of the Sahara. I will attend to these three and then I will see to the fourth if you should still want his dismissal."

"What you wish will be done. Your remuneration is already in your bank account in Amman."

"Yes. I know. I am giving to you these six cell numbers. Each day starting today I will use one of them, as noted, per day. Then they will be destroyed at the end of that day. I will stay at a Motel 6 for a few days, then I will go elsewhere."

Faisal said, "But do you not need something more elaborate, classy?"

"No. Being elaborate has its costs. Being where I am tells me of my lessons from youth."

"So be it," Faisal said stoically.

Jack Scholz had a surveillance team on Ali by the next morning. One of his men, Yousef, an ex-SEAL and fallen-away Moslem, had already entered the Center. Within five minutes, he had identified Ali and had passed on a picture via his cell to Scholz who was in a van parked at a Dominick's grocery store, two blocks from the Center.

Yousef had engaged Ali in conversation. The entire conversation was wired into the van to the listening Scholz.

Yousef: "Pardon me. Are you the one in charge of the Center?"

Ali: "Yes. Can I be of help?"

Yousef: "I am a fallen away Moslem. My family is from Egypt. They wanted me to be American more than Americans do. I was in the service. SEALS. I have come to be troubled by America. Iraq, Syria, Afghanistan, Israel, all of it. I was driving by here and I said to myself why not? So, I came."

Ali: "Do you speak Arabic?"

Yousef: "Of course."

Ali: "That is a big advantage to have. I am gladdened. How about the Koran? Have you read it?"

Yousef: "Of course. But not recently."

Ali: "The SEALS. These are tough, are they not?"

Yousef: "The toughest of the tough."

Ali: "Not many of us in that group."

Yousef: "No. When I left they were trying to get me to go undercover into Baghdad."

Ali: "And?"

Yousef: "And!? I left. There is just so much a man can do against his own people. This I won't do."

At this point Scholz called McAbee. He was proud of Yousef and especially how close his story mirrored what he was saying. There was a big difference, however. Yousef was a confirmed atheist and had a deep hatred for the radical Islamic clergy and their superstitious followers.

McAbee said, "Jack, are you having any luck?"

"Luck is with us. One of my men is not only talking with Ali right at this moment, but he has already phoned over two pictures of the bastard. I think that he'll become a fixture at this center and he'll be able to keep pretty close tabs on our friend Ali. I'll forward the photos to you. Has the runt found anything?" He knew that McAbee detested his name calling and epithets about Barry Fisk.

"Barry is not having many breaks. Ali seems to know how to hide. To Barry, that's a good indication of his guilt. He's also been sent a warning by Israeli intelligence to stay out of their networks."

"They gave us Ali. Are they hiding something?"

"Probably. But I was surprised that Barry tried to access them. They're so damn security conscious."

"What about the twins?"

"Nothing yet. Keep me informed on what happens out there."

"One other thing Bertrand. Did the Israelis mention that they had live cover on Ali?"

"No. The word I got was monitor. Why?"

"I'm concerned about a double operation. They can get messy. Also, they tipped the feds. We don't need a party out here."

"I'll call my brother. Maybe he can find out about a double op." He disconnected.

Scholz raised the volume in order to pick up again on Yousef and Ali.

Ali: "We have services frequently. Good groups who talk and meet. You're welcome to stay here. You might, once again, feel the power of Allah, my brother."

Yousef: "I will do that. I will sit in the mosque and reflect."

Ali: "This is good. If you would like to talk, come anytime to me."

Ali went to his office after speaking with Yousef whom he saw as an example of youth all around the world who were being challenged anew by their faith. If it came to be that this seedling ripened into a true believer, his background and training would be quite usable in the future.

But he was once again obsessed over his ill treatment by Faisal. Trust had been severed because he was so intent on protecting Mohammed and Othman. Why did they have to send that senseless note to Chamberlin? That coy and obese fool's murder in itself re-righted the scales of justice. Their foolish arrogance and his poor oversight had now come between him and Faisal. Being told, so bluntly, not to call Faisal indicated to him that what was once there between them was now gone. He was also alarmed that the French woman's killer was dead at the hand of Faisal, not directly by his hand, but by his order. There was no denial that this wealthy Saudi could with the movement of a finger have him killed also. He decided to call Othman and Mohammed for a meeting. Perhaps, there was a way to reconcile with Faisal. Othman answered the telephone and vowed to Ali that he and Mohammed would be in his office within the hour.

Yousef used a public telephone in the lobby of the

building. He called Scholz in the van. When Jack answered, Yousef said, "Did you get a clean read on our conversation?"

"Yes. Nice work. What's up with him?"

"He's for real. Under the surface he's mean, I think. But right now he's being a nice guy, friend of the dispossessed. I'll hang here for awhile. Don't see any twin-like guys."

Barry Fisk entered the website of the Islamic center. He found little of interest, until he hit the patrons list. In there, he found the names of 25 individuals and twelve organizations. His work was cut out for him.

Simon had his driver follow Othman and Mohammed from River Forest. He decided to make them his first target as they were known killers and thus dangerous. Ali wasn't. The two brothers were impressive. They strode as warriors, unafraid of enemies or obstacles. They acted as though blessed by God. Simon thought that some were blessed by God, but that those few should never act so. God was ultimately a trickster, neither Moslem nor Christian, both of which religions he respected, although he loosely adhered to the latter out of respect for his parents and family. The only other part of this theology that he could explicate was the justification for his vocation. To the few who had the nerve to ask, he would simply state that life on this earth was a passage and what was ordained was ordained. The separation from this world was painful but it was only temporary. Death was a cause for weeping and in the end, tears would be shed as they always were by him, tears for the other.

The brothers glided into the Islamic Center and parked at the far end of the lot. They backed it in as though preparing for a fast escape. It was as though they feared contamination from the other cars although no car was near them. Simon guessed that while he would weep, the brothers would not have such a release.

It was his guess that they were to meet with Ali. A momentary temptation passed his way, the killing of all three in one swoop. It did not feel right though and he rejected the impulse. However, a pipe bomb in the back of their car did seem right.

He told his chauffer, who had not spoken to him except to say 'yes' or 'no,' to pull up alongside of their isolated car. He said, "Snap our trunk lock," in Arabic. Simon heard the release noise as the trunk lid of his limo popped up about six inches. He said to the driver, "When I close the trunk lid I will need about 15 seconds. When I reenter this vehicle I want you to leave this lot slowly. We will then stay in the neighborhood." He answered, "Yes." Simon liked his professionalism. He left the vehicle and went to the trunk which he opened halfway. He removed from it a paper bag with hand-handles. He quickly scanned the lot and saw nothing inauspicious. He slammed the truck lid down and in a matter of seven quick steps was behind the vehicle of his prey. The chauffer pulled the car ahead and stood ready for Simon's re-entry. He removed from the bag the pipe-bomb of about 12 inches and placed it into the tailpipe of the car with an abrupt arm twist. It was fortuitous that the pair had backed in the car, thus negating their chance of spotting the protuberance of the pipe bomb that extended about two inches from the end of the tailpipe.

With the empty paper bag in hand, he was back in the car in a matter of seconds. He saw nothing unusual as he once again looked quickly at his surroundings. He said quietly, "Please, drive." They were probably out of the lot before Ali, presumably, met with the doomed pair.

Scholz sat in the van awaiting further details from Yousef. One of the items that he was most interested in was where this Ali lived, or where he went after work. Yousef would hopefully be able to to supply that detail.

His cell rang. "Yeah?"

"You won't believe this. It has to be these twins that you've referred to. They're here. Just came in through the doors. What do you want me to do?"

"Pictures, pictures – if you can."

"OK. Got them from a distance."

"Just stick around there. Don't expose yourself. Stay in touch."

"Will do."

"Bertrand, it's Jack. Your twins seem to be in the building. I've got a pic that I'm forwarding to you. What do you want me to do?"

"Cut the audio surveillance for now and follow them when they come out, Jack. I'll leave now from the Hyatt but it will take me a good bit of time before I get there. But I'm on my way. My cell will be on, of course."

"I'll head over toward that lot so that I can get a glimpse of them on their way out."

"OK."

Othman knew at once that a change had occurred. Ali's usual calm disposition was gone. He was fidgety. Was there a small band of perspiration across his upper lip and brow? The brotherly kisses were tense, watchful. They were beckoned to sit. He wondered what his brother Mohammed was thinking? Perceiving?

Ali spoke, "There is news my brothers. Our patron and his patrons have asked me to once again review with you the circumstances surrounding the note that was sent to the dead Chamberlin. And, what do you think has become of it?"

Othman looked at Mohammed whose features darkened noticeably. Between the pair, it was always understood that Othman would speak for them. "It is as I have said before, my friend. We felt that this cancerous dog should sit in apprehension and fear before his time came."

"The actions of our movement will be declared publicly to all at the moment when it is deemed best by those above us. This note is seen as a violation of our discipline and has caused disruptions. The fact that the note has not been recovered furthers the problems that our masters see in front of us. No permission has ever been given to go to this extreme."

"We are in Allah's fold. We have felt the protective hands of Allah through our acts. We are confident that what we did was right. That this Chamberlin suffered for his wrongs."

"Listen to me carefully. You can not do anything unless it is approved by our masters. This is what discipline requires. It is what will make us great and unstoppable."

Othman looked down at his shoes. He was not about to argue with Ali who was so often a supporter. Mohammed's shoes shuffled, a sign that he was on the very edge of restraint.

"I must have your assent to what I am saying. I must report back."

"We say yes. If it comes to be that we can no longer give our agreement then we will tell you and leave the organization." He said this as explicitly and as uncontritely as he could.

Ali stood. He said, "I will inform them of your decision, then, my brothers. Good day." He turned and walked away. No kiss, no respect. Othman was furious. He reached toward Mohammed who shook his arm loose. They strode angrily from the center and back towards their car.

Ali knew from this point forward that the lie he had told Faisal would never be alterable. His hope was that it would eventually become forgotten, a thing of the past.

CHAPTER XXIV

Jack Scholz was about 200 feet from the entry to the parking lot of the Islamic Center. Two events caught his attention, one his consciousness, the other his intuitiveness. He had seen many explosions in his day; what he saw barely affected him. He surmised a car bomb. He saw smoke in a far-off section of the lot, that, combined with the noise, led him to this conclusion. But there was another incident. A black Cadillac coming toward Scholz had crossed almost parallel to the entry to the lot when the explosion occurred. It slowed almost to a stop for about three seconds before hurtling out of the area at tremendous speed. Scholz caught three letters on the Illinois plate, NVD, the rest was lost. The very dark windows of the Cadillac offered a glimpse of a smallish mustached man with an impassive and, was it sad, face.

Scholz did not drive into the lot. He rather went forward two blocks and pulled into a Walgreens drugstore. He parked the van and started to walk to the center. His phone rang, "Yes?"

"Jack. Yousef here. I'm watching Ali as I speak. He is frantic. Those two, the twins, were in a car that just exploded, at least he's yelling about his two friends. I saw them leave the building about five minutes ago."

"Confirm hard on the twins. I'm walking toward you right now. We have to make sure on this. When I am convinced, I'll go back to Dominicks. Be careful. Ali might think that you caused this."

He called McAbee and told him of the events. McAbee said, "Make sure on the twins. I'm going to head over to Rufus and try to get a take on the pictures that you celled to me from Yousef. Ali is now a big key here. I wonder if he did it?"

"Yousef's take is no unless he's an extraordinary actor. I'm in the lot now. Closing on the scene. I'll tell you this, if they were both in that car they're both dead. I'm wondering if you can get the midget to run a check on a late model, black Cadillac, four door, front letters Nora, Victor, David, and three more letters, numbers, combo, I'm not sure. The vehicle did strange things in the midst of the bombing. Probably nothing, but who knows?"

He saw the ravaged corpses of two individuals. They were burned beyond recognition, their bodies still smoldering. Because their car had been backed in, a vision of both was clear. One of them had plunged through the blown out windshield. He face pointed out, grotesquely, part way onto the hood of the car, straight out like a hood ornament. The remains almost totally charcoal in color. The other in the passenger seat sat erect as if waiting for the accursed car to proceed forward. The smell was familiar to Scholz, so hardened to these things. He searched for Yousef and saw him standing a few steps from Ali who was still beside himself in dismay. Scholz could not understand him as he was speaking in Arabic. On the other hand, he reflected, his body language pretty much spoke for itself. He caught Yousef's eye, turned around and walked out of the lot as fire engines, squad cars and ambulances converged on the scene. He could not tell if it was the twins, but he saw nothing that told him no. He managed to get the plate numbers of the destroyed Lexus. The midget had more work to do.

McAbee entered Rufus' apartment. Duke looked at him sadly but his expression picked up as McAbee patted him. Rufus still moved slowly, and there was unsteadiness to his gait.

"Rufus, I have some news. Some events. Nothing is certain but some things are showing clarity. Let me first show you two pictures from my cell phone. I can have these blown up and put on paper later but for now tell me what you see."

One attempted look from Rufus had him scrambling for his reading glasses. "Here, now, let me see what you have there. Color, nonetheless. That's who they are, those two bums. They're the ones who beat me. No need to blow this up, do you have them? Have they been arrested?" He took off his glasses and looked expectantly at McAbee.

"No. No arrests. There's more Rufus. I think that there's a very good chance that they are both dead from a car bombing about 30 minutes ago. Not positive, but pretty sure."

Rufus sat there. He bit his lip and shook his head. Nothing was said for several minutes as he took to petting Duke who sat with his mouth open and with pale joy in his eyes. "I don't know what to say to you McAbee. It's all so out of my range of experiences. If it's true that they are dead and that they were the ones who murdered Regis, then good riddance to them. They lived and they died in a manner that befits them." He shook his head and stared out into his living room. Then, he said, "Does this mean that it ends here? Or is there more?"

"Oh there's more Rufus. But whatever else there is will hopefully be far removed from you and this building. I do believe that you are out of harm's way. But just in case, stay alert. I've got to go now." Once again, he found Duke irresistible and petted him. Duke was a happy dog as McAbee left Rufus' apartment.

Barry Fisk grumbled under the increasingly strident demands of McAbee. He was still in the midst of the patron's list for the Islamic Center when he was pressed twice within five minutes to track the two license numbers. He knew that breaking into the Department of Motor Vehicles and Licensure in Springfield, Illinois, was becoming harder to do. Not impossible, but they had developed a series of shrewd traps. He was also surmising some interesting conclusions from the patrons list for the Center. But McAbee had spoken and it was his dime.

The burnt-out Lexus was pretty easy. He had the full license plate. The vehicle was registered to the Islamic Center. Why was he not surprised?

The incomplete NVD on the late model Cadillac was another story. He had seven hits on possibles. The nice morsel noticed by the fascist, Scholz, helped a bit. Four doors. It knocked down the list to three candidates. The registrations probably told the story, 1) Gino Maggiano, 2) Douglas McIntyre, and 3) Saleem Zharib. If, in fact, Scholz was on to something it was probably this. Hate him as he did Scholz was a damn effective agent. While he knew that brains would eventually destroy brawn such as Scholz, he knew that Scholz wasn't just brawn. He was even more dangerous because of his dual skills, intelligence and menace.

He called McAbee and told him of his findings on the plates. McAbee complimented him for his quick work and disconnected. He wondered if his quick work would be rewarded by a bonus or whether McAbee thought that he received information on sale. But then he thought the better of his sullen thinking and went back to the patron's list for the Islamic Center.

Simon called Faisal. His message was direct, "The pair you wanted is gone. One remains. Should I know anything?"

"No. May Allah remain with you."

Simon dismissed his driver for the remainder of the day, a man named Saleem Zharib.

McAbee called Augusta Satin. She was in Rock Island, about 170 miles west of Chicago, on the western border of the state as Chicago was on the eastern border.

"Augusta, I'm in Chicago. I need some help up here. If it's not possible, I can use one of Jack's men. No pressure."

"Yes Bertrand. No pressure. I love your no pressure," she laughed into the phone.

McAbee loved that laugh. It was always worth the price of admission. He smiled, "Augusta, really! I don't want to interfere with your life. Now come on give me a break will you?" he said lightly.

"When do you need me?"

He paused purposefully. He said, "That my dear, dear friend is a loaded question."

"Oh sure. Here comes the Irish jive. You guys don't need any lessons from the brothers Mistah!" she said in a taunt. "But come on, tell me when and I'll be there. The kids are OK. I can get cover."

"I'd like you up here tonight for dinner. How's that? I'll tell you what's going on. The job is for tomorrow. I need a tail on a hired limo. It was a longshot observation by Jack, but now I'm inclined to say that it has merit. I'll reserve a room at the Hyatt tonight. Let me know when you get in. I'll take you to a nice place if you promise to keep your hands off me."

"Hah! I'll be gone soon. Probably will get in around seven. Should I be armed?"

"Yes. There are some dangerous critters around here."

He next called Roberta Chamberlin. "Roberta, Bertrand."

"I thought you had skipped the country," in full sarcasm.

"I'd like to stop by to see you. I have some news. I think that you'll find it interesting. Are you available in, let's say, a half hour?"

"If it's important, I'm available right this instant."

When he got there, he found her pacing in her large living room. Her maid withdrew quickly, McAbee noticed. Roberta had to be a cross to work for; he sympathized with the maid. Roberta looked at her watch, twice within 10 seconds. McAbee figured there was going to be trouble right at the start of the meeting and he wasn't in the mood for it. It had been, all told, a fruitful day with some excellent breakthroughs.

"When you say a half hour, I expect you to be here. You're 10 minutes late," she said with maddening arrogance.

"Yes I am. Thanks for keeping the time. Now, are we going to talk or not, Roberta? Or are you going to revert to a difficult place? There are many things going on right now. I'd like to share them with you in a civil manner," he looked at her sternly.

"OK, OK Bertrand. You're right. But, in my defense, do you have any idea of what I've been going through? And you haven't exactly been the update champion of the world you know."

He started to talk, intent upon giving her a thorough overview of the case. He was surprised. Not once did she interrupt what had to be a solid 20 minute description of where things were at this time in the affair. His conclusion was, "So, Regis can not be brought back Roberta. For that I'm most sorry. I know that your pain is deep and that your frustration must be extraordinarily intense. But I do think that the two dead men were quite involved with the murder of Regis. So some justice has occurred. I know that they probably had help for what they did. I don't know if we'll ever get them. My best guess is that they are turning in on themselves. It's possible that we may only have to sit by on the sidelines and watch them self-destruct."

There was a long silence as she collected herself. She gave three false starts before finally saying, "I can't tell you how impressed I am by what you've done. I'm sure that you're three steps ahead of the rotters in the Chicago PD," she stroked her chin and looked skyward for a few seconds. "You know I think that if these two were the killers they were probably very much under the thumb of some even nastier people. As you suggested. So, now what? You're on to this Ali-person. But is he where the buck stops or does it go higher? And, if so, is it even in this country? Poor Regis never stood a chance against them. I told you this once before, Regis was an innocent. He thought that humor was the yeast of life. If he's in heaven I'm sure that he's still trying to figure this all out."

McAbee hesitated to pursue this thought, however he found it to be an uncanny comment about Regis, a man so innocent that it blinded him to the harm that he was causing. Certainly, it made him a figure to pity. Not a particularly uplifting piece of thinking and it had even more pathos to it because his mother saw him for what he was. Lamely, he said, "Whatever the case nothing justifies what was done to him."

"Yes, yes, I know," she said distractedly. "So now what happens?"

"We're going to try to move on Ali. He's a piece of this puzzle. I just don't know if he's on the edge of the puzzle or in the middle. He's very upset. It may be possible to manipulate him into a mistake of some sort."

"Mistake?"

"Doing something that gives us new leads, directions. I'll pursue this, Roberta, until you tell me you've had enough."

"I can see that now. It gladdens me. Finally, someone takes the bull by the horns. Don't worry, I'm ready to take this to the bitter end."

"As long as you realize that it may come to a bitter end."

McAbee returned to the downtown Hyatt and immediately took a shower. Just as he put on a pair of shorts, his room phone went off. He walked toward it, hesitating to pick it up. He needed some down time to think. The almost frantic happenings of the day caused him to feel besieged. He picked up the phone on the fifth ring, "Hello?"

"Bertrand, my dear, dear brother. Did you turn your cell off – what's going on out there? Hey, it's a 24/7 world that we live in," Bill said with his most acerbic edge.

Bertrand didn't need a hectoring brother. Roberta had probably called him as soon as he had left her place. "Bill, easy, easy," he said with a warning edge that he hoped his brother caught.

He did. He softened immediately. "Roberta called. She's thrilled with your work. But I'm sorry to say this isn't primarily why I'm calling you."

"Is everything all right?"

"Uh, yeah. Everyone's alive out here if that's what you mean."

"OK Bill, let's hear it. What's up?"

"The two asses, Flotsam and Jetsam? The goons who were cooked today in the parking lot?"

"Yeah?"

"95% sure that one of the burnees was the rabbi's killer. When they came in to the center some photos were taken. The tape quality at the Marriott was poor but the match is pretty close. When you asked about other ops I didn't get to it right away. I have some news for you. It's a hornet's nest at that center. There's a joint surveillance, FBI and Mossad. Tell Scholz that he's radioactive. They went ballistic when they saw him in the parking lot. This isn't the first time that ex-marine Jack Scholz has been in and around bombings, car explosions, and other disasters. Just to make sure on this, Scholz didn't do this, did he dear brother?"

"No, no way. He was engaged in a watch. Ali is on our list, compliments of you and the Israelis."

"Well, there's more. The CIA and FBI in a rare show of collegiality have been cooperating on dealing with Ali. Apparently, Mossad was behind on this one. Not in front which is what I assumed."

"Scholz expressed concern about this."

"For good reason. They want you off of this, N…O…W," he spelled out.

"Who's they?"

"All of the cooperating parties."

"We may have a man inside. Do they?"

"Talk to me about that."

Bertrand told him Jack Scholz's placement of Yousef.

"Pretty skimpy placement. He's been in the place about four or five hours and the two best friends of Ali are blown up. If Ali isn't a good causal thinker, he might blame your guy," Bill said sarcastically.

"Might not too. He is vulnerable; someone like Yousef might look good. By the way, did any of your friends see the placement of the bombs?"

"No. Your twins parked on the other side of the building."

"Did they see anything else?"

"Not that they're sharing."

"What about Ali?"

"They're on to Ali. The big question for them is who is running him? They've dug up some of his background. Seems like he doesn't have the education or the skills to be very high up. Arabic societies are very hierarchical. The assumption is that it's ultimately run by some higher ups. That's what makes for a cell. They think that this is one."

"Bill, I'm not in this for the rabbi. That's a Mossad issue. Who's in this for Regis?"

"It's not important to them. Well, maybe the FBI if there's a connection between Regis and the rabbi. I will say this, however, Jack Scholz has their full attention."

"If I pull off on this, Bill, I pull off of our best lead. What about Roberta?"

"I'm sorry Bertrand. But remember, Ali was given to you by Mossad. He who gives can take. It's a tacit rule in this game. Do you have other leads?"

"Yeah. A few. Tell me about Yousef. Should we discontinue his use?"

Bill paused then said, "No, keep him in. If they have a problem, I'll call you back. Not to do that would be an unnecessary variable for Ali. But tell him to be very, very cool. I can't tell you how relieved I am that Scholz is innocent. There would have been one ugly scene if he was involved," Bill said with gravity in his voice.

To Bertrand, this was Bill coming in again on the issue. Apparently, he still had lingering doubts about Jack. "Bill, again, Jack had nothing to do with the whole thing. He was monitoring Ali by way of Yousef. Case closed. Please pass this on to them. Also, his continued presence near the area is to monitor Yousef on Ali. We're not trying to interfere with their game."

"You just made a distinction with a hair of a difference, but I'll pass it on to them. Stay tuned…you know, if you stay in the business long enough you're going to get to be pretty damn good." He hung up.

Bertrand smiled to himself and then shook his head. Getting a morsel of praise from his brother was quite a feat.

CHAPTER XXV

Augusta parked a block away from Saleem Zharib's residence. She had purchased a cup of coffee from a 7/11. She was tuned to WBBM, the all news station out of Chicago. She heard, "At six a.m. we go to CBS national news." She heard the dull click and voilá she was listening to details about Iraq and the insurgency. She shook her head in frustration as she listened and sipped from the still very hot black coffee.

Zharib lived in the upscale area of Maywood, about seven miles from downtown Chicago. Augusta found Maywood to be sociologically schizophrenic. The first half of the township was mired in black poverty. Augusta was not comfortable when she took the First Avenue exit off of the Eisenhower as she proceeded through that area as fast as she could. Suddenly, she found the better part. It wasn't a subtle shift, it was sudden and shocking. She found Zharib's residence, a medium bungalow. The lights were on in the house. She noticed that his garage was in an alley that bisected the street that she was on. She had a good view of the garage. At 6:45 a.m. she saw a full furl of light and then the unmistakable limo slowly backing out of the garage.

She called Bertrand, who seemed pretty alert for this time of the morning, and she told him that she was tuned in on Zharib. Slightly annoying, but forever Bertrand, he told her to be careful. She was about to say, but didn't, 'No, today I'm going to be reckless.'

Ten minutes into the drive, an easy follow given that traffic was still pretty light, she saw the limo pull into a Motel 6. She thought of a pig with a diamond necklace.

She drove directly into the motel complex and parked near the office. The limo was waiting outside the motel office. She could see into the office. A sister was at the counter dealing with a smallish, thin, mustached man. He went to the entrance door and made a gesture to the limo. She removed from the floor of the car a camera with a telephoto lens. She turned off the automatic flash and sequenced six shots. When the small man came to the door of the motel, he motioned for Zharib who came out of the vehicle and soon picked up two bags which he carried to the trunk. Augusta timed her entry into the motel foyer when the limo pulled away.

She rushed to the woman and said, "I need your help. I want his name and I want you to quarantine his room for the day. Here is $100. I'll call you soon. OK?"

"Hey! Yeah."

"Your name?"

"Raven."

Augusta saw the limo turn right as she tore to her car and picked up the chase. It wasn't hard. The limo was about three blocks ahead. Within a minute she was at a correct following distance. She called Bertrand and told him of the motel and the match to Scholz's description of the man in the limo. "Can you get someone over there to turn the room?"

"I'll call Jack. Get me the info on the room number and tell this Raven to be prepared. Where's the limo headed to?"

"We're heading back over to the Ike." She hung up.

Ten minutes later she called McAbee with news given to her by Raven: the room number (214), the name, Harry Jones, and the fact that Jones paid in cash for the room. He had given a $100 deposit. The delay in the office when he was there was due to the fact that Motel 6 owed him $3.27. Raven owned that she thought he'd say to hell with it and she could cop the $3.27. He didn't and he wouldn't. "Dis the same sonofabitch who was picked up yesterday by a limo. And he ain't no Jones – he's some kind of Turk or something," Raven said in disgust.

Scholz would have, McAbee reported, a team of men there within the hour. They would comb the room for prints, hair samples, and the like.

"Looks like we're heading back to that Islamic Center that you told me about last night. I'll be in touch." Augusta disconnected happy not to hear that she should be careful, then she laughed at herself. She was being a bit of a bitch toward Bertrand who last night had been so damned abstract and mentally removed that she wanted to kick him under the table at that nice Italian place that he took her to.

The weeper, Simon, took out another cell. He called Faisal who answered on the second ring of this call. "Good morning. I am heading to the Center to remove the other problem. From there, I am going to Detroit. I have just made reservation to leave from Detroit this afternoon at

4:30 p.m. I felt something at the motel this morning on my way out. As you know, I was moving to another, but that is not necessary. I wish for you to call and tell the party that I am to be expected with a message of the utmost secrecy. I will let you know when it is done. As to the other, it is not the time."

"I understand my brother. May Allah be with you," Faisal said unquestioningly.

Chauffer Zharib had already been told by the man that they were going directly to Detroit after the visit. The man's plan was to leave at 4:30 p.m. for Amman, Jordan and from there on to Beirut, Lebanon. He had been told to watch for a tail. He had, but he didn't pick up anything obvious. He had never quite seen the likes of this man, whose name was never given. Energy effused from him. His attentiveness and focus was a bit frightening in fact.

He was confused by the man's fuss at the Motel 6. Some woman had apparently come into the parking lot either in a way that made him suspicious or she did something, but whatever it was, it bothered the man so much so that he was on the phone to a travel agent and had secured a changed reservation within two minutes. He certainly had a way about him that brought others to his command. Zharib purposefully and obstinately refused to dwell on the parking lot doings of yesterday and the subsequent massive explosion that had come from that area. The man was not an angel of mercy.

As they came near to the Islamic Center he heard from the back of the limo, "Slow down, go by once and around the block, then again, the same. On the third time I want you to drive in and drop me at the entrance, a few steps from the door. Then, I want you to leave, go down the street and wait at the edge of the next street after a right turn, near the mailboxes. Notice I am wearing a baseball hat, Yankees I believe. When I am in the vehicle I want you ready for Detroit. Break no laws and be observant for anything unusual."

Zharib tipped the beak of his cap. There was nothing else to say.

As he came up on the center it was 7:55 a.m. He did as instructed. The parking lot at the Center was still very lightly parked, but the Center was open as he saw a woman enter. He caught the man's face in his mirror. He had a way of looking at things that reminded him of a wolf. It was as though he had a grid in his mind. Everything on the grid had to have a reason to be there and to be properly placed. A quick pick up of Zharib's eyes by him in the rearview mirror brought instant fear. He would not look that way again. He proceeded by the Center and made a right at the next street. He eyed the mailboxes where it was stated that he would wait. In about two minutes, he was again near the Center. Nothing appeared to have changed. He, again, went by and turned at the corner. Midway down that street the man said, "Pull over!" He did. A quick glance at the rear view mirror caught the man's head fully turned, facing back. A car had just come into the street from the corner. As it passed, Zharib noticed that it was a black woman. She didn't seem interested in them.

From the back of the limo, "That car has followed us from the motel. See to it that you are aware of it. Proceed."

The Islamic Center was housed in an old movie complex. The building had been re-arranged to accommodate the handicapped and had developed a roundabout that allowed for people to be dropped off a few feet from the entrance to the Center. Zharib drove up and parked within six feet of the entrance. The man wore his Yankee hat low to the eyes as he slid out and was through the door in what seemed to be less than a second.

"Yeah?"

"Bertrand. I've been made. The limo is in the Islamic Center area. They got me on a side street. Seems like Jack had a hit yesterday. I'm going to float for a few minutes and come back onto the scent. Sorry. No way to avoid as far as I can see. It's a sign that they have a high IQ."

"Do your best, I'll call Jack. Be careful."

She disconnected.

When Simon entered the Center he took out his cell and dialed Ali's number.

"Good morning," he said shakily.

"Ali. I have come from Faisal. I have a most important message. I am in the building. We will need maximum privacy."

There was a short, but too noticeable a pause. "Yes. Yes, indeed. Where are you?"

"In the entryway. Tell me how to proceed."

Ali gave him instructions to his office. He was brought up short by the man. "No – more private than that. There is concern."

Ali gave him directions to a seldom-used room off of the prayer center.

As Ali reached the door to the room and was searching for his master key, Simon came toward him. Ali in his haste and nervousness didn't seem to know that he was behind him. He opened the door and threw the light switch to a compact room that was no more than nine feet by twelve. Simon touched his hand as he was withdrawing the key from the lock. He said, "Good morning, Ali. My name is Simon."

Ali jumped and staggered backwards in obvious fright. Simon shut the door as Ali tried to recover his bearings as his forehead dampened. "Ah, oh, yes." He stepped forward as if to kiss Simon.

Simon reached out with his left arm, keeping Ali at a distance. "I have come with no hostility toward you." He felt his eyes watering as he looked at this scared, little man who knew in his heart that no good would come to him from this weeping man. "In the story of us all we have a place on the stage of events. It is my job sometimes to change the characters. It is not a fate that I welcome. I just accept." Tears started to flow uncontrollably from his eyes as he saw Ali realize what was to occur. He moved toward a now semi-paralyzed Ali and with a quick thrust upwards plunged a dagger into his heart. Ali felt little if anything. He was dead as Simon withdrew the blade and gently dropped the man to the floor. He wiped the blood from the dagger on the robes of Ali and he placed the weapon into a scarab on the inside of his right pants leg. He withdrew a handkerchief from his back coat pocket and wiped the tears from his eyes. He then took the keys from Ali's curled fingers, opened the door and then locked it. As he proceeded toward the entryway of the building he noticed a strong young man who carried himself like a soldier. He was talking on a cell phone. He had an odd sensation, but he continued on out the entrance to the street and then forward down the block. When he turned at the corner the limo was waiting. The driver left immediately. Simon looked back to see if the limo was being followed. It didn't seem so. But there were to be a number of foils used as they drove to Detroit.

He called Faisal who answered immediately. "The third is gone. Some other time, perhaps, we can attend to the other problem."

"Allah be praised."

"Yes, yes indeed," he responded stoically.

Later in the day, the Northwest airplane left Detroit International for Jordan. Simon had a window seat deep in the economy section of the plane. He breathed a sigh of relief when the plane's flight monitor showed them to have passed into Canadian airspace.

Ali's body was discovered at 8:50 a.m. by the Islamic cleric who had come to manage services. Screams erupted in the complex. When Yousef ascertained the cause of the screaming, he left the Center and walked briskly toward Jack Scholz's van. He explained what had happened.

Scholz was not given to shows of emotion other than varying ranges of anger. Yousef had worked for him on several jobs. Never had he seen anything of the anger that he saw in Jack's eyes. His fury was extraordinary. If Yousef got too close to it, he was sure that he would be burned badly. Jack gave him $2000 in cash and said, "You did well Yousef. No one else did. Thanks." Yousef got into his Mustang and drove away, happy to be out of the circuit of things.

CHAPTER XXVI

Bertrand asked Augusta to accompany him to Roberta Chamberlin's place. He knew that Roberta and Augusta had bonded from the time past. He had also asked Roberta, if she would be so kind, to invite both her daughter, Sybil, and Rufus O'Hanlon. She had consented.

As they drove toward Roberta's domicile, Augusta noticed the strain on Bertrand's face. The two of them had spent many hours last night trying to get a handle on what had happened, what had not happened and what they would probably never know. During their dinner, by room service, he had taken two calls from his brother Bill. He had come out of both of the calls shaking his head in some kind of dismay.

She broke the silence that hung heavily in the Explorer. "What will you tell these people?"

"As much of the truth as I can share. There are some things that I can't divulge, of course. But you know what hurts the most? We stumbled into something, we carried ourselves pretty well and then it all evaporated. There were players in this game that we could never have known were there. And they're still there, but we can't go any further.

The agencies are thrilled by what you did at the Motel 6, some possible prints were picked up, some DNA and now they're saying we were as close as anyone had ever come to an assassin of legendary skill and daring. The pic that Jack's Yousef got was extraordinary. So, in that sense, we made a big impression. Bill was thrilled. But they all want us to stop dead in our tracks. They say it's not al-Qaeda but there's something out there that we touched, but we are to never touch it again," he said resignedly.

"I feel lousy about being made."

"I should have had two or three cars on it. I underestimated Jack's hunch."

"Well, you did and didn't. You actually gave it a run. Most chief investigators would have dismissed it. Most cops will tell you, Bertrand, that there's never a perfect solution. There's always a glitch somewhere. You're being very hard on yourself. Remember the two who did in Regis were snuffed and this Ali was probably in the middle of the whole thing. They're all dead."

"And this assassin?"

"What can you say? Somebody brought him here to shut down these operations. Maybe it was the note that you found in Regis' walking stick. A datum, a hanging shard. We'll never know these things. But it seems that all of the pressure you put down on this case yielded some good."

"Yeah, I can tell Roberta that some kind of justice was served. But a whole other type wasn't. I'm convinced that there were people pulling strings in this thing who are free and clear."

"I know, I know. It's too bad that the limo driver was murdered. He could have helped a lot."

"The assassin knew that he had been outed somehow. That we'd go after the chauffer. If he hadn't been outed, the chauffer would still be alive."

"And don't forget Bertrand, it was your team that outed him," she patted him on his arm. He didn't seem to be very consolable.

They were all there when Augusta and Bertrand were shown into the living room. Rufus noticed right away that Bertrand McAbee was uptight. He was struggling with some force inside himself even as he shook Sybil's hand, and oh my God, hugged Roberta, and then finally came to Duke and him. Funny thing. Duke seemed to shake him out of his introspectiveness, as McAbee stooped down and patted the dog energetically. He went over to the loveseat and sat next to that stately black woman who worked for him.

He started out slowly. "I think that Regis was murdered for a cause. The cause is radical Islam. Later, a rabbi was murdered in the downtown Marriott. Same cause in operation. I think that the murderers who killed Regis and the rabbi were in a cell of radicalism. I think that the intent of the cell was to murder those whom they found most aggravating. Somewhere in the future, maybe after a few more killings, they would make a grand announcement about their victims. The point of the matter is this: Regis was so good at what he did that I think they made him their first victim. Almost surely, the twins killed your son, your brother, your friend. They had help but we'll never find that out. Probably other members of the cell. The twins are definitely dead. So some justice was served. Add to this, the man who was involved somehow with these twins was also killed. We can only speculate about that. As to the assassin, he has come and gone. Our CIA, the Israeli Mossad, and Interpol are currently moving on that score. But there is no thought that he had anything to do with Regis' murder. He was brought in to stop a hemorrhage. As to the cell, I've been called down by Homeland Security. There is nothing further that I can do without getting myself arrested. I have gone as far as a PI can go under the circumstances. Homeland Security will take this case into another stratum beyond my reach." He stopped and looked around.

Rufus thought that Bertrand had probably been a damn good lecturer when he taught those years back.

Roberta asked, "Your brother Bill. He has been apprised of all this?"

"Yes."

"He agrees that you must stop?"

"Yes," Bertrand said evenly.

"Well, then, the matter is closed. I have one consolation."

"What's that Roberta?"

"That Regis got under the collar of these intolerant bastards. He would have enjoyed the spectacle of the whole thing," she smiled sadly.

Sybil went toward her and placed her arm around her. Rufus was glad to see them at a peace of sorts. He remembered some wry comments from Regis relative to how Roberta clashed regularly with her daughter, Sybil.

As for Rufus, at least he had been given some kind of answer for this terrible affair. And he had met McAbee, a most interesting man. But, surely, did McAbee belong doing what he was doing? A PI? Really!

AFTERWORD

- The cell, according to the best of information, still exists. But it has morphed into a new form. The various services wait with trepidation.
- The weeper, Simon, underwent facial surgery in Switzerland. He has wept on three occasions post-Detroit. Four victims are beyond weeping.
- Roberta Chamberlin gave a huge bonus to McAbee. He shared it with Scholz, Fisk, and Satin.
- Faisal is close to completing an organization that he sees as wreaking havoc on America.
- Bertrand McAbee is back working his usual cases. But every time he thinks of Regis and the outcome of that case he shakes his head and whispers, "Jesus."
- Duke the Boxer died, suddenly. Rufus O'Hanlon died a week later. Roberta told McAbee that she thought Rufus' heart broke. McAbee believed it.

Printed in the United States
By Bookmasters